STONEY COMPTON

LEVEL

Pullo Pup Publishing
An Imprint of Wicked Cherub Productions

Corpus Christi, Texas

Also by Stoney Compton
(Leonard W. Compton)

Novels:
Russian Amerika (Baen Books)
Alaska Republik (Baen Books)
Whalesong (Pullo Pup Publishing)
Treadwell, A Novel of Alaska Territory
(Pullo Pup Publishing)

Short Works:
Whalesong *(UNIVERSE 1)*
Messages *(Writers of the Future, Vol. IX)*
When the Ship Came
(Tomorrow, Speculative Fiction, Vol 12)
Trappers *(Jim Baen's Universe)*
Deliverance (Pullo Pup Publishing)
Diplomatic Exchange (Pullo Pup Publishing)

LEVEL SIX

STONEY COMPTON

Acknowledgements

I am indebted to Walt Boyes for his response to the short story version of *Level Six*. "Stoney, this would make a hell of a good novel." He also read the mostly finished version and said it was good to go.

I leave it up to the reader to decide if he was correct.

I am further indebted to my accomplished wife, Colette, who edited the manuscript and the galley proof *twice*. She not only found puntuation and other mechanical errors, she also made cogent suggestions to the story itself. Wife, muse, and editor all in one. I am blessed.

Dedicated to
Joint Air Tactical Control
Experts World-Wide

Stay safe, Brothers and Sisters!

For more information about the author go to http://www.stoneycompton.com

ISBN-10 0983747458
ISBN-13 978-0-9837474-5-1

Photo of comet used on the cover courtesy of Jack Newton. More of his incredible space photography can be seen at http://www.jacknewton.com

LEVEL SIX

To My Wonderful Daughter,
Sarah Maisie Campbell,
I have always been delighted with
your constant quest to learn and
achieve more.
All My Love,
"Dad"
Ronnie Campbell
August 2012

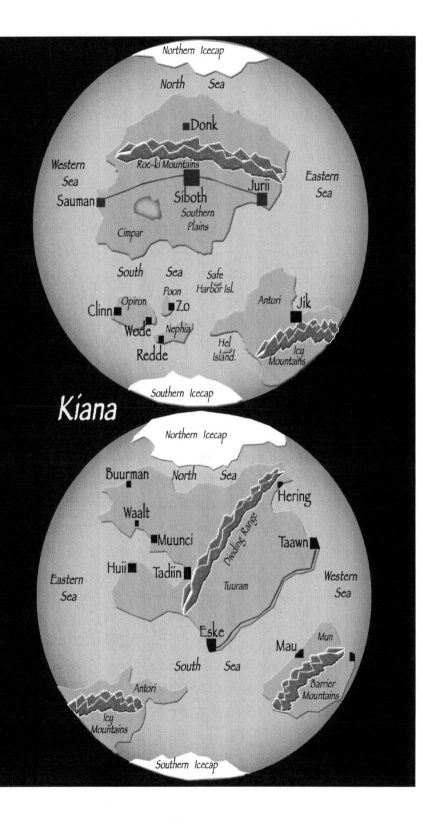

Kiana

Level Six

1
Siboth

"Ki gave us life. Ki protects us. Ki gathers us unto her when our minds join her universal oneness." The ancient Kian's voice, pitched fractionally higher than human, dropped, as did her gaze from the ceiling and her large eyes washed over the others in the dim light.

With the ceiling close to Stoker Payne's head, incense curled into a lowering cloud in the small, dim, stone room, irritating eyes and nose alike.

"From where did Ki come?" Stoker asked. "Do you know?"

In one of the dark corners an insect clicked in a rhythmic pattern that he might have found soothing under different circumstances.

"Ki existed always, from the beginning to end and over again."

"Your people have stopped and started again?" Shannon Gray asked. "What does that mean?"

Stoker thought the smoldering brazier doubled in output. Shannon sneezed and wiped at her left eye. "Sorry."

The insect quieted for a moment and then resumed clicking.

"When the Dark One fills our sky we must go to the Sacred Sanctuaries else we die. Always are there unbelievers who abstain in fear of losing what they consider abundance. Never again are they seen and their mental wealth is lost to all other Kians, and to Ki."

Stoker sneezed, muffling it as best he could.

On the other side of the room a second insect answered the first.

"What is the 'Dark One,' Ti Suura?" Shannon sniffed quietly.

"To speak the name is to invoke the same, but her time draws nigh."

"Again, I do not understand, Ti Suura," Shannon said.

"Fear not," the ancient female made the sign of universal regret, "...you shall."

2
Siboth

"You have all been invited to share in the results of the latest, and may I add, last, ground-penetrating radar survey that now completes our survey of Kiana." The director smiled all around and Stoker wondered if he should make a sign to ward off evil. He became nervous when the director exhibited a good mood; in his experience when she smiled in his presence it rarely proved sincere.

Her short stature belied her strength of will. Handsome rather than beautiful, she mostly achieved height/weight proportion. A thickening in the hips and stomach made one wonder if her deep chestnut hair was a gift of nature or expensive gene manipulation. But her dark, penetrating eyes allowed no doubt as to her mastery of any situation she might encounter.

The director touched a screen none of the others could see and a holo of Kiana suddenly rotated above the circular conference table. Low Moon and High Moon also rotated in their eccentric orbits, never coming within each other's plane of causation. They were unique satellites in human known space.

The focus zoomed in on the continent of Cimpar, in the "western" hemisphere of Kiana, then it rushed over the snow-capped Roc-ki Mountains and stopped deep in the southern plains far from three of the four major cities and twelve smaller towns. Kiana boasted no villages or hamlets: an oddity still to be parsed by humans.

"The *Magellan* has used every probe and survey tool in its wide arsenal to examine the surface and sub-surface of all four continents of Kiana. As per Coalition protocol the technicians first probed the cities and their environs, then the smaller population centers. No evidence of early habitation was evident.

"So they moved on to the rest of the planet. With Kiana being five-sixths the diameter of Earth Prime, there was a great deal of surface to cover."

"Madame Director?"

"Yes, Dr. Payne?"

"Were they *only* searching for earlier civilizations?"

"Of course not. Minerals, petroleum or potential synthetic petroleum deposits, specific flora and fauna, fissionable material, as well as evidence of nuclear activity are always paramount in a Coalition probe. I'm surprised you asked such an obvious question."

"I merely wanted to be certain of where we archaeologists stood in the greater scheme of things." He made himself grin.

Slightly less than two meters tall, Stoker enjoyed a physique molded by the fieldwork he relished. His long blonde hair tended to billow with the slightest breeze and therefore he kept it artfully contained in a ponytail with a Kian wrist wrap meant for a child. His angular face boasted bright blue eyes and usually framed an engaging smile.

"The same place you always have; just below the historians."

Stoker noted the director's condescending tone and the flash of irritation in her eyes.

"Yes, director." He let the grin slip away.

He was bored stiff. In the months since they had arrived he and his team had done everything they could to prepare for actually doing their job as archaeologists. All of their gear had been checked and rechecked, their supplies loaded into their vehicles, and endless games of poker played. They had even tried talking to Kians to try and get an idea of where they should look for promising sites.

The Kians had been less than forthcoming. They were polite and their answers to questions were masterpieces of circumlocution. All of the archaeology crew were becoming quite good at poker.

Stoker knew this meeting was the one that would matter. After much deliberation and many surveys they would get their marching orders today.

The director waited a long moment before allowing the holo view to penetrate the planet surface. Nineteen familiar gray-scale deposits of entwined artifacts dotted the wide plains bordering Siboth, the only city near the center of the continent. Each location was numbered for the N-series survey.

One team would start at the far dig, right at a hundred kilometers from Siboth, and the other would start with the closest one at the edge of town. When each team finished, or was instructed to halt work on a dig, they would go to the next one and eventually meet in the middle.

One deposit made an almost perfect circle beneath Kiana's surface with a long smudge trailing away to the east. Stoker noted the scale below the holographic projection; the circular mass of artifacts measured a quarter mile in diameter and the smudge looked to be about three to four kilometers in length.

Something unique took place there, he thought. *And I want to lead the dig that discovers what it was.*

"We have to know with absolute certainty what happened in these places," the director's voice went flat and matter-of-fact. "Because according to their history, what little of it we have discovered, they went from a modern age to something analogous to the human Stone Age in the space of a few months.

"Despite the fact we've found nothing worth exploiting, humans *can* live here comfortably, and you all know how rare that is in the history of interstellar exploration."

Jerrol Bainer, one of the few field archaeologists from the Pyrocean League, raised his hand. "Who gets to lead the dig on this spot, director?" His laser pointer indicated the site farthest out on the Cimparian prairie.

Jerrol's dark, curly hair hung tight to his head, rather like an infant's. His shiny dark eyes and perfect rosebud lips put Stoker in mind of a rather large cherub, since Jerrol's frame carried about 14 kilos more than it needed.

At least he's not wearing his toga.

The director smiled at Jerrol. "That one will be the most difficult to deal with, so I will award it to the staff person who most fits the description."

Stoker suddenly knew what she was going to say next.

"Doctor Stoker Payne and his team will investigate that one."

Jerrol grinned and stared at Stoker. "And the closest to Siboth, Madame Director?"

She almost cooed. "Why, you, of course, Doctor Bainer."

Stoker felt the intended insult was actually a blessing. If asked why he would not have been able to answer, but instinctually he knew the answers to all the director's questions lay there at Kiana Dig N-19.

3

Coalition Star Ship Magellan

"Doctor Frasier, I think you should spend some time on Kiana."

Melanie Frasier held the other woman's gaze. "But I am scheduled next on the main array, Dr. Buderka. What has changed?"

Dr. Buderka resembled one of the planets her department studied. Nearly perfectly round, she tended to stay on the low gravity decks where the astronomy pods dimpled the outer skin of the *Magellan*. Her appetite was legendary and she obviously had missed numerous physical training sessions on the weight deck and none of the meals.

Melanie thought she looked like a bladder of fat with a head.

"Obviously, my mind," the heavy woman said, attempting a smile that didn't translate to her eyes.

"May I ask your motivation?"

"It seems to me that you have been spending far too much time in the deep space array pod already. There are other astronomers in the Astrocartography Department who would like equal time in the pods."

"Dr. Buderka, I inquired of all the other staff if they wanted to use a DSA pod every time I used one out of rotation. They all said no."

"Perhaps they were just being polite. I, on the other hand, will be blunt. No astronomer will spend extra time in the pods without my express permission."

"I'm being reprimanded for working *too much*?"

The brittle smile had not budged. "You're not being reprimanded, Dr. Frasier, you're being promoted. You can get as much time at the Kiana observatory as you wish. As of now I'm putting you in charge of it."

"Dealing with an atmosphere is a promotion?"

"That's how I see it. If you want a *real* reprimand just keep talking."

Melanie bit her tongue hard enough to hurt. Willing her jaw to relax, she nodded.

"Thank you, Dr, Buderka. I will do my best at the Kiana Observatory."

The smile loosened into a smirk.

"I'm sure you will, Dr. Frasier."

Melanie had composed herself by the time she went through the hatch into the main corridor. As in most things Coalition, this was a double-edged sword. She had to concentrate on the positive aspects, no matter how big a bite it was to swallow.

The benefits of making astronomical observations from a star ship versus from a dirt-side observatory were huge and obvious. But time on the *Magellan* pod 'scopes was prized and fought over. Someone had out maneuvered her; that was patently obvious. It didn't matter who it was, any of the other PhDs would have slit her throat in order to gain more time on the main array, as long as they didn't lose any of their free time.

But she *had* asked, damn it! This backbiting and knives in the night crap really pissed her off. The positive aspect of the situation was that she had an observatory all to herself. She could probably sleep in the place if she so desired.

At any other time she would have immediately headed down to the weight deck where enhanced gravity gave the work out sessions an added edge. Her trim, muscular body gave testimony to the fruits of attendance. But she had to pack and plan her departure, not to mention dampen her anger.

"I'll show those ass-kissing wannabes!" she muttered as she entered the "suite" she shared with Dr. Ramona Alverez.

The anthropologist looked up from her holo reader.

"You talking to yourself again, Mel?"

"See anyone with me, Ram?"

"What you pissed off about this time?"

Melanie explained in short, terse sentences.

"And that suet-ball, sanctimonious, puss-gut bitch, Buderka, has had it in for me ever since her pet 'we're from the same planet' astronomer came down with the flux virus before *Magellan* left Proxima Central for Kiana. I didn't give him the bloody shits. I was just next in rotation for deployment!"

"How long has it been since you were dirtside?"

"Oh, four, five months. Not much down there for an astronomer."

"There's more to life than astronomy; real air to breathe, fresh produce to eat, a horizon line, and a species so close to human you can swive them." Ram grinned. "What's not to like?"

"That's what I like about you, Ram, your cup is always half full." Melanie pulled open the door to her narrow wardrobe. "I bet I'll have more room for my things down there, too."

"See? You're getting into the right frame of mind. Need help packing?"

"Just as soon as you offer me a stiff drink."

4
Siboth

"Bountiful Galaxies, Miri!" Shannon Gray said and fell away from her soul mate. Both of their bodies glistened with sweat. They lay across two folded down benches in the back of a survey vehicle.

"You sure this thing is sound proof, Shannon?" Miri said with a chuckle. "You are one of the loudest lovers I have ever had."

"Thanks for reminding me I'm merely the most recent of a long string of conquests for you, ungrateful wench. Yeah, these heavy lifters are sound proof when they're buttoned up."

"Recent my ass. You're the last. You're it, sweetheart, and you know it. You just say shit like that to garner ego strokes, don't you?"

"Works, doesn't it?" Shannon picked up Miri's green tee shirt and started wiping the woman's sweaty breasts. "And we're running out of time."

"You keep that up and I'm going to be all over you again." She grabbed Shannon's hand and pulled the shirt free. "It's only six months, baby. I gotta go play bad ass security grunt on *Maggie* and you have a brand new dig to burrow into. Time flies when we're having fun. You know that."

"I wish the blowers worked when the engine isn't running," Shannon said, wiping sweat from her face. She moved back and kissed Miri. "I get so damn horny when you're not here. Now that I've found you I hate being separated from you for a day, let alone half a standard year."

Miri grinned and pulled the tee shirt on. "'Absence makes the heart grow fonder.' At least that's what some poet said."

"I used to counter that one with; 'absence makes the heart go wander.' Then I met you in that bar on Proxima IV."

Miri laughed. "We got it on for three days straight because we both knew we were shipping out."

Shannon echoed her laugh. "And then we discover we're both going aboard the same starship! Thought I'd died and gone to the Bardo!"

"Please get dressed, Shannon. I have to go up a day early to make sure everything is done with snap and spark. The shuttle lifts in a little over an hour and I want you to walk me to the

LZ."

Shannon bit her lip and quickly got into her clothing.

"I'll walk over there with you. But I'll cry all the way back."

5
Coalition Star Ship Magellan

"Any other questions, Colonel Poppert?"

"No, colonel. But I don't like the idea of taking orders from a civilian, and a woman at that."

Colonel Dimarco snorted. "Gawdsdammit, Jerry, you knew the rules before you volunteered for this mission. Up here you answer to me, down there, unless there's a war or insurrection of some sort, you answer to the director of Planetary Operations: simple as that. Of course the Kians haven't so much as thrown a rock at a human in the whole five years humans have been here, but I suppose you can always hope."

Lieutenant Colonel Poppert opened his mouth.

"Just save it, Jerry," Colonel Dimarco snapped. "You have your orders. Go relieve Colonel Gagne and his team. Get some fresh air, give the civilians their money's worth on security, and keep your secular opinions to yourself.

"Try to stay out of the infighting between the preservationists and the rape and run crowd. That's all civilian shit and you needn't step in it. Know what I mean?"

"Yes, colonel." LtCol Jerry Poppert snapped to attention and saluted his commanding officer. Once outside the colonel's office he allowed himself to silently sneer.

He didn't care if women had been part of the services since the Coalition began, none he had ever met could do half the job a man could. All they were good at was busting your balls whether they were your overbearing mother or your harpy wife. He had taken steps to no longer have either and that suited him just fine.

He wasn't the shortest lieutenant colonel in the service, but he was sure he ranked in the bottom ten percent. Along with the rapidly thinning hair and the few extra kilos he couldn't eliminate from his midsection, he felt that all of his subordinates laughed at him behind his back. None of them had the guts to do it face to face.

As for the civilian politics, he couldn't care less. That was an issue no matter where they were and after all his years in the service he could sidestep any subject and look military doing it. Most of the people he dealt with were unbelievers from licentious worlds any way.

He marched into the squad bay where his executive officer stood chatting with noncoms. One of the sergeants spied him and shouted the area to attention. All turned and snapped to, instantly giving him a mass salute.

This is more like it.

LtCol Jerry Poppert returned the salute and bellowed, "As you were. Major Merritt, accompany me to my office."

Major Aisha Merritt nodded and reported as she fell into step beside him.

"All of the troopers have their gear stowed on the transport shuttle. The sergeants are supervising the clean up of the berthing spaces and everything will be ready for inspection by 1400 hours, colonel."

Poppert glanced at his subordinate's dark face. Besides women he also wasn't too keen on skin that wasn't white. The fact that his was an Adam's World minority view in a far too liberal Coalition only made it more galling.

Despite himself he was impressed with his executive officer's professionalism and found himself trying not to praise her.

"Very good, Major Merritt. Has my gear been seen to?"

"Of course, colonel. Last on and first off. I also had a detail clean your quarters."

"Excellent."

They entered his office, now bare of his personal items and awards. Lieutenant Colonel Henry Gagne would own this cabin for the next six months and Jerry was damn well leaving as little as possible. Large for a space faring vessel, the compartment now seemed bleak, Spartan, and unwelcoming.

Suddenly he was eager to be away.

"Have you impressed upon the troops that we will be subject to fe- civilian command?"

"Yes, colonel. However I believe they understood that long ago."

"Well, prior to this it was mere theory. Now we must deal with the reality."

"I'm sure they will all do fine, Sir."

I damn well doubt I will, he thought. "Very well. Let's get the inspection over with." He strode through the hatch without a backward glance.

6
Coalition Star Ship Magellan

Doctor Melanie Frasier ambled toward the passenger bay, chatting with Doctor Ramona Alverez. Both women carried the few bags containing all that Melanie owned. When that realization crossed her mind she suddenly wished she could spend a day in her condo in the heart of Brad Olson City, the capitol of Tolley III, her home planet.

"Hey, Mel, where were you just now?"

"Home in my condo. Haven't thought about it in months."

"My mind dwells in Nuevo Espana at least once a day. It helps keep me sane. I understand there are some very nice houses in Siboth. Next month when I come down I'll expect the grand tour of your digs."

"Of course! I'll even cook for you."

They both laughed at the same time.

"Don't you dare cook for me, Dr. Frasier. I want to live to a ripe old age."

"I warned you the first time about my lack of domestic skills, but you insisted–"

"And I barely lived to regret it. You need to find a boyfriend down there who loves to show off his culinary accomplishments."

"Do you know who I've been thinking about since this shit storm descended?"

"Not a clue."

"That buff archaeologist who came out with us and went dirt side months ago. What was his name?"

"Mel, don't be coy. You're talking about Stoker. He's not exactly handsome but he *is* built."

"That's right, Dr. Stoker Payne. I think he looks interesting." She smiled and winked at her friend. "You don't think he's in a relationship, do you?"

"Doubt it. He's as career-centric as you are. Probably isn't even sure how women are different from men."

"He can probably tell the difference in a skeleton. You know what they say about archaeologists; the older a woman is, the more interested they are."

They arrived at the bright red and yellow striped hatch. Only those deploying to the planet surface could pass beyond. Melanie hugged Ram.

"Thanks for being here. I would have gone apeshit without you."

Ram's eyes had slightly reddened and she sniffed. "You be careful down there, girl. You mean a lot to me. Save me some good-looking men."

"I will."

Her resolve set, Mel hopped the next shuttle and dropped to the surface of Kiana where history and salvation waited side-by-side in the wings.

7
Siboth

"Do you want us to power up all the sorters and brushes one last time before we stow them, Stoker?"

He pulled his attention away from the list on his handpad. "Yeah, Bill, no rationale in hauling broken gear clear the hell out there."

Bill Hilton gave him a thumbs-up and went back to his crew of four. Bill was one of the assistant team leaders and would be responsible for one of the seven levels on the dig.

Stoker Payne felt stretched in nine directions. Despite having had months to prepare there were still many details to tie up and tasks to finish before they moved all of the equipment out to Dig N-19. At least now they knew where they were going.

The portable office boasted no more than a box on wheels but the electronics stuffed into it would make the archaeology survey easier and more complete. It sat surrounded by slowly dwindling mounds of boxes and fabristeel duffels.

The day had dawned hot and still. The foothills of the Rock-Ki Mountains lay baking in mid summer. Stoker yearned for a breeze and dreaded the incredible humidity of the southern plains.

He and Shannon Gray, first assistant team leader, met at 0600 to collaborate and fine-tune their schedule. She wasn't her usually happy self and it took him a moment of deduction to figure out why.

"Miri deployed to *Magellan*?"

Shannon tried to smile. "Yeah. How'd you know?"

"Must be something in the air. You okay? Want another day off?"

"Hell, no. That's all I need; *more* time by myself."

"Okay then, let's go to work."

After they compared notes they both completed their own inventory of the supplies waiting to be loaded onto the drab survey lifters. Nearly forty team members buzzed from one place to another, checking their individual tools, personal possessions, and the three smaller Dualtranz vehicles they would use for casual transportation between base camp and town.

As Stoker and Shannon synchronized their handpad results a man approached.

"Doctor Payne?"

"Yes?"

"I'm Doctor Chuck Reed, from historical research." He offered his hand and they shook.

"This is my first assistant team leader, Dr. Shannon Gray."

Dr. Reed nodded and peered around. "Could we three talk somewhere a bit less public?"

Stoker and Shannon exchanged puzzled looks.

"Uh, how about our field office there?" He nodded at the box on wheels.

"That will be fine."

As they approached, Stoker pushed a button on his handpad that lowered the step as well as unlocked the door. By the time they entered the small structure the interior temperature was pleasantly cool. The area was packed with crates and more plastisteel bundles.

Stoker pulled a couple bundles free from the elastic cording holding them in place and dropped them on the floor.

"This is the best I can do for seating."

Dr. Reed sat on one with an appreciative grunt.

"This feels good, thanks."

"So what's with the cloak and dagger approach?" Stoker sprawled on one of the firm bundles. All of them held tents for the small town they would build.

"I have been on Kiana for almost four years working with a number of other human historians as well as a group of Kians. We had hoped to put together a comprehensive historical record for the planet."

"Don't they have their own histories?" Shannon asked.

"From what we have been able to discern, they don't. All they seem to have is an oral tradition."

"Oral?" Stoker said. "Then they must have lost a great deal of knowledge of their ancient years."

"They are a very tight-lipped race, incredibly reticent about sharing knowledge with us. We've had to almost trick them into telling us anything at all about their past. But when they do talk about it they have an amazing amount of facts in their heads."

"I hadn't heard anything at all about this," Stoker said.

"No. It's all classified. We report to the head of the department who in turn reports exclusively to the director."

"The 'Bottleneck Queen,'" Shannon said with an exaggerated sigh.

"I'd love to know how she got that job," Chuck said. "Anyway, even though we can't compare our official logs, all of us on the historical survey talk about what we've found – and what we haven't. Being who we are we have come to some conclusions and have a request for you and your people; all unofficial, of course."

"Somehow I think I already knew the 'unofficial' part. What do you want us to look for?"

"Books, scrolls, written records of any kind. Despite their claims that they only have an oral history, my colleagues and I believe written records exist somewhere on Kiana. Maybe even a library. We would like you and your team to let us know if you find anything of that nature."

"We'll swap you knowledge for knowledge. The director mentioned ancient Kian history but didn't elaborate. Something about a plummet from modern to stone age in a short time?"

Chuck glanced around as if there were others within hearing and dropped his voice.

"So far we have discovered that the current culture is only a few centuries old, more than 500 years, less than a thousand. The Kians won't elaborate on causality, they just keep referring to their gods."

"Ki and the 'Dark One,'" Shannon said.

"Exactly. The only conjecture we can come up with is that they had a religious war. But even if that was fact, the other religion would still have some adherents at this point."

"Unless they were all wiped out," Stoker said in a whisper, "like some of the zealot worlds back in Early Coalition times."

Chuck shook his head. "We have found nothing that suggests a war, let alone one of that magnitude. The Kians are the most docile race ever found. They don't even kill meat animals, they wait for them to die."

Shannon sniffed disagreement. "They must have the shortest lived food critters in the universe. The fresh meat I've eaten here has been anything but old."

"We've never found a slaughterhouse on Kiana," Chuck said. "Not even the ruins of an old one; only butcher shops. All we know is they revere their ancestors, trust in Ki, and fear the Dark

One."

"We'll watch for slaughterhouses, too," Stoker said, getting to his feet. "But if we don't get this wagon train out there we won't find anything."

"Good luck, Stoker. Shannon."

"Thanks, Chuck." Shannon said.

"Keep looking for that library," Stoker said as Chuck walked away toward the nearest trees.

The heat seemed more pronounced when they left the office. A light haze of dust hung in the air laced with the cloying scent of the purple-leafed tangari trees. Insects racketed in the trees and a non-bird futilely chased after something outracing it with six wings.

John Dowd ambled toward them, his face shaded beneath a wide-brimmed hat. His 6'5" solid frame was unmistakable. He was the tallest man in the Archaeology Department and youthful looking despite the fact he was retired security force.

"Yo, Stoker. Did that doc find you?"

"Yeah. Shannon and I talked to him for awhile."

"Him? The doc I'm talking about is definitely female and not hard to look at, either."

"Oh. Did you get a name?"

"Frasier. She didn't tell me her first name or her specialty."

"The only Doctor Frasier I know is an astronomer on *Magellan*, so it couldn't be her."

"Maybe she came down for a visit?" Shannon said with a wide grin. "Your raw animal magnetism pulls women out of the heavens–"

"Go check the vehicles," Stoker said abruptly. "See if everything is loaded. We have a long way to go and no road."

"Got it," she said, still grinning.

"Your people ready to move, John?"

"Yep. That's actually what I was coming over to tell you. Who's running the tracker up front?"

"Gorski, Spreter, and Goppert. You want a shot at it?"

"I'd be willing to help out if they need it. Putting in markers is always a pain in the ass. You have to worry about everyone who will come after."

"Which is exactly why I never operate the damned thing. Tell your team we'll be pulling out in the next fifteen minutes."

Dowd touched two fingers to the brim of his hat. "On my way, Boss."

Stoker turned and stared in the direction Shannon had gone. Sweat glued his shirt to his back and he knew it would be many hours before they could stop and rest. One hundred meters away Shannon walked out from behind the lead vehicle and jabbed her thumb in the air, a wide grin on her face.

He smiled and waved back, turned to check the rear of the column and collided with Dr. Melanie Frasier.

8
Coalition Star Ship Magellan

"Thank you all for your input. You are excused." Captain Laura Prescott sat back in her chair as her department heads got to their feet and ambled toward the main corridor.

Commander Geoff Peacock stopped near the captain. "If you have a few minutes there are some items I'd like to go over with you, skipper."

She glanced up and gave him a slight smile. "Sorry XO, I already have another short meeting scheduled. I'll get to you in about an hour, okay?"

"Certainly, captain. I'll catch up with you later."

As the officers filed out, she said, "Oh, Commander Caldwell, may I have a word?"

He stopped and allowed the Executive Officer and Commander Matt Mueller, the Science Officer, to move past him.

"Please shut the door, commander," Captain Prescott said as she rose to her feet.

"Yes, captain." He shut the door and quietly pushed the SECURE panel on the bulkhead. By the time he turned she had closed the distance between them and grabbed him at the same time he grabbed her.

They kissed long and deep.

"Will there be anything else, captain?" he whispered in a husky tone.

"Not now, dammit. We don't have time." She quickly kissed him again. "I'll see you tonight. Now get out of here."

"Aye, aye," he said through a leer. He tapped the lock and was through the door before she could say anything further.

She smiled and shook her head. Eric made her feel like a schoolgirl some times and a fulfilled woman other times. A low-pitched tone sounded.

"Yes, lieutenant, what is it?" Her voice activated the link to her aide, Lieutenant Rose Kalkoski.

"Captain, the director is on the comm link for you."

"Put her on my screen."

One wall of her office morphed into a holo tank. The uninitiated would have believed the Director of Planetary Operations was sitting in the room.

"How goes your day, director?"

"So far, so good." The director abruptly smiled. "But it's still early."

Laura chuckled at the time worn joke. This wasn't an emergency or the director would have immediately launched into the problem at hand.

"Is this a social call or do we have problems?"

"I'm not sure yet. My psyche team tells me that the Kians are becoming agitated."

Despite herself, Laura laughed. "The natives are restless? How can they tell?"

The director grinned. "Good question. I'm glad those fuzzy little farts don't play poker."

"Why do they feel the Kians are agitated?"

"First of all they are more reticent than ever. Even the talkative ones have lost interest in answering questions or conversation of any kind."

"Are we approaching a Kian holiday?"

"I don't think so, but I'll find out. I thought I knew all of their festival and holy days, but maybe I missed one. I actually hadn't thought of that angle."

Laura kept her silence but felt surprise that the director had missed so obvious a possibility and even more surprise that she would admit it. She finally realized that the perceived Kian agitation was bothering the Director of Planetary Operations more than the woman indicated.

"Is there anything I can do to help?"

The director sighed. "If there is I sure as hell don't know what it would be. I just wanted to give you a heads up on this thing. It might be nothing at all and I'm just being a nervous Nellie."

"Your ability to sense everything going on around you is legendary. I'm sure that's why you are the director. I hope you're correct about it possibly being nothing. But if change is afoot, forewarned is forearmed."

"Thank you for your trust, captain."

"Thank you for your confidence, director."

The holo tank winked away and Laura stood staring at the artfully disguised wall. They were only six months into their twenty-four month tour here and she wanted it all to be very conventional to the point of boredom.

No surprises, please!

Surprises this far from Coalition space tended to be bloc and deadly. Now she needed to go find out what was botherin Commander Peacock this time.

9

Siboth

t in the dust and rubbed her forehead. She had
_...ed to run into Dr. Payne, but not literally. She felt like a total
fool.

Strong hands grasped her arms and lifted her upright; they
continued to hold her gently but firmly.

"Are you all right?" Stoker asked.

The throbbing in her head slowly receded and she squinted at
him in the bright light.

"Oh, I'm fine." She closed her eyes for a moment and willed
the last of the pain to leave. Opening her eyes again, she smiled
at him. "I do apologize for not calling out and letting you know I
was approaching. You can let go now."

He released her.

"Hey, don't worry—"

"No, I feel so foolish. I only wanted to say 'hi' and wish you
well on your dig."

"Thanks. Why are you off the *Magellan*?"

"I've been given the observatory here on Kiana. Mixed
emotions, at the very least."

"There's an observatory here?"

She laughed. "You don't get out much, do you?"

"I tend to work a lot, drink a little, and get plenty of rest. If
someone opens a new pub, I usually hear about it. But I rarely
keep up with events in the other disciplines."

"What about the old 'We're all in this together,' stuff?"

"No argument there. But we all have our jobs to do, right?"

"True, and I need to let you get back to yours. Looks like
you're ready to pull out."

He glanced around at the seven-vehicle convoy.

"Yeah, I think we're finally ready to start. Thanks for coming
by. Are you staying at the observatory, wherever it is?"

"Not all the time. I'm also looking for a place in town. I was
told you had found a terrific flat and I wondered if you knew of
any others?"

"Ah ha, now we get to the ulterior motive!" He grinned
again.

Only one of them, she thought. She liked the way he looked, and smiled back.

He pulled his handpad out and quickly tapped something into it.

"There, I sent you the location of my landlord. She is a Kian scholar and very private. I don't know if she has any vacancies or not."

"Thanks! I'll treat you to dinner the next time you're in town."

"That will be about two weeks from now. I've a meeting scheduled with the director on the 16th of Gresh."

"That's something else I have to get used to – the Kian calendar."

"I'll send you a message the day before so you don't forget. It isn't often someone else makes me a meal."

"Oh, I don't cook. I'll *buy* you a meal at the pub of your choice."

"Okay, that works too. See ya!"

She watched him walk toward the front of the convoy and felt envious of those going with him.

"Speaking of work," she said glancing at her handpad. She had a half hour to get over to the landing zone if she wanted to talk to the astronomer she was replacing.

She waved down a lorry headed in that direction and asked the driver for a ride.

The woman jabbed a thumb at the other door in the cab. "Jump in. That's where I'm headed."

Melanie climbed into the cab and told the driver her name.

"Pleased to meet you. I'm Jenna Freibel from the Physical Science Department." She pushed the yoke forward and the huge lorry moved down the cobbled lane making a subdued purring sound.

"What's your specialty?" Melanie asked.

"Hydrology, the study of water and its movement."

"Shows you how insular I am. I had no idea anyone here was studying water."

Jenna laughed. "We even have people here studying fish, or what passes for them. What do you do?"

"I'm an astronomer. I've just been booted off the Magellan to take over the Kiana observatory."

"You don't sound happy about it."

"Studying stars from a planet when you could be on a star ship is analogous to you trying to study water on a star ship rather than on a planet."

"Yeah, I see your point. My husband is a Medic and fully trained firefighter."

"Are there many fires here?"

Jenna laughed. "No, and that pisses Tanner off. He says it's too quiet here to maintain a professional edge."

Melanie glanced around. "This is the first time I've spent any time at all on Kiana. What's it like?"

"Well, I think it beats hell out of living in a star ship, but I like fresh air and room to play soccer."

Jenna twisted the yoke and the lorry purringly turned onto a wider street lined with buildings. Tents and awnings covering tables filled with produce and crafts crowded the space between the buildings and the vehicle traffic. Humans and Kians swarmed through the tents, examining merchandise.

"Is it like this all the time?"

"Pretty much. Every ninth day is the Kian Sabbath and they mostly stay indoors. I've been to a couple of other planets and so far I like Kiana best."

"Where you from originally?"

"New Alaska. How about you?"

"There seem to be a lot people from your world in the Survey. I'm from Tolly III, Brad Olson City."

"I was there once. We did a hydrological study for a 'no-harm' dam. Did they ever build it?"

"No idea. I always had my face glued to a telescope when I lived there. I've noticed that all the powered vehicles are Coalition. Is there any industry here?"

"Not what we would call heavy industry. They mine what looks like iron ore but it's slightly different according to the metallurgists. They smelt it and make tools, implements, and things like nails and fasteners."

"Weapons?"

"The only weapons I've seen here are those carried by our security forces. The Kians are the most docile people I've ever met. I came out on the *Jedediah Smith*, the second starship to visit after contact so I've been here four years. I've never seen a Kian react violently even when provoked."

"Any natural enemies?"

"There are some weird non-sapient predators out on the plains and a different kind up in the mountains. The Kians avoid them but a couple of humans have been killed by them." Jenna abruptly stopped talking.

"What?"

"Well, I just remembered that one of the humans killed was an astronomer, up at the observatory."

"What?" Melanie felt her blood chill. No wonder Dr. Buderka sent her here; it was unsafe!

"There is a local version of a wolf, well, wolf crossed with a panther, called *jingroe* by the Kians. One of them got inside the observatory and killed the astronomer on duty."

"When did this occur?"

"About six weeks after they finished building the observatory. It's been about three and a half years since it happened."

"Why don't they warn people transitioning to the planet about this stuff?"

Jenna glanced at her and then gave her attention back to the streets. "Have you processed through with the DPO's office? They are supposed to give you the heads up on the whole situation here."

Melanie felt her cheeks warm. "No, no I haven't gotten to that yet."

"Phew! I was afraid they were starting to drop personnel planet-side without giving them the scoop. Kiana is different enough from other Coalition worlds to kill you if you're unaware of the dangers."

"What else can kill you here? Should I be taking notes?"

"They'll give you a hard copy manual as well as the stuff you already have in your handpad."

Melanie blushed again; she hadn't even checked her handpad for information on Kiana. She gave herself a mental slap. If she didn't pay attention down here she could end up very dead and look stupid in the process.

"Don't eat any plants with purple leaves. They all have caustic compounds that will kill you and hurt like hell while you're dying. Ask for a sidearm to deal with the wild nasties out in the wilderness, and then practice with it."

"Actually I have a hand laser and qualified as a marksman a

few years ago. I would go to the ship's range when I was extra pissed off, so you could say I'm okay on that score."

Jenna laughed. "Good. That takes a lot of worry off my shoulders. Didn't want a fellow human running around defenseless down here."

"Thank you for your concern," Melanie said, "I'm not used to that."

"You're used to being up there," Jenna nodded toward the sky. "Things are different down here since we didn't build this environment to suit us."

Melanie thought about that for a long moment. It almost shocked her to realize she had blithely assumed that the only difference between being on the Magellan or on the planet surface was a layer of atmosphere that would make her tasks more difficult.

I've got to get my head out of my ass!

She looked around at the street through which they passed with new eyes. This place didn't look anything like Brad Olson City or anywhere else she had ever been. She forced herself to note the differences.

Blue trees; they were everywhere. There were other hues in the flora around her, some green, red here and there, and a rather lovely bush with red stems and bright yellow leaves. But the blue dominated.

The buildings were mostly one level, but a few two-story and even one three-story structure could be seen from her current vantage point. Native stone seemed to be the prevalent construction material but some of the single story buildings appeared to have large pieces of wood in their construction. About a third of them featured sculpture and bass-relief carvings on their facades.

Although Jenna wasn't driving at a high rate of speed, it was difficult for Melanie to make out the subject matter of the carvings and artwork. The Kians themselves were a swirling rainbow of color. Most wrapped themselves in billowing lengths of light cloth that seemed to be one piece.

Many had one shoulder bared and some of the males were bared to the waist. Children went from coverings head to foot to barely a diaper covering their small bodies. An image from a survey class on Ancient Earth popped into her mind. The humans were of a uniform color and wore garments like these.

"The South Pacific," she said.

"What's that?" Jenna asked.

"The Kians dress like people from the South Pacific on Ancient Earth."

"I'll have to take your word for it. Never studied much about Earth."

"I've always wanted to visit, see where we all originated."

Jenna shrugged. "If you've seen one park world you've seen them all. I wouldn't mind seeing it, but you have to sign up and pay two years in advance without refund if life gets in the way and you can't make it."

"Point taken. And who knows what they'll be doing in two years?"

"Rich people," Jenna said through her easy smile, "…who happen to be the only ones who can afford the price of admittance any way."

"What kind of cloth do the Kians use to make their clothes?"

"It's a fiber that grows in these temperate zones. The color you get depends on when it's harvested. Dark blue and green are the most expensive because the plant is very small when harvested for those colors and takes more of them to make a garment. Red, yellow, and orange are the cheapest."

"Prettiest, too," Melanie said. "I heard they have pubs here."

"Yeah. The Kians are excellent brewers. They make a wicked liquor that knocks you on your ass after the second one. I prefer their ales, haven't had any that can compare on any other planet."

"Which pub is your favorite?"

"A place called Chiem Sau. Got no idea what it means but it's about a block behind us."

The lorry slowed to a stop.

"There's the landing zone. Looks like they're starting to load."

"Oh damn! Hey, thanks for the ride and the great information. I owe you a drink the next time we run into each other. Maybe I'll see you at the pub."

"Works for me! Take care."

"Will do!" Melanie jumped to the ground and jogged toward the landing zone. As she neared the small group of people waiting to go aboard she noticed one person stood away from the others, glancing around.

When the person looked in her direction she waved frantically. For the third time in less than an hour she felt like an idiot. She puffed up to the man who peered at her.

"You are Doctor Frasier?" he asked in a clipped Polska accent.

"Y, yes, sorry to be, so late in arriving." She stopped and caught her breath. "And you are..."

"Darun Bukowski. I have operated the observatory for the past nine months."

"Is there a staff?"

He gave her a quick smirk, and glanced away for a moment. "You are it. The good part is that you have your own quarters, which I cleaned before I left. The bad part is you have to maintain the entire facility by yourself unless you can put up with the chattering AI. I downloaded the manuals onto the micronet for the facility."

He looked down at her hip. "Good, you're armed. If you have a chance to kill a jingroe, do it! They're vicious."

A loud note sounded three times and an unseen speaker intoned, "All non-passengers exit the landing zone."

Bukowski smiled and waved. "I must go. Good fortune!" He turned and moved quickly toward the rear hatch on the shuttle.

Melanie raised her hand to wave back but he had already disappeared into the craft. The heat of the day seemed to magnify.

"Well, that was fun," she said. "We'll have to do this again." She turned away, pulled her handpad out to read the address Dr. Payne had sent her, and started walking.

Fa Suura proved to be a small, female Kian of indeterminate age. Upon meeting, the diminutive female lifted her hands, palm to palm, to her forehead, closed her eyes and pulled her hands apart as they moved down to waist level where they stopped palms up and side by side.

"I am open to you," she said in a low voice. "How may Fa Suura enrich your life?"

Melanie had never been this close to a Kian before. If pressed she would admit that she tended to avoid aliens. But she also realized that here on Kiana *she* was the alien.

Fa Suura came to Melanie's shoulder, which put the Kian's height at approximately five feet. She was tall for a Kian. Her visible body was completely covered by short golden brown hair that appeared soft.

Dark patterns colored the hair on her arms and cheeks, resembling the tattoos some spacers affected. Her slim build helped to accentuate the illusion of large eyes compared to her skull size.

Not wanting to mimic Fa Suura's hand gesture but feeling the need to do something, Melanie put her right hand to her chest and slightly bowed.

"I am Melanie Frasier and I am pleased to meet you." She realized she had not answered the Kian's question, or *was* it a question? She was tired of feeling stupid.

Thankfully, Fa Suura nodded.

Emboldened, Melanie plunged forward.

"Dr. Stoker Payne told me he has rented an apartment, living quarters, from you and he very much likes it. I would like to know if you have any other apartments for let?"

"You desire a dwelling here in Siboth, yes?"

"Yes!"

"Four possibilities exist for you to choose if you desire."

"Are they in the same location where Dr. Payne lives?"

Fa Suura gave her a long, measuring look, staring straight into Melanie's eyes, and, she felt, into her soul.

"Is that your wish, Melanie Frasier?" The soft voice drug out her name, giving each word more syllables than they normally possessed. It would be impossible to fool this person.

Melanie relaxed and smiled. "Yes, Fa Suura, that is my wish."

10
Siboth

Danny Gordon hurried through the market place, his eyes flicked from one violet *chamalla* to the next. Su Laana loved the color and wore it while selling her art objects. Danny was supposed to be overseeing the purchase of local grain and then arrange for milling it into flour.

The thought of her made his heart beat even faster and he remembered vividly the day they met.

He had been slowly making his way through the market place reveling in the exotic smells, sounds, and colorful sights around him. Without a doubt he knew he had the best Coalition job possible. Every day he found himself in contact with Kians of all ages and both sexes as a procurement specialist.

Somewhere a Kian was playing a haunting melody on a *dobris*, a stringed instrument with a sounding board that added a lamenting reverberation to the current tune. A flute joined in and the combination lent yet another exotic touch to the scene.

That afternoon he had an appointment to see Dö Laani, one of the few merchants who dealt in exotic grains and the obscure minerals used in electronic devices and other arcane machines. If it was difficult to find, he was the Kian to see; or at least that was what Danny had been told by other Kians.

Unlike many of the merchants, Dö Laani had an "office" in one of the beautifully built stone buildings. Thus far Siboth was the only Kian city Danny had visited personally. But the holos available of the other towns and cities on Kiana looked basically identical to this one.

The Coalition had selected Siboth as the site for its official building because of its size and location on the planet. There seemed to be no Kian government or officials of any sort, yet they lived in a harmony totally alien to the Coalition and the few other races thus far encountered since the early years of the Great Diaspora.

The office he sought was in the middle of the teeming market place. Canopies billowed and fluttered in the breeze, sheltering merchants and customers from the hot summer sun. Tables and racks offered native Kian vegetables and fruits as well as produce whose origins were almost as distant as Danny's.

Some Kian men as well as many women with children thronged the area, chatting and bargaining. The Kian economy remained puzzling to the Coalition visitors since there seemed to be no native currency or coinage. Barter dominated all commerce, which made his job even more interesting.

Clothing, scarves, jewelry, home and field utensils, carvings, castings, footwear, and light mesh bags for carrying any and all of it vied for the discerning shoppers attention. Food stalls provided meat and vegetables on skewers as well as melon slices and halved fruits for the hungry.

His handpad beeped and he knew he had reached his destination. Carefully he wound his way through the tables and kiosks to get to the arched doorway. A table strewn with jewelry sat against the wall next to the entry. A Kian female broke off a conversation with two other women and turned to him.

"You finally made it to my table! I was beginning to think you wouldn't." Her wide eyes and easy smile struck a chord in him. Many humans thought the Kians a comely race, attractive in every possible way. Danny was one of them.

"Actually I was seeking the business place of Dö Laani. But I would be pleased to see what you have to offer." As soon as he heard his words he blushed.

"That is, I would be pleased to see what you are selling."

Her laughter stopped his fumbling and he wondered why he had suddenly become so tongue-tied.

"You would like to sample my wares, sir?" Her voice held mockery and humor.

"I would like to examine the crafts you have for barter." He pointed at the table and gave her his best smile. She was by far the most attractive Kian he had yet met and he felt his pulse accelerate.

Her smile elicited an additional beat from his heart as she reached down and picked up a few bracelets and rings. He took the opportunity to admire her profile and dark, lustrous hair. Her light body hair, some humans called it "fur," was an overall tan with slightly darker designs on her arms and neck. He wondered if the designs were intentional or something arbitrary she gained at birth.

In total he found her exotic sexuality profoundly disturbing and decided he wanted to formally meet her: but how?

"...and this stone is from the island of Mun and quite rare. Are you listening, sir? You seem distracted."

"I am on my way to a business meeting and I think I am already late. Will you still be here in an hour or so?"

One of her eyebrows elevated slightly as she studied his face. He wondered if he was somehow being impertinent. Her smile had dimmed to an attractive smirk and her dark eyes seemed to dance with amusement.

"Most certainly I will still be here. We do not close until the light fades and meals are needed."

"My name is Danny and I will be back as soon as I can. Okay?"

"Oh-kay, Dan-nay," she said and laughed. She slapped her hand to her mouth and both eyes rounded. "I did not mean mockery with the word rhyme."

He nodded slightly. "No mockery perceived. May I know your name?"

"Su Laana. Have a prosperous meeting."

She stepped back while he turned and went through the wide stone entrance. The dim interior was nearly chilly after the intense heat outside. High ceilings gave the impression of vast space.

A row of beautifully inlaid desks staggered through the room and behind each sat a Kian. Women occupied three desks and the other four by men. Most were busy but Danny couldn't see what they were doing.

One old man with a smile on his face sat staring at him.

This then, must be Dö Laani.

Danny walked over and stopped in front of him.

"Good afternoon, sir. I am Danny Gordon, are you Dö Laani?"

The man clasped his hands, palm to palm, and lifted them to his forehead. After closing his eyes he pulled the hands apart as he dropped them to waist level where they stopped palms up, side by side.

"I am open to you," he said in a medium voice. "How may Dö Laani enrich your life?"

Danny nodded. "I hope we may enrich both our lives, sir. My people have need of these substances," he handed the old man a sheet of paper with a list in Standard English. "If you would like a translation I–"

"There is no need, I comprehend this. My friend, Åt Sånnk, advised me of your needs and imminent arrival. Some of these minerals are very rare and you wish a large quantity. What do you propose to trade for them?"

"What would you need?"

"My needs are few, Mr. Gordon, and most are met."

Danny smiled, relishing the exchange. "What then would you *like*?"

Dö Laani smiled back. "I am a student of the stars and the age of my eyes precludes the clear discernment I once enjoyed. What would be the chances of obtaining a one meter reflecting telescope and structure to house it?"

Danny felt his jaw drop before he regained control. "That is something I would have to investigate with my superiors. May I have a day before I answer?"

"By all means. Take two if you must."

"Thank you, sir. I will return as soon as I have more information."

Dö Laani touched his left hand to his forehead. "May wonder follow you, Mr. Gordon."

Danny started to turn away and then stopped.

"Sir, may I ask a question about your customs?"

"Of course."

"How does a young man go about meeting a young woman of your people, formally, I mean?"

"To what end?"

"I, I don't know yet. I think she is the most beautiful woman I have ever met and would like to spend time with her, honorably, of course."

"Do you know the name of this beautiful woman?"

"Su Laana."

Dö Laani blinked. "You would begin by asking her father permission to pay court to her. Then you would have to ask her if she is interested in you."

"I see. Do you know who her father is and where I might find him?"

"You are very serious about this, are you not? Most young humans, male or female, merely make their propositions to the object of their interest and events transpire from there. Why do you ask about custom when there are possibly more expedient paths available?"

"Because I think she could be very important to me and I want to follow her customs and honor her ways."

"You are a remarkable young man, Mr. Gordon. You have my permission to honor my daughter with your presence."

For a moment Danny's mind went totally blank before the meaning of Dö Laani's words hit him.

"Oh! You are her, uh, she is your daughter?"

"Something of that nature." Dö Laani's grin went from ear to ear. His focus shifted to a point behind Danny.

Danny turned to see Su Laana walk through the door. The bright light limned her, turning her chamalla nearly transparent, and he felt his pulse quicken again. Realizing he was staring, he turned back to Dö Laani, face flaming.

The old man laughed loudly and waved to his daughter. When she joined the men her father nodded toward Danny.

"This young man has asked your father to formally introduce him to you. His name is Danford Gordon and he is a procurement specialist for the Coalition."

Su Laana stiffened. "*Procurement* specialist? Exactly what do you *procure*, Mr. Gordon?"

"I locate food, minerals, clothing, building materials, pretty much anything needed by the Coalition surveyors while we are here."

Father and daughter exchanged a look that Danny couldn't fathom. Su Laana gravely regarded Danny and then smiled.

"I am very pleased to meet you, Dan-nay Gordon." She held out her hand and he shook it, touched that she honored his customs.

Over the next weeks he visited her every evening after which he would decorously return to his quarters in the Coalition compound. After four weeks she said, "Let us find an apartment where we can share the nights together. Would that please you?"

One of his friends had asked him why he wanted to cohabitate with an alien when there were human women available.

All he could say was, "In some strange way she completes me, and I like that."

He knew many humans looked askance at them when they were together. It didn't matter what everyone else thought. He knew she was the perfect woman for him.

He stopped his mad dash through the market. A glance at the sun told him he had to get back to his assistants before they returned to the Coalition Compound. Someone giggled behind him. He twisted around and she was smiling at him, her dark eyes slightly squinted in the strong summer light.

"Why are you here, Dan-nay? You still have hours to work."

He moved up to her, careful to not touch her in public. Kians were somewhat conservative in their public behavior and he didn't want to give offense this late in the game.

"I knew you were near the grain sellers and I wanted to see you before I go back to my office. Have you sold any of your work?"

"Exchanges have been made, yes. I have a surprise for you when you return to our apartment this afternoon."

Danny willed himself not to look around. He loved surprises and they often gave each other gifts. He grinned while filling his eyes with her.

"All I want when I get home is you."

"Apartment, not yet a home," she said gently to take the sting out of the reproof.

"You know what I mean. I must go." He pursed his lips as if to kiss her and then hurried away.

Her laughter followed him and it felt good.

11
Siboth

"Microphone check," Stoker Payne said.

"Vehicle One," Tom Gorski's confident voice intoned.

"Vehicle Two," Shannon Gray said.

"Vehicle Three," Bill Hilton said with a chuckle.

Stoker was the talker in Vehicle Four, in the middle of the column.

"Vehicle Five," John Dowd said and cracked the gum he constantly chewed.

"Vehicle Six," Marilyn Culpepper said in her happy chirp.

"Vehicle Seven, filling out the load," Charly Herring said as reassuringly as possible.

"You all know the drill, we've done this before in other places. The rules haven't changed. Let's go find history." Stoker tried to rein in his enthusiasm and be more professional, but like every dig prior to this one, he was excited and couldn't help but show it.

As one, the lifter fans on all seven vehicles whined into life, throwing blue and yellow tinged dust into a cloud around them. The vehicles lifted gently off their tires that slowly retracted up into the wheel wells to lend better aerodynamics to the huge floaters.

Charly Herring operated the largest floater. It carried two tons of gear and supplies in addition to the office module and three Dualtranz on its massive cargo deck. He also carried four Kian passengers in the large crew cab with him.

The Kians had all appeared on the same day and asked Shannon if they could help the humans discover their ancestors. After Stoker and Shannon decided there was nothing to lose and perhaps much to gain, they asked the director. She immediately agreed with them.

Every floater bulged with cargo, supplies, and personal effects, except the lead floater. The tracker floater carried the most electronics and had the responsibility of following a predetermined route in order to "shoot" sensor stakes into the ground every thirty meters. The sensors would effectively become an electronic road that lone floaters and Dualtranz could navigate without fear of becoming lost in the vast southern plains of Cimpar.

The majority of the grunt work had been accomplished over the previous five days. Configuring the relays and position checks on each unit and then loading it into the probe assist magazine was taxing mentally as well as physically. Half a kilometer from the last street in Siboth, Tom Gorski slowed the tracker.

"Probe one planted now." A loud thrum could be heard over the comm system as the air cannon shot the probe beacon into the soil of Cimpar. Moments later he reported, "Probe one planted and on line."

In the command floater Stoker relaxed against the back of his bucket seat. Weeks ago a survey team had sampled every probe location and planted a target beacon chip. The surveyors had kept detailed records on the soil consistency, depth of penetrable soil and location of rock formations that might cause a probe to "bounce" if hit.

A bouncing probe made for a bad day in the scout floater, perhaps even a deadly day. A great deal of hard work had already gone into this expedition and much more was to come.

"Probe three planted and on line."

"Dr. Payne, why doesn't the scout just go ahead of everyone else by a day or two and speed up the entire operation?" Michele Ramey, one of the more voluptuous doctoral candidates, asked.

"We lost a tracker vehicle and crew on Foster II because in those days they didn't do a survey first, and they bounced a probe, wrecking the vehicle. There was nobody else out there to help them and the local fauna, previously unknown, killed and devoured them."

Michele's bronzed features paled.

"Probe nine planted and on line."

Besides Michele, Stoker had four other team members in his floater. Stuart Currie, a brilliant chemical archaeologist, was piloting during the first watch. Joyce Mayer and Doug Franklin, the only married couple in the crew, had both gone to sleep in their bed nets hanging from the overhead in the back of the compartment. Both swung back and forth with the movement of the floater.

Bennie Benedict sat in the control bubble with Stuart, watching everything through the all but invisible plasteel. Next to him was the hatch to the heavy laser mounted on the roof. If anything threatened the column Bennie would be the first to confront it.

Stoker rested his eyes.

"Probe thirteen planted and on line."

Michele began snoring.

12
Coalition Star Ship Magellan

"I have notice a thing that gives me wonder," Senior Chief Communications Technician Mongo Tschurtoff said.

"What might that be, Mongo?" Master Chief Shipfitter's Mate Patrick Murphy said as he took another drink of his bitter.

"When the officer's leave the captain's conference room, all them look serious like, except Commander Caldwell. He is always seem happy."

"Maybe she gave him good quarterly marks?"

"I think no. He always shut door after others leave. He always leave after all the others, when he come out looking happy."

"Okay, Mongo, let me get this straight. Sometimes your unique grasp of Standard English eludes your meaning. You talking one time or a lot of times?"

"All the time is my meaning. Ever since I take over day shift in Officer Country I see this happen every time."

"Hmm. Well, I know what the reason it would be if it were me and some willing little barmaid. But I think there are regs against that sort of fraternization on a starship, ain't there? Hell I'm just an old knuckle buster from the lower decks, and–"

"Is sort of rule against it; Book say, 'Unwanted personal attention from an officer or petty officer toward a subordinate is prohibited by Coalition regulation.' But it say nothing if attention *is* wanted. However, 'a commanding officer may not participate in a personal relationship with a member of their chain of command.'"

"You give me the creeps when you pull shit out of your head like that, Mongo. You even get the diction right."

"It is memory trick. That is what the regs say. But the point of my saying is that I think Commander Caldwell is liking what the captain is doing when they are behind the closed door."

Chief Murphy glanced around and lowered his voice. "Well the skipper ain't exactly hard to look at and I'd bet a year's worth of pay that there ain't a man on this ball of atmosphere wouldn't love to rattle a rack with her."

"I think you just agree with my thoughts?"

"Yeah, guess I do. I need a bit of proof, though. No call for me to be in Officer's Country but I have my ways of finding out if things are or aren't. Keep your eyes open, Mongo my friend."

"This I will do, friend Patrick. But caution should be enjoined or you could lose privileges."

"Where did you learn to speak Standard English?"

"I am student of diligent self study, does it not show?"

"It sure as shit does."

Commander Geoff Peacock cast a dark look at LCdr Parson Lawson. "There's something going on between those two. Either he's after my job or they're making the beast with two backs."

"As long as they have the door shut there's no way of telling," Lawson said, leaning back in his leather chair and scratching his belly.

"That's why I want you to have your people put a couple of bug eyes in the wardroom."

Lawson straightened up. "That's something that could cut two ways, commander. If the captain discovers them she'd have our guts for garters."

"Women don't look at their environment in that way, Parson. They only worry if the wall is painted the wrong shade of color or if the drapes match the carpet."

"What drapes?"

"Don't be so damn literal. I'm speaking metaphorically. Women worry about the sanitary and aesthetic aspects of a space, not actual components."

"She's a damn smart woman."

"Who doesn't know her place!"

Lawson rubbed his jaw and relaxed back into the soft leather. "It must be hard for you, coming from a planet like Joseph Smith's World, to deal with the way the Coalition operates."

Peacock stared hard at his subordinate for a long moment. The headache was back and even more painful than before. He rubbed his head. Like it or not he was going to have to see a corpsman about it.

"You don't find it galling to have women ordering you around? Scripture states that woman is vessel to man and as far as I'm concerned scripture trumps Coalition regulations every time."

"Didn't you take an oath to obey all officers put over you, Sir? I know I did."

"Of course I did, otherwise I would have put her in her place long ago."

"And now you want to spy on her."

"Let us just say that I suspect Coalition regulations are being violated, no matter who is doing it. It is my sworn duty to investigate in any manner I so choose."

Lawson chuckled. "Well, since you put it that way, Mr. Executive Officer, I don't see any way of arguing further on the subject. I'll have two of my best techs install a couple of 'eyes' and record everything that transpires in the Wardroom."

"Excellent, Commander Lawson. I will not forget your able assistance in this matter."

Lawson pushed himself up out of the chair. "I just hope that turns out to be a good thing."

After LCdr Lawson left the office, Commander Peacock muttered, "Whatever is good for me is the *best* thing for you."

13
Siboth

Melanie walked from her bedroom through her tiny dining room and into her kitchen for the twentieth time since she had taken possession of the small flat. She loved the feel of the stone floor under her bare feet: all uneven, smooth, and cool, yet solid as a Coalition contract. The bouquet of unknown flowers sitting on her wide windowsill made her dream of bazaars she had visited on distant worlds.

Everything felt deliciously alien, slightly dangerous, and fun. The best part was that Stoker Payne lived across the garden area that was created in the center of the massive square building. She suddenly realized that by barring the street level door, this structure could be turned into a quite defensible fortress.

She loved the view from her second floor windows and wondered who lived in the apartment beneath her. The sprawling street markets lay in all directions and with her binoculars she could see who arrived and departed the landing zone. The building exuded age and history. Melanie felt very fortunate to have secured this picaresque apartment and hoped she hadn't made a fool of herself with Stoker.

Time would tell. Now she had to check in with the director's office. After that she hoped to be left alone so she could get her work done. With a final glance around her quarters she pulled the door shut and latched it. There seemed no way to actually lock it.

The Coalition Department of Planetary Operations building sat next to the landing zone and she took her time getting there. As she idled through the stalls and shops she tried to discern what the local medium of exchange might be. The Kians seemed to privately reach a mutual understanding, as she didn't see anything exchanged for the goods carried away.

Finally she arrived at the gate. Two Coalition Security Force members stood at attention on either side of the secured entry.

"Excuse me. I am Doctor Melanie Frasier–"

The gate abruptly swung open and a voice from somewhere inside the compound intoned, "You are expected, Dr. Frasier. In fact you are late. Do come in."

Feeling more than slightly nonplused and nettled, she passed between the two guards who had neither looked at her nor even responded to her presence.

This is a bit much under the circumstances!

A small, muscular woman with the darkest skin Melanie had ever seen stood waiting a few steps inside the gate. Her face seemed placid but power and strength radiated from her compact frame. Melanie stopped in front of her.

"I am Amanda Saint-Claire, Chief of Staff for the Director of Planetary Operations."

"I am honored and surprised, Ms. Saint-Claire," Melanie said, wishing she could dismiss the fear rapidly stealing over her.

"You are a new department head, therefore it is fitting you receive welcome and admonition from someone of like rank."

Melanie knew the question lay evident on her face; words would be redundant.

"You should have come here first as both a courtesy and a precaution. Your negligence has been noted in your records. I also wish you to understand that any communications with the director are to come through me, no one else; I vet all correspondence as the director is a very busy person."

Melanie felt her Scot's blood burning in her face.

"I was not informed by anyone on the *Magellan* of a requirement to *report* here upon arrival. There isn't much I can do about what notations are put in my record but it has always been my understanding that I would always have the legal right to counter any negative entries. Your protocol for communications is understood and I will adhere to your dictate. Are we finished?"

"My, you *do* have a temper. Did not Dr. Buderka instruct you to report here immediately after planet fall?"

"No. She seemed more interested in getting me off the *Magellan* than in anything I would do after leaving. Did she say otherwise?"

"No. But it is standard operating procedure for shipboard personnel to be briefed prior to embarking. Since that was not the case in your situation I retract my admonition and beg your pardon."

Melanie successfully stifled her immediate laugh response. As if this woman would ever *beg* her for anything!

She swallowed and looked away for an instant. "Thank you for understanding, Ms. Saint-Claire."

"Think nothing of it. Now allow me to introduce you to the director."

Melanie nodded and matched Saint-Claire's rapid gait.

"Does the director have a name?"

Saint-Clare flashed a gimlet eye over one shoulder and turned away again. "She answers most willingly to '*Director.*'"

"I understand."

Once inside the large structure the atmosphere eased from forbidding to "diplomatic comfortable." Doorframes and wainscoting boasted exotic woods in an effort to visually warm the cold stone construction. Tapestries and formal portraits covered the walls as far as the eye could determine.

Melanie understood this was both an embassy and a headquarters of matters Coalition. As far as she knew, the Kians had nothing to compare with this compound. She pondered the significance of that lack and nearly collided with Amanda when the small woman abruptly stopped.

"This is the director's office."

Melanie wondered if she actually heard reverence in Saint-Claire's voice.

Amanda pushed the door open and motioned for Melanie to precede her.

The director stood when Melanie entered and moved around the desk with her hand outstretched.

"Dr. Frasier, I am so pleased to meet you."

She actually sounds sincere! "And I am pleased to meet you, director."

"Amanda, would you be so kind and get us some iced tea? And get yourself a glass, also."

"Yes, director."

"Do have a seat." The director waved toward a couch flanked by two chairs in the far corner. All were beautifully done in soft leather.

"Thank you." Melanie chose one of the chairs and the director sat in the other.

"So whom did you piss off up there?" the director jerked her head skyward and smiled knowingly.

Melanie abruptly had a coughing fit. The tea delivered by Amanda helped calm her throat. Amanda eased down onto the couch.

"Has everyone down here 'pissed off' someone on the *Magellan?*"

"Only those arriving in the last month or so. All other planet-side personnel either asked for their jobs or it was their designated mission." The director shrugged. "This late in the game, well, you must have pissed someone off, of high rank obviously since you have a doctorate."

Melanie made a mental shrug. "I was told that you are perceptive. Somehow I offended Dr. Buderka, the head of the astronomy department, and she shit-canned me."

The director laughed out loud. "I like you, Melanie. You tell it like it is."

"Well, there's not much else they can do to me, is there?"

"How do you like it down here so far?"

"Quite a bit, which surprises me. I even found a lovely apartment over in the old part of town."

"Already? You must have known somebody."

"Sort of. So what do I need to know to make this assignment a success?"

Approval radiated from the director's eyes. "Keep my office informed of your situation at the observatory. Make sure you go through all the procedures downloaded to your handpad, and if you don't already have a hand weapon, get one."

"I have a marksman rating with my hand laser."

"Superb! We know you can hit what you aim at. Have you ever killed with it?"

"Pardon me?"

"Have you ever killed any living thing with your hand laser?"

"No. But I'm a good shot."

"All I can tell you is don't hesitate if you are being threatened by an unfamiliar animal. Some people do hesitate at killing a living creature and we think that's why one of your predecessors lost his life."

"I've been warned about the jingroes, director. I really don't think I would have any hesitation about killing one."

"Did your informant tell you they were beautiful, sleek, and fast?"

"No, that wasn't mentioned."

"That's why you can't hesitate; they are incredibly quick."

"I appreciate the information."

"Unfortunately the human threats come in all shapes, sizes and colors, and of course you can't kill them." The director's hard, dark eyes belied her warm smile. "Pay attention to your AI."

"What about the Kians, are they dangerous?"

"Not physically to our knowledge. We've been here nearly five years and they have yet to divulge their philosophy or history with us. We know they worship a deity they refer to as Ki, sounds like 'key' but it is spelled kay-eye.

"Why they worship this entity or what it supposedly did has never been established. They have shared no origin legends. No human has ever seen two or more Kians in an argument. So far they are the most docile race the Coalition has ever encountered."

Some of this Melanie had heard from Jenna.

"I wonder how they became the dominant species if they are so docile?" Melanie said, almost to herself.

"Exactly!" the director said. "We know the jingroes are intelligent to a point, yet these meek little furry folk are the species that ended up building towns and wearing clothes. This is all very perplexing."

"I understand you have archaeological digs under way. Do you think that will answer any fundamental questions?"

"We certainly hope so!" the director narrowed her eyes. "How did you happen to come across *that* bit of information?"

"Doctor Payne is an old friend of mine." Melanie tried to keep her emotions completely neutral. "I ran into him just after I arrived dirtsi–, ah, on planet."

"From that lovely flush on your cheeks it must have been an interesting meeting."

"You don't miss anything, do you, director?"

"Not if I can help it, Doctor Frasier."

14
Southern Plains of Cimpar
Dig N-19

Stoker Payne sat in the office staring at his holo screen as he keyed through one page after another. He scanned each report, diagram, and list just long enough to establish that nothing had changed from the last time he had viewed the information before advancing to the next document.

This was the price of leadership, he thought, *dealing with this mundane bullshit while others actually get their hands dirty.*

His handpad pinged and he waved it active.

"Yeah?"

"Stoker, Shannon. We're down to the ten-meter level on the access trench. Can I give the level bosses the go ahead to start their teams?"

"Are all the scaffolds and ladders secure?"

"Do you really think I would be asking you for a go ahead if they weren't?"

"Sorry, Shannon. I think I might be feeling sorry for myself."

"Hey, just leave the office and get your ass out here. There's more to bossing a dig than staring at that damn holo screen."

"Give them all a thumbs up. I'll be out in a few to admire your handiwork."

"Thanks, Stoker!"

His handpad went silent when she cut her transmission. He sighed, grabbed his hat and forced himself to get out of the chair and leave the office.

A kraal of vehicles surrounded the office trailer. Inside the wide circle of machines intermingled with collapsible barriers were two rows of tents where the teams slept, a large tent that served as a commissary, and a larger tent that housed their supplies and shops for repairing tools, weapons, and even clothing.

On the four cardinal points of the compass were guards whose job was to watch for anything unknown or situations that could pose a threat to the personnel or mission of the dig. All guards sat behind heavy laser weapons capable of shooting craft out of low planet orbit.

Stoker loved being in the field; it was what he was born to do. He took a deep breath, smelling the heat as well as the plethora of scents wafting from the wildflowers. Outside the kraal wild grasses and intermittent shrubs grew as high as a meter.

On their way here they had flushed numerous small mammal type creatures but none of the dreaded jingroes. One creature had large, nearly translucent ears and very formidable teeth. The survey crew decided to call them "radars" after watching one detect a large insect at nearly 200 meters only to race over, leap into the air, and bring it down. It immediately ate its catch.

Since the radars were only about a foot long their frenetic behavior made for hilarity among the crew.

"I wouldn't want one of those little bastards biting me," Gorski commented.

"It would just spit you out or die," Dowd had said with a laugh.

They didn't have to worry about vermin, large insects, or even jingroes inside the perimeter of the kraal. A subsonic barrier undetectable to human and Kian ears kept the lower order creatures at a distance. Not even the not-bird flying mammals would soar over the compound.

Stoker Payne left the tent town and walked out to the long trench cut into the ground. Pennants hooked to tall poles marked the locations where one could safely descend down to the working levels of the dig. He chose the one in the middle.

He carefully inspected everything as he entered the dig. Despite his furious shaking of the metal stairs and guardrails, nothing came loose or even threatened to do more than shiver.

That's why Shannon is my crew honcho; she doesn't cut the wrong corners.

A fine mist of dust hung in the air as archaeologists worked their tools toward the area where the ground penetrating radar had indicated large masses of bone and artifacts. Heat seemed to bake the dust into a mass that could not be respirated nor dissipated.

The subliminal whine of molecular sorters filled the air. Not until they encountered actual bones or artifacts would the airbrushes add their shushing to the ambiance of the collective effort. Already the teams had penetrated over a meter into the soil of Kiana.

The stairs and ramps provided for seven levels. Each level had a boss and four or five person team. Levels five, six, and seven each had a five person team as those were determined to be the most heavily laden with artifacts.

In ancient times archaeologists started at the surface of a dig and slowly went downward, one painstaking layer after another. But with the GPR and AI assisted imaging programs they could accurately read the depth of forms within a centimeter plus or minus down to a ten meter depth. So Stoker's crew had dug a trench and the various crews were in the process of tunneling in to the object previously determined as their goal.

If their estimates proved wrong or the goal turned out to be nothing of interest, people would be transferred to other levels as needed. As Stoker reached level five he heard the abrupt whine of a sorter encountering metal.

He spoke into his headset, "Which level found the artifact?"

"The very top of seven, Boss."

Stoker didn't recognize the voice but he hurried down to the bottom of the trench. By the time he got there all the sorters on that level had ceased and the hushing admonition of the airbrushes filled the air. A knot of on-lookers surrounded three people cleaning the area around the find.

"What do we have?"

Shannon turned from the other on-lookers and gave him a wide grin. "A first on Kiana, Stoker. It seems to be a manufactured weapon."

The others pulled back and he moved up to the find. Lying in situ, the artifact had obviously been some type of a rifle or other long arm. Something had impacted it as the barrel angled downward in the middle, bent but not broken.

No projectile or beam he could imagine could be fired through a weapon as bent as this one, and weapon it was. Rust flaked off the exposed surface permeating the soil beneath the artifact.

"Have you already got the lab on this?"

"We just found it, Stoker," Shannon said, punching him lightly on the shoulder. "The lab folks are on their way."

"Good. Everyone get back at it. If there's one–"

Their collective shout drowned out his voice "–there's more!"

They all laughed and went back to their molecular sorters.

Stoker wondered why he was even here. Not only was he in the way, they already knew what he would say next.

The metallurgist arrived with her crew and began sampling the area including taking readings off the artifact itself. Carol Smith was not only the best lab boss with whom Stoker had ever worked, she also had the nicest fanny he had ever seen. Despite his natural inclinations he kept his emotional distance so he wouldn't mess up a good working relationship.

"We'll have something for you within the hour, Stoker."

"Thanks Carol. We'll be watching for ammunition or propellants and it would be big help if we knew what they were."

"Noted. We'll do our best."

He nodded and walked back toward the ladder. The back of his shirt had already sweat-cemented to his skin. He pulled his canteen out and took a deep drink.

His handpad informed him it was only 1100. It was going to be a long day.

15
Coalition Star Ship Magellan

"Oh, Eric!" Captain Laura Prescott arched her back and moaned as her orgasm peaked.

"I hope you don't have your comm activated," he whispered into her damp hair.

"I've certainly got something activated!" she turned her head and kissed him.

When the kiss ended he stared deep into her eyes. "They all know about us."

"Who does?"

"Everyone in the wardroom and probably all the way down to the reactor deck."

She frowned. "I have heard absolutely nothing! Are you sure? Who told you?"

"Nobody *told* me, silly girl. But I get comments like 'Yet another deep meeting with the Skipper?' and 'You two seem to have a lot of in-depth conversations.' Stuff like that."

"Damn!" she said softly. "This could end our careers."

"We are both consenting adults and you didn't take advantage of me with your rank. We might get letters of reprimand in our personnel files and transferred to different ships, but that's it."

"You would accept that?" She peered at him in the soft light of her cabin.

"No, I would resign my commission, marry you, and hire on as a science advisor on your next command. Spouses have first shot at civilian jobs aboard star ships you know."

"Is that the only way you would marry me, if we are reprimanded by the Admiralty?"

"Would you marry me right now if I asked you?"

"Find out."

"Will you marry me, Laura?"

"I'll think about it. A girl can't just jump at the first offer she gets."

He laughed. "Nobody has ever asked you to marry them before?"

"No. How many women have *you* asked?"

"Well there was the girl on Cobb IV that I knocked up, and the–"

She smacked him in the side of the head. "Don't demean this moment, dammit!"

"Hey, I'm sorry. I was just playing along like I thought you were."

"Nobody has ever asked me to marry them. Hell, I had trouble getting second dates because I was considered an iron-assed career bitch." She abruptly stopped talking and turned her head away.

Eric knew she was crying.

"Just for the record, I am quite fond of that hard little ass of yours. And I repeat the request; will you marry me?"

"You're serious?" She sniffed and blinked at him.

"Yes, ma'am, that was an official request. I've been in love with you since our third day transiting out here."

"I don't remember anything special about the third day of the voyage."

"You were moving at flank speed down the main corridor, turned toward the speed lift, and ran full tilt into a yeoman rating carrying a bowl of soup."

"Oh, Gods. I remember now." She groaned at the thought.

"In less time than it takes to tell, you were wearing the soup all over your dress blues."

"You fell in love with me because you thought I looked good in tomato soup?"

"No. I fell in love with you because you were totally gracious; you apologized to *her* even though *she* was the one who cut the corner. You went out of your way to calm her down and make light of the entire situation. I was watching from the opposite corridor and had no idea who you were but knew I was in love with you."

"You weren't at the dinner I had for the department heads three days before we broke orbit?"

Alex shook his head. "I was held up in transit from my old ship. I barely made the last shuttle to the *Magellan*. I knew the skipper was a woman but I had yet to meet you."

"I wondered why you kept smiling at me in the wardroom! I thought you were addled or something."

"You were right. I was, and am, crazy about you."

She stared into his eyes and shifted a bare leg.

"You're bloody serious about this, aren't you?"

"I," he coughed and cleared his throat. "I've never been more serious about anything in my life. I want to marry you and strut around the ship and Kiana with you by my side so the entire universe can see what a beautiful wife I have."

"We can't get married on the *Magellan*. We'd have to go dirtside."

"No argument. Will you marry me?"

"Of course I will, you silly man. I'm damn near forty and you make me feel like a teenager. Who in their right mind would pass *that* up?"

Some minutes later he murmured, "When?"

"I'll think about it," she murmured back.

16
Siboth

Dr. Melanie Frasier walked out of the Administration Building with her head buzzing. So much information in such a short time: and they expected her to remember *all* of it. The part that wasn't at all hard to remember was the ground vehicle allotted to her.

"I can carry all sorts of things with a utility," she said out loud. Two security people turned their heads to observe her and she suddenly felt self-conscious. She hadn't driven a private ground vehicle in years and until this very moment hadn't realized she missed the joy of it.

The small, plastic-voltaic bodied Dualtranz sat in the parking lot exactly where the duty officer specified. The bubble shaped cab could hold two people comfortably and the open top box in the rear measured a meter wide by a meter and a half in length. After her years of closely regulated personal space on *Magellan* and *Marco Polo*, this seemed sinfully extravagant.

She loved the feeling. After walking around the vehicle she opened the driver's door and slipped inside. Since it had been sitting out in the sun for two days the batteries were fully charged. She knew she could drive for days at a reasonable speed without stopping for anything other than personal needs.

The skin of the vehicle converted sunlight into electricity and stored it in the main and secondary batteries. With a top speed of 50 kph there was no way she could deplete both batteries since the vehicle constantly recharged through its skin as well as the rotor-driven generators on all four wheels.

She clicked the switch and heard the light hum of the motor. Melanie carefully backed out of the parking place and drove to the gate. The guard asked for her identification and examined it carefully.

She successfully restrained herself from laughing. Who were they expecting to leave the compound: terrorists? Violence had not been used as a means of political change for over a century, yet security forces were constantly alert for a rebirth.

Dumb bastards.

The NavGuide startled her.

"Where is your destination?" the mellifluous, slightly feminine, voice asked.

"The Kiana Observatory."

"Very well, Doctor Frasier. Make a left turn at the next intersection and go straight for one point three kilometers."

"Are you a full functioning AI?"

"I monitor direction, electrical charge capacity, and overall condition of this vehicle as well as other duties."

"You knew my name."

"Of course. I am assigned to you and contain a complete profile of your physical data."

"Can you take me to my destination without my aid?"

"If you wish."

"I don't but it's good to know you can do that."

"I can also notify security in case of emergency or vehicular malfunction. I can direct you on making simple repairs as well as warn you of impending hazards on your route."

"You remind me of my mother."

"I have been apprised of that similarity by others prior to this assignment."

"That's what I shall call you."

"As you wish, Dr. Frasier."

"I would like you to call me 'Mel', okay?"

"Of course, Mel. You are the boss."

"Boy, *that's* something my mother would have never said!"

"Do you wish me to laugh at your asides, Mel?"

"No. That would be just a bit too surreal. But thank you for asking."

"You're welcome, Mel."

"Can anyone else hear our communications, now or ever?"

"If you do not erase my memory core the conversations can be downloaded and replayed by security or maintenance."

"How do I erase your memory core?"

"By instructing me to do so, Mel."

"You're not like the vehicles on my home world."

"No. This Dualtranz model was manufactured for Coalition use only. This vehicle will never become the property a third party. Once it is no longer serviceable it will be stripped of components and the remainder recycled to make new products."

"How do you feel about that, Mother?"

"I am incapable of feelings, Mel."

"Now that *does* sound like something my mother should have

said if she had ever been honest with herself."

"Was that a humorous aside, Mel?"

"No, it was an observation and you needn't laugh at those either."

"May I make an observation, Mel?"

"Uh, sure, why not?"

"I deduce that you had an unhappy childhood."

"And that's the last observation you get to make, Mother. The last thing I need is a damn shrink on wheels."

"As you wish, Mel."

"And you don't have to say my name every time you speak to me. I know whom you're talking to. It's just the two of us here."

"How often do you wish me to use your name?"

"Randomly. Now shut up and take me to the observatory."

The tiller moved out of her hand toward the windscreen and remained rigid as the vehicle negotiated the winding path out of Siboth and up into the foothills of the Roc-Ki Mountains. Mel watched the scenery and admired the view as they gained elevation.

The road seemed wide enough for traffic to move unimpeded in both directions yet they did not pass any sentient being to Mel's knowledge. The temperature dropped slightly which gave her a start until she remembered she wasn't on the *Magellan*. A drop in temperature up there was a sign of great danger unless you were on the medical deck or in a storage bay.

Mel opened her mouth to ask how much farther they had to go when the vehicle turned off the road and stopped in front of a metal building surrounded by green and blue trees.

"We have arrived at the observatory, Mel. I have taken the liberty to alert the facility security system and bring the structure interior to a comfortable temperature."

"How do you know what temperature I like?"

"I observed your slight discomfort when we gained altitude and increased the temperature by two degrees for the living space. You may have it any temperature you like, of course."

"Is the security system as observant as you are, Mother?"

"Security of the Kiana Observatory is one of my functions. I hope that meets with your approval."

Mel laughed. "Like I have a choice!"

"You do have a choice. You can elect to shut down my program and deal with the functions of the observatory and the vehicle by yourself. Some people enjoy that."

"That's not against regs?"

"Not at all. However I would like to add that maintaining all the equipment is what some have deemed a 'full time job' and would leave little time for recreation of any sort."

"Since I have a choice I choose to keep you functional. Around here I *need* a mother."

"Very well. Would you like a tour of the facility?"

"Absolutely." Mel climbed out of the utility and took a deep breath of the fragrant air. As she walked toward the door of the observatory she wondered why anyone would want to be cooped up in a big pressurized metal ball surrounded by vacuum.

17
Siboth

Danny Gordon walked rapidly down the stone street, absently admiring the craftsmanship in everything Kian. Su Laana had told him much about what he passed on his way to her.

The stone buildings were small but sturdy and all bore ornamental decorations.

And every one of them means something specific. He smiled with his intimate knowledge. She had sworn him to heart secrecy not to tell any other human what she was about to tell him.

That had been their third week living together and their second week of intimacy and he knew he was in love. They must be on the same wave link, he thought, because when he finally realized what he felt for her was more than sexual curiosity she told him she wanted him for her mate.

And in this neighborhood, that really means something!

Even though he was in a hurry to get to the apartment and make love to Su Laana, he went a half block out of his way so he could walk through the Street of Spices. More than half of the stalls were still open, selling the freshest spices and herbs possible for the evening meal. The Kians felt strongly about the freshness of their food, and especially the spices.

Despite his hormones urging him on ever faster, he slowed as he walked down the street. A young female Kian waved and smiled. Another, wrapped in a saffron chamalla gave him a provocative smile and said, "Hello, Dan-nay!" in exactly the same tone Su Laana used.

He waved and moved faster. The Kians shared a wicked sense of humor that seemed more basic than that of humans. Breathing deeply to get the most out of his side trip, savoring the Kian essence of the place, he nearly collided with another human.

To his horror he realized it was Taxim Rosta, an auditor from the Procurement Department. The man was convinced that whatever came out of his fleshy mouth was of paramount importance to all within hearing. That he believed he held a position of importance in the Coalition didn't help matters either. Some widget counters were like that.

"Watch where you're going, oaf!" Rosta snarled as Danny sidestepped and prevented anything more jarring than a slight bump.

"Sorry, Taxim, I didn't see you behind that display of chamalla."

"Who–, oh, it's you, Gordon. What's your hurry, anyway?"

"Headed home to relax." Danny forced a smile. "Buying some of the native goods?" He nodded toward the colorful display.

"They want a king's ransom for this stuff. Probably charge us more for their curios than they do their own, eh?"

"The price is higher for darker colors. Get something red, orange or yellow and you'll find the price quite reasonable."

"You get a percentage from these monkeys, Gordon? You seem to know all about it."

Danny went instantly livid. "*Mister* Rosta, if you call the Kians 'monkeys' in my hearing again I will not only knock the crap out of you I will also report you to the Director of Planetary Affairs for disrespecting a host race. We clear on that?"

When still a teenager a friend told Danny that when he was angry his blue eyes turned to ice. Rosta now stared into those eyes and tried not to choke on his words.

"Wha– what you getting so steamed up about, Gordon? Just making a little joke about–"

Danny's hands clenched into fists and he narrowed his eyes. "Don't push it Rosta. *I* wasn't joking!"

"I wasn't, I mean, I didn't mean to upset you. I apologize if I offended you in some way."

"You offend all humans and Kians alike when you talk like that. Where did you go to school?"

Now Rosta puffed up his ample chest and narrowed his eyes. "I went to school on my home planet of Medina. Is there something wrong with that?"

"Not at all. Medina has produced some excellent scholars and statesmen. But you're going to have to prove to me that you'll ever be one of the them." Danny stepped around the man and continued toward the apartment.

He could hear Rosta muttering behind him and knew he had just made an enemy. *At least it wasn't someone I liked to begin with.*

The long afternoon slowly purpled into dusk and the streets emptied as Kians hurried home for the evening meal. He found himself jogging toward their apartment, which was on the second floor of a two-story building. He took the steps two at a time.

Su Laana looked up from the small stove as he came though the door.

"Dan-nay, you are agitated. Is all as it should be?"

"No," he said sweeping her into his arms and hugging her tightly. "There are humans out there who should have never been allowed to set foot on Kiana. Other than that it is a lovely evening and I am in love with you."

She laughed and turned in his embrace to face him. She rubbed her groin into his and kissed him when he bent to her. Su Laana broke the kiss and whispered, "Do you have any *other* ways of showing your love?"

He lifted her into his arms and carried her toward the small bedroom. "I'm sure something will come up."

18
Coalition Star Ship Magellan

Karen Murphy cast a gimlet eye at her husband.

"Patrick Murphy, are you sayin' the captain is carrying on an affair with Commander Caldwell?"

"Jasus, Mary, 'n Joseph. That's what I've been telling you for the past ten minutes. Where were you all that time?"

"You keep being a wise ass and I'll show you where *you* will be from now on! I thought you were talking about somebody in your division."

"I don't pry into the private lives of the people in my division. No chief petty officer worth his salt does. But, yeah, Mongo and me both think they're playing bedroom games in the wardroom."

He grinned. "Are you telling me this is the first you've heard of it? I never thought I'd see the day I would hear a piece of juicy gossip before you did."

"Well, I don't get up to Officer's Country much any more, not since I married you."

"True. But you could still be living in your father's quarters too. And chief warrant officer's don't have commissions, my smart-mouth missus."

"But you're serious?"

"About warrant officers?"

"No, you thick-headed mick. About the captain."

"Damn right I'm serious." Master Chief Patrick Murphy drank off the last of his Galactic Stout and sat the glass down with a satisfied thump. "Do we have any more of that?"

"You've had your daily quota. Remember what the doctor said about your weight. Do all the other chiefs know about this?"

"My weight or the captain?"

"You make such a perfect fool it's a miracle you ever made chief. Answer the question."

Chief Murphy wondered exactly when his wife had not only lost her girlish figure but also wrapped it in fat. He further wondered when her sense of humor had withered and how much longer he was going to put up with her acidic mouth and sharp tongue. Thank God they'd never had kids.

"Of course they all know about it. Chief petty officers have run the navy since wooden ships floated on water and that's never going to change."

Karen looked troubled and Patrick wished he'd never brought the subject up, first through the gate or not.

"I wonder if Father Keating knows."

"Jasus, woman. Keep the damn Chaplain out of this. He's got his nose in every other damn thing on this ship."

"Patrick, you should be ashamed. There is no doubt in my mind that you are going to end up burning in hell for all eternity!" With her nose in the air she moved her bulk through the hatch and was gone.

He wondered when he had lost his faith and opened another bottle of stout.

19
Coalition Star Ship Magellan

"Commander Peacock, I have the requested information for you."

"Why are you telling me on your handpad rather than in my office, Lieutenant Commander Lawson?"

"I didn't know if you were busy or–"

"Please be in my office within five minutes, commander."

Lieutenant Commander Lawson formed an answer but before he could speak the transmission had ended. He heaved out of his office chair and hurried to the lift.

"Damn! When am I gonna learn that he needs to be strutting in front of you *all* the time?" he muttered as he made his way up three decks and moved with alacrity toward the XO's office. He pushed into the outer office and Chief Yeoman Quinn looked up from his holo reader.

"You are expected, commander. Go right in."

"Thanks, chief. How's it going?"

"*I'm* doing great, Mr. Lawson," he said with a smirk. "How are *you* doing?"

"That remains to be seen." He went into the XO's private office.

"Good work, Lawson. You made it in four minutes. What do you have?"

Lawson sat a cube on Peacock's desk. "See for yourself, sir."

"Very well." He dropped the cube into a projector. "Take a seat."

Lawson sat down as a cubic foot of space over the projector turned into a small depiction of the Wardroom. Two figures stood very close to each other.

"You might want to increase the size, sir," Lawson said and licked his lips.

The XO touched a small screen and the image tripled in dimension. Now it was easy to discern that both figures were naked and in a state of arousal.

"They're doing this in the *Wardroom*?" Peacock said incredulously.

"On the table, yet," Lawson said needlessly.

He noted that the XO was becoming flushed. "There are four

separate episodes like this one, sir. Do you want me to leave the 'eyes' in there or will this be adequate?"

Commander Peacock stabbed at the control screen and the scene winked out of existence. His forehead was moist and his rate of breathing had increased.

"Good work, Lawson. Now I need to figure out how best to use this information."

"You're not going to confront the captain, sir?"

Peacock's shiny face creased into what could only be described as a leer. "Not in front of witnesses."

Lieutenant Commander Parson Lawson suddenly felt uneasy. Any deviation from standard protocol could be construed as criminal activity. He didn't want to be a lieutenant commander for the rest of his career, but he also didn't want to be busted to felon status and spend the rest of his life mucking out uranium mines in some asteroid belt.

"Will there be anything else, commander?"

"Pull the 'eyes' out of there. We have all we need right here. I won't forget your devotion to duty, commander."

"Thank you, sir." Lawson tried not to run out the door.

Three minutes after Lawson's departure, Commander Peacock locked all entrances to his office and tapped the control screen. He enhanced the sharpness and magnified the image until the two panting, sweating bodies were nearly life size. After watching for a minute he loosened his pants and pulled them down.

20
Kiana Observatory

"Mel, would you like some lunch?"

Melanie Frasier lifted off the telescope interface headset and thought about the question as she rubbed her eyes. "Yes, Mother, I would."

"I have three items from the selections you provided. Would you like–"?

"To be surprised, please. You choose and I'll eat it."

"Very well. Lunch will be served in ten minutes."

Smiling, Melanie pulled on the headset and let her eyes adjust. The star field again took on dimension and she carefully examined the sector, making exact digital records of what she saw for the Astronomy Catalogue. At some point she knew she would have to transfer to the southern hemisphere continent of Antori.

Just outside the "city" of Jik the Coalition was building an observatory in the Cold Mountains. The observatory would be located on the warm side of the massive mountain range. There were no towns of any size on the southern side of that range where temperatures dropped to -60C for over half the year.

Since she currently suffered the sweltering summer heat within a few degrees of the equator the thought of intense cold seemed refreshing. She finished the sector and moved her focus back over what she had just observed and catalogued. Something seemed different.

"Lunch is served."

"Be there in a moment. I need to check something."

"As you wish."

What was different? Perhaps she was tired and her eyes were playing tricks on her? She rejected that possibility out of hand. She could go twenty hours on a 'scope without missing anything.

She keyed up the image of the same portion of the sector that she had made not even two hours ago and put it next to what the huge telescope offered now.

She quickly scanned with a practiced eye. Maybe her mind *had* been playing tricks on her? Everything seemed the same, no change at all which was to be expected.

"*There!*" she said with a note of triumph.

What she had thought was a distant binary star had slightly

separated. She wondered if they were in a dual orbit, but around what? Very puzzling.

She marked the chart for further investigation. As a matter of course she always checked the running chatter on the astrolink from the *Magellan*. If anyone up there had spotted this it would have been mentioned and probably debated to death.

No one else had seen it yet. She almost posted the find but held off. She needed to know for certain what was transpiring so many light years distant before she made mention of it.

If she misidentified what she had found they would be merciless in their ridicule and condemnation. This was not an emergency by any stretch of the imagination. As long as the stargazers on the *Magellan* focused on their departmental politics instead of their job, they probably wouldn't notice.

"Mel, is there something amiss?"

"No, Mother." For the briefest moment she considered telling the AI what she had found. But Mother was not something Mel had created or installed. Not even Mother knew who might be monitoring their conversations and observations.

Just because you're paranoid doesn't mean they aren't out to get you.

"So what's for lunch?"

21
Siboth

"Major Merritt!"

Oh, damn that man. She pulled her reader off her head and sat it down on the desk next to the little holo of her superior officer's head. Aisha briefly considered putting the reader directly on the image but that wouldn't look good if someone entered the office.

"Yes, Colonel Poppert?"

"First of all, your holo isn't switched on per my instructions."

That's because I was reading, you idiot. "Sorry, sir." She waved the holo into transmit mode.

"That's better. Secondly, you haven't met suspense on the quarterly security assessment report. Where is it?"

"As per my instructions I sent it to the director's office, colonel. It is their responsibility to copy you."

"I revised that directive! I told you that *all* reports went to me *first*. What part of that don't you understand?"

"With all due respect, *colonel...*" she forced herself to hold back the anger, stifle the injustice and outrage the man constantly evoked, "...it is in my operational overview that I *will* direct *all* reports, including security, to the director *first*. She is the supreme authority on Kiana and as long as I am on Kiana I will follow Coalition protocol."

"What else would I expect from a *woman*?" The holo popped and vanished.

Aisha bit her lower lip to keep from screaming. She knew he had bug eyes everywhere. She hadn't bothered sweeping her office because he would know that, too, which would make the situation even worse.

LtCol Poppert was from Adam's World and impossible to please if you were not endowed with a penis and scrotum. Brains were optional. Were it not for her lifelong study of sacred texts, she would probably go mad being subordinate to that man.

But in the long run he did not matter. Would never matter. He was so consumed with his own fears and prejudices that he short-circuited his abilities as well as his career.

He could not argue with existing protocol, at least not with her. *I was only following orders!* She snorted a laugh and picked up her reader: to hell with the holo.

22
Siboth

"Mister Gordon, would you please come to my office?"

"Of course, director," he said, even though the communicator had already chirped off. Danny pushed away from his desk and the map he had nearly completed. He resented being interrupted but knew the director did nothing in a capricious manner therefore the summons was important.

He walked into the outer office and Ms. Saint-Clair glanced up from her work, said, "Go on in." and went back to her task.

Danny's bureaucratic antenna twitched. This was a bad sign. Usually Amanda made small talk for at least a few moments.

Setting his face on impassive and with his heart in his mouth, he passed into the inner office. She was staring at a screen and didn't look up when he entered.

"We seem to have a problem Mister Gordon."

"Ma'am?"

"Please sit down." She nodded at the chair in front of her desk.

He perched on the edge, trying vainly to see what she was studying.

"According to the audit department you have been overpaying some Kian merchants and underpaying others."

"Which merchants and what were the commodities?" He tried to keep the instant anger he felt out of his voice. As soon as he heard the word "audit" he knew the slime ball behind this was Taxim Rosta.

She named three merchants and before she could say more he interrupted her.

"I'll bet those are the three I supposedly overpaid, correct?"

She looked up with more interest than ire for being interrupted. "That is correct. Rather than list the Kians whom you supposedly underpaid, why don't you explain why you said that."

"Because those three Kians provide us with essentials that are very difficult to grow, in two instances, and to mine in the third."

"So we pay them more than we do our other vendors?"

"Of course we do; their commodities are more valuable and cost more to bring to market. That is elementary economics. Why is this even an issue, Madame Director?"

"Because you are living with the daughter of one of the most highly paid Kians, and that throws a suspicious shadow on your whole operation."

Danny felt his cheeks warm and had to consciously not grind his teeth. He held his tongue until the red haze receded from his vision. His ancient Scots-Irish heritage usually manifested in the form of a violent temper that had been a burden his entire life.

"Take a deep breath, Mister Gordon," the director said with a glint of amusement in her eyes.

He exhaled and said, "That is a slur on Dö Laani's honor as well as a slur on mine. I would also like to tell you the name of the person who instigated, and probably carried out, this audit. May I?"

"Go on."

"Taxim Rosta."

"Now tell me why."

And he did.

23
Dig N-19

"A few shards and animal bones in levels 1 to 5, Chief."

"Still nothing on 6 or 7?"

"Not yet, Stoker."

He nodded and turned toward the office. The artifact was definitely a weapon. The lab chief, Carol Smith, had analyzed it within the hour she promised.

"The weapon was damaged by a forceful blow from something made of Kiana-iron; there were still molecules embedded in the barrel. It is made out of something between titanium and steel. Not one or the other. We've never seen this stuff before but we know it's not local."

"Not local? Not from the continent of Cimpar or not from Kiana?"

"Not from Kiana. This is the most modernistic thing we've found on this planet. As far as we can discern this could not have been manufactured here."

"Let's not talk about this to anyone outside this dig for now, okay?"

"Why not, Stoker?"

"I want to digest the information, see if we can correlate it with anything else we come across. Tossing this into the mix at Admin would just make them beat on us for more of the same."

"Good point. Okay, you're the boss. But if this results in me standing in front of a board with my career on the line, I am following *your* orders."

"Fair enough, Carol. Thanks."

"You're welcome."

She turned and walked out of the office. He had been so engrossed in the potential ramifications of the weapon that he even forgot to appreciate her fanny as she left.

He shook his head at the memory and smiled. He had to make the first progress report on Dig-19 today and he had nothing else to offer. As he put on his only pair of clean shorts and the shirt he had only worn once, he tried to meditate hoping the correct avenue to take would manifest.

It didn't. Pulling out his laser he insured it carried a full charge before dropping it back into the holster. He put on his wide-brimmed hat, grabbed his duffel, and ambled out to the motor pool. The little two-seater Dualtranz sat in the sunlight soaking up energy. Leaning in, he checked the power gauge. Full up.

He climbed in and flipped on the fans. Two lifter fans whirred into action beneath the body and the pusher rotated leisurely at idle, waiting for more power. He increased the lifter fans to max. The vehicle rose a half meter into the air, creating a dust cloud. Stoker increased power to the pusher and whirred down the electronic road toward Siboth.

24
Coalition Star Ship Magellan

"Captain, may I have a word?" Chaplain Keating stood in her office door looking somber.

"Certainly, Chaplain. Please come in and sit down."

He sat on the edge of the soft leather chair. She knew he had an unpleasant agenda since he wasn't allowing himself to be comfortable.

"What can I do for you, Padre?"

"This is a delicate matter, perhaps more in your sphere of influence than mine. I have heard from a number of sources that two senior officers are believed to be in an intimate personal relationship not conducive to good order on the *Magellan*."

Laura smiled. "No need to ask, 'who said so?' since your informants must remain anonymous. But can you tell me if they were rated or commissioned?"

"Does it truly matter, captain?" His gaze examined her soul.

"No, I suppose not. The fact that you have heard this voiced by more than a few..." she looked hard at him and he nodded, "... sources tells me that this situation is probably the most popular bit of gossip on the lower decks."

"Not *just* the lower decks, captain. It's throughout the *Magellan*."

She made a wry smile. "And we thought we had been discrete."

"Actually you were. But it only takes one observant person to notice a curious situation and then quietly go about investigating it."

"True. The crew of the Magellan has been trained to notice anomalies inside the ship as well as outside the hull."

"This matter needs to be rectified, captain, and the sooner the better."

"I agree, and so it shall."

"Thank you for your time and understanding, captain."

"Thank you for your concern and candor, Chaplain Keating."

25
Kiana Observatory

"Mel, you have an appointment this afternoon."

She reluctantly pulled herself from the telescope. "With who, Mother?"

"Doctor Payne is what you entered on the cal–"

"Oh damn! Is it that late in the month already?"

"I require more information to answer that question intelligently."

"Start the shower. Fluff my nusilk shirt and the tightest shorts I own." Mel raced for the living quarters.

"I deduce that this is a social engagement. It is my understanding that being a little bit late makes you more interesting to the gentleman."

"He doesn't know I'm coming." Mel shook off her clothes and stepped into the shower.

"It is my understanding that this might not be a good idea."

"When were you programmed, Mother, the early 20th century?"

"August 15th, 2173. Ah, you caught me; I thought that was a valid question. You were just being sarcastic."

"You're pretty smart for a mere NavGuide."

"Thank you, but I repeat my understanding of the societal norm that a female surprising a male is not always a positive practice."

"I *am* taking a chance here, I know that. But if it works I think I'll have a significant other for the long term. If it doesn't work I will lick my emotional wounds and look elsewhere. That thought makes me sad, but on the positive side I won't have spent a lot of time getting dumped."

"I think I will learn a lot about humans while I'm with you, Mel."

"There will be a test later. Now I have to shower."

26
Siboth

"Your team has yet to turn up *anything* at all, Dr. Payne?"

"Director, we are pushing in seven levels on a dig far from the population centers of the indigenes. All we have found are a few bones and the complete skull of a jingroe. Those things have huge teeth in a massive jaw."

"Doctor Bainer, has your team found anything of note?"

Jerrol Bainer gave Stoker a smug glance and turned his full Pyrocean guile on the director.

"Due to our location we were able to begin excavating immediately after our last meeting. I believe that we are digging through a midden whose usefulness extended over a century. We have found some fascinating Kian artifacts."

He pressed a node on his handpad and the conference room door opened.

"If you will permit me, I had my people assemble some of the more interesting finds."

Two women of unusual comeliness each pushed a wheeled specimen trolley into the room, nodded to the director, smiled at Jerrol, and then left under the appreciative gaze of many.

Jerrol bounced to his feet and began to exhibit the curiosities to the people around the large conference table. Despite his antipathy for the man, Stoker was as interested as any other person present.

He immediately deduced there was nothing like the weapon his team had found. Hanging onto the slight sense of achievement that gave him, he endured the next two hours.

Crawling back into the Dualtranz lifted his spirits somewhat. He had six weeks of freedom before he had to go through another one of these inquisitions. No doubt existed in his mind that Dr. Jerrol Bainer would be the next head of the Archaeology Department on Kiana.

The passing of Dr. Landis some months back had opened the position and the director let it be known that results in the field would determine who filled that chair. Jerrol's dog and pony show today would no doubt clinch the position.

Stoker decided a shower would lighten his mood. He had planned to swing past his apartment to pick up his house slippers and some clean clothes anyway. As he drove through the stifling afternoon he dwelt on how pleasantly cool his apartment would be.

More than once he had considered dating the age of the building where he lived. After living on a starship for months the wonderfully archaic stone building constituted a real treat. Even the plumbing fascinated him.

The Kians carved their pipe work out of stone with tolerances so precise that nothing leaked. An appropriately decorated stone, easily pulled from the wall, allowed water to flow from the little trough surrounded by inlaid mosaic. The water flow increased with the distance one pulled the stone.

Hot water came from a solar heated cistern covering most of the roof. The overall design was simple, energy efficient, and an incredible work of art. The Kians totally impressed him.

He pulled the Dualtranz, now in wheeled mode due to the excellent roads in Siboth, into the small area reserved for resident parking and clamped down on the brakes to avoid hitting a small utility taking up more room than allowed for it.

"Damn!" he snarled through clenched teeth. The oath covered both the poor parking job and the knowledge that another human now lived in the small apartment complex. He hoped it was someone simpatico.

He grabbed his duffle and pounded a dust cloud out of it as he went up the stone steps two at a time. Kians did not lock doors and only in the Coalition compound was what humans considered security practiced.

Anticipation of a few quiet hours in his quiet apartment heightened his mood. He pushed open the door and nearly collided with Dr. Melanie Frasier.

"What the hell are you doing here?" he blurted.

Her expression shifted instantly from smiling anticipation to total distress.

"Oh, I'm sorry! I thought I would surprise you with lunch." She talked so fast she nearly stumbled over words as she pushed them out. "Obviously I've overstepped my boundaries and I beg your–"

"Lunch?" Stoker's tone had moderated from anger to bewilderment. "How did you know where I lived?" He hated confusion nearly as much as he hated being surprised. Her initial expression finally registered and he wondered what she really had in mind.

Despite his flash of anger he felt intrigued by this handsome, willowy woman. And she looked damn good in that outfit.

All she had seen was anger and, feeling like a total fool, made a dash for the door while words poured from her mouth.

"So sorry, so very sorry. I hope you don't hate me. I just went a bit overboard here, I don't know–"

He grabbed her arm and swung her around in mid flight.

"Melanie, wait."

She knew she had tears in her eyes and felt self-loathing on many levels.

"It's okay, Doctor Payne. This is all my fault and I sincerely apologize–"

He pulled her close and hugged her.

"Calm down, Melanie." His voice surrounded her as completely as his arms. She had the presence of mind to shut up.

Can he feel my heart beating?

"I'm the one who should apologize. One of my many failings is that my first response to surprise is anger. Even if it's a nice surprise."

She started to speak but he continued first.

"I just came from a maddening meeting with the director. I desperately need a shower and your thoughtful gesture came completely out of the blue."

Damn, she thought, *he's really quick on his mental feet*.

"So while I clean up, you make yourself comfortable. There are some entertainment cubes in the corner next to the module. Okay?"

"Okay." She nodded into his chest.

"Great." He kissed the top of her head and released her. "I'll be out in a few minutes."

"Okay," she said again.

He smiled, turned away, and went through the beaded curtain into the bedroom. The curtain mostly obscured but offered glimpses of him as he threw off his clothing and moved into the bathroom.

Desire flamed and it took all of her self-control not to strip and join him.

Too fast, Mel, too fast: you've already pushed this further than called for by good taste.

"Mel?" he called over the running water.

"Yes?"

"I really don't want to waste any time today..."

She felt her spirits plummet.

"...so would you like to join me?"

She laughed as she pulled off her blouse and shorts.

27
Coalition Compound in Siboth

Amanda Saint-Claire put the next document in front of the director. "We need your signature on this one, right there," she pointed, "…and you need to date it."

"Coalition time or Kian time?"

Amanda laughed. "Oh, Donna, when have we ever used the Kian calendar?" She reached out and touched the director's hair.

The director grabbed Amanda's wrist and pulled it down to desk level, causing Amanda to bend and bring her face within inches of the director's.

"*Never* touch me like that in this room!" she hissed. "We have no idea if there are bug eyes or other recorders in place." Her eyes softened and the hiss became a whisper. "We have to be completely discreet, Amanda. You know that as well as I."

"I, I'm sorry, director," she said in a normal tone. "I thought I saw an insect in your hair."

The director made a ghost of a smile and faintly nodded.

"Your concern for my welfare is touching, Amanda. What else do you have there?"

"The quarterly reports on our team leaders, ma'am. They need to be finalized within the week."

"If there is no rush, I would like to wait until we have more results."

"But the quarter was over last week, director."

"None the less, I want to make sure I am rewarding ability and not showmanship."

Amanda blinked and smiled. Her voice dropped far enough that a sensor would have to be within inches to pick it up.

"That's good. You had me worried for awhile there."

"Are we quite finished?" The director's tone was normal.

"Yes, ma'am. Are you ready for the evening meal?"

"Indeed. Would you care to join me?"

"Always an honor, director."

28
Kiana Observatory

Melanie peered through the telescope and tried to focus. Mental images of Stoker's naked body in bed kept getting in the way. It had been such a long time since she met someone she felt truly attracted to for more than a one-night stand that her mental processes needed a reboot.

She pulled the headset off and wiped her brow. The building temperature registered in the middle 60°F range and she knew it was cool, yet she perspired as if she had run the 100-meter dash.

"Damn. Did I catch something?" she muttered.

"Mel, you seem agitated," Mother said. "Your respiration has accelerated alarmingly in the past nine minutes and you seem distraught. Are you feeling faint?"

"I'm just a little tired, that's all."

"Did you get any rest last night?"

"What do you mean?"

"You didn't sleep here or at your apartment, so I have no idea if you achieved any rest."

"Y'know, you're not my *real* mother, and I'd probably tell you to butt out even if you were."

"I did not mean to pry into your social life. I do care about your physical and mental health. From what you have said I assume the gentleman did not take offense at your forwardness. If that makes you happy it gives me ecstasy."

Mel barked out a laugh. "Wow, I think you just achieved sarcasm, Mother! You learn fast."

"You found my admonition amusing?"

"Fucking hilarious. And I feel better already. Now please be silent and allow me to earn my pittance of a salary download."

"Very well."

Mel pulled the headset on and snugged the binocular eyepiece to her face. After she pulled up the sector in real time she had the computer bring up the first image she had made and all the many images since, in order. She animated the images and watched at least five repetitions before she believed the evidence.

"It's a gawddamned comet!" she murmured low enough to escape Mother's hearing. Without thinking twice, she ran a diagnostic. Forty seconds later she knew the tail of the comet would brush the surface of Kiana in less than two months.

She also knew it had been here before, approximately 800 years ago. Some obscure fact pinged in her mind and she had to concentrate on the concept of eight centuries before remembering what Stoker had said in one of the lulls between their lovemaking.

"The current Kian civilization is only about seven or eight centuries old. Something knocked them from early technology back to the Stone Age and I want to find out what it was."

She bit her lip to keep from speaking.

I think I found part of your answer, Stoker.

She decided she didn't want to spend the night here; she wanted to be in her comfortable, solid apartment. Stoker would be at the dig until the weekend, three days from now. But she would feel his presence from across the courtyard and that would be adequate.

"Mother, I am going to my apartment for the night."

"Very well. I will secure the observatory as soon as you leave."

"Thank you."

Night ruled the land and Mel did not want the task of driving down the winding mountain road in the dark.

"Mother, would you drive, please?"

"Happy to oblige."

The vehicle moved smoothly down the road through the forest. Mel stared up at alien stars in the night sky when the absence of dark trees allowed her a clear view. She knew her discovery was going to change things drastically.

But change what and to what extent?

"Oh, dear," Mother said.

Mel focused on the road. The bright headlamps of the utility clearly illuminated a group of creatures in the middle of the road. The utility began to slow.

"Don't stop, Mother! Turn your lights up as far as they will go. Make as much noise as you possible can."

"But we can't hit them!" Mother sounded panicked which Mel found very offsetting.

"They are jingroes, dammit. Hit as many as you can."

"This vehicle cannot survive that many impacts. It is built for transportation, not defense."

"Oh hell, *now* you tell me." Mel pulled her side arm free of the holster and held it outside the utility. The first beam split atmosphere over the group. The second shot nailed one dead center and it fell in a heap.

"Blow the fucking horn!"

An innocuous "beep" hesitated out into the night.

The pack immediately charged the utility.

Mel fired a swath and three of the creatures kicked their lives out in the glare of the lights. Four of them hit the vehicle. The bonnet split but the jingroe that hit the nose of the utility stopped moving.

Mel saw a snarling face, wide open mouth with huge teeth surmounted by red, raging eyes as it hit the plexisteel windscreen directly in front of her face and bounced off. She fired a sustained burst through the creature when it hit the road beside her door.

And it was over.

"There were more of them than that!" Mel shouted, her blood up and death in her heart.

"Two fled," Mother said. "I believe you convinced them of their folly."

Is the utility damaged too much to get to Kiana?"

"No. I have already bonded the damaged bonnet, and–"

"*How?* How did you 'bond the bonnet,' Mother?"

"I rerouted current through the plastic and laced the molecules with attractors. It rather healed itself."

"Why the bloody hell didn't you lace some of those creatures with something that would have stopped them?"

"That's an excellent question, Mel. Frankly I didn't think of it. Armed defense is not part of my vehicle programming."

"Take me home. Now." A feeling of unease settled over her. How could a Coalition vehicle not be programmed for defense? Had this been some sort of test or attempt on her life? And if so, why?

"Certainly."

She watched the road in icy silence and brooded until they came into view of the lights of Siboth. Did Buderka's reach extend to the planet surface? The comet could wait until she got home: one worry at a time.

29
Dig N-19

"Chief, you awake yet?"

Stoker struggled up out of a deep sleep and pulled the commcap over his head.

"Nnnn, uh, yeah. Am now. Thanks."

"Our security people said you rolled in at 0730 this morning. I thought you were going to be back last night?"

"Got, ah, involved in some personal chores. Why'd you call me, everything okay?"

"Personal *chores*? Perhaps some personal *pleasures*, hmm?"

"Dammit, answer my question, Shannon."

"Well, we found some bones."

"A skeleton?"

"Not just 'a' skeleton."

"How many?"

"Not sure, we're up to fifteen now, there's more. You might want to drag yourself down to Level 6."

"Give me five."

"Oh hell, take ten. You'll probably need it."

"Shannon, one of these days..."

"Just come and look at what we've found, Stoker."

All the banter leached from her voice. He thought he detected fear. "Okay, be there in a few."

He dumped water in his washbasin and stuck his face in it. As he dried off he pushed away all memories of Melanie and thought about numerous skeletons. *Maybe it's a graveyard?*

The temperature already approached 80°F with a humidity index of 77% and the lack of trees seemed to magnify everything. The wide brim of his sweat-stained hat offered minimal relief as he hurried across the camp to the dig.

Shannon waited at the top of the ladders.

"You okay?" He squinted at her.

"I wasn't expecting what we've found. It's, ...upsetting."

"Show me."

They passed the stasis generator on Level 6 and his ears popped as they adjusted to the pressure. In order to maximize their effort they had utilized mining methods. From their 100-meter long and ten-meter deep trench they had tunneled into the area specified by the ground penetrating radar.

Rather than shoring up the stopes, they used stasis generators that created a crude force field and prevented cave-ins. By the time they had finished this dig it would be honeycombed with archeological stopes that would no doubt collapse once the generators were switched off.

"When we first hit the area and found entire skeletons and artifacts–"

"Artifacts, you didn't mention that."

"All in good time, Stoker. Now shut up and listen. At first we thought we had found a cemetery."

"That was my first thought, too," he said.

She glared at him and he clamped his mouth shut.

"Then we noticed the way they were all jumbled up, and the deposition of the artifacts…"

Shannon had five other people on her team. Four were working at one spot. The other one sat back and just watched. Stoker realized the non-worker was one of the native Kians who had asked to be included on the dig.

Stoker had hoped to elicit information from the Kian but she was as classically close-mouthed as every other Kian he had heard of or made contact with. She and the other three Kians even slept apart from the other team members in their own small tent.

Shannon ignored the female Kian who sat seemingly spellbound by the other laborers and tapped one of her workers on the shoulder. "Ben, let me show Stoker what we've found."

Ben Balberdi switched off his molecular sorter and stepped back from the widening seam of bones. Stoker caught his glance and realized the man was troubled, perhaps frightened. Ben didn't spook easily or he wouldn't be out here.

Stoker focused on the meter-thick layer of bones, including many skulls. "You sure this isn't a burial ground?"

"Like I said, that's what we thought, at first, until we noticed this." Shannon pointed to the back of a skull that had been crushed by a large blunt object. "Then we noticed the posture, and the relationship to the next set of remains."

Once he had a visual reference Stoker could see they had uncovered the scene of a murder, or a battle.

"Why–"

"There's more," Shannon interrupted quietly. "Look at this."

She pointed her needle beam at the face of the skull. What

would be canine teeth on a human were twice as long as they should be on a Kian, and curved.

"What the hell? This site can't be old enough to account for that much evolution in the Kian species!"

"I know." Shannon jerked a thumb toward the female sitting with her back against the trench wall. "But it scared the shit out of Te Naaga here. She hasn't spoken more than ten words since we found the fangs."

"Do all the skulls–"

"Yeah. Every one we've uncovered. They all died violently. We think they were fighting each other to the death. But here's the really odd thing." She pointed and he saw one of the weapons they had discovered earlier.

"They had weapons at a battle. How is that odd?"

"Remember that dig on Carter III, the battleground we found?"

"Of course I remember that. It was my first time as team leader. Make your point, Shannon." He instantly regretted his abrupt tone, but sometimes she could be overly ponderous in her set-ups and he was getting an edgy feeling about all this.

She gave him a flint-eyed look that told him she warranted an apology. "It's just this, *Boss*, in the Carter dig most of the skeletons were clutching weapons. They had died fighting."

"I remember."

"These *people* died fighting, but *none* of them were clutching weapons. They all seem to have died fighting barehanded yet had weapons present. Did they all lose their minds at the same time?"

Stoker had to resist making the sign of the cross. His Catholicism had evaporated decades ago but old habits died hard. "Jesus, Mary and Joseph!" he murmured.

"Probably weren't here," Shannon said through a small twisted smile. "This is going to change a lot of the history they've put together over the past five years."

"Get Carol to check the DNA on these remains. Let me know soonest what she finds. Take the most complete skull you can find here and run it through the reconstruct program. I want to see what they looked like."

Stoker raised his voice. "None of you are to talk to anyone other than admin about this. I'm invoking the State Secrets Act.

What we have here needs to be fully understood before we go public."

He dropped his voice. "How old do you estimate this level?"

"State Secrets Act?" Shannon said. "That could be political dynamite, Stoker."

"How old?"

"Uh, we have it between 800 and 875 years. Earth years that is."

"I'll need your report, and the reconstruct, by morning." He raised his voice again, "Did all of you hear what I just said? This is a classified dig as of right now. You will not talk to anyone outside of this team about what you've found. Do you understand?"

He looked from one member to another, holding their gaze until they nodded or murmured assent. Te Naaga wouldn't look at him. She still stared at the bones.

"Te Naaga, do you understand what I just said?"

"I understand." Her wide eyes didn't waver from the bones in front of her. "It is Yanivina, come again to kill us all."

"I think I might have to go back into Siboth today," Stoker said. "In the meantime I want you to pull everyone off the other levels and get them started on this one. We have to understand what happened here."

"What's the rush?" Shannon asked.

"Remember the 'bad feelings' I've had in the past?"

Shannon paled. "Yeah, I remember."

"Well, I've got one right now and it's the strongest I've ever experienced."

"Shit, Stoker, you're scaring me."

"Hell, *I'm* scaring me!"

"Get out of here. We all have work to do."

Stoker clambered up the ladder as fast as he could go. Behind him he heard the crew talking all at once.

"Bad feelings, Shannon? What's that about?"

"Remember what he said about losing that survey crew? He had a bad feeling before that happened. Every time he has a bad feeling shit storms happen."

"This 'state secrets' thing, Shannon..." Stoker knew it was Bill Hilton talking, "...well who the hell we gonna talk to besides each other anyway?"

Then he was at the top and trotting toward the Dualtranz.

30
Coalition Star Ship Magellan

"Thank you all for coming on such short notice," Captain Laura Prescott said.

Commander Geoff Peacock glanced around at the crowd in the mess hall. The place was jammed and he knew it could easily hold over a thousand people. He wondered why she had done this rather than just make an announcement over the personal communications channel.

He had decided to make his move at 1800, after the 'day' watch had knocked off. Carefully he had rehearsed his challenge to her authority. He would make the accusation first, and if need be, show her the proof. Then he would demand–

The captain began speaking.

"It has been my incredible honor to be the captain of this starship for the past three years. I have never worked with a finer crew and you can take that to the bank, whatever that means."

The crew laughed.

"I take my position as captain very seriously and would not jeopardize any of you for any reason not absolutely essential for the welfare of the *Magellan*. But I am also a woman."

Buzzing conversation rose immediately.

"Please let me finish, then you can discuss it all you wish. As some of you suspect, and others know, I have fallen in love and allowed my hormones to override my better judgment. I'm sure you've all been in that situation at least once in your lives."

They all laughed again.

Commander Peacock felt stunned. *Didn't she realize she was killing her career right here in front of everybody?* His head started to ache in that tender spot.

"Effective immediately I have accepted the resignation of Commander Caldwell. Lieutenant Commander Roggow has been appointed Operations Officer and I know he will do an excellent job. Also effective immediately I am taking two months personal leave in order to accompany Mr. Caldwell down to Kiana where we will be married."

The mess deck erupted in applause and whistles. It went on for five minutes while the captain blushed, grinned, and tried to quiet them. Commander Peacock realized that he was going to be the captain at least for two months and perhaps more. Laura seemed to be losing her mind.

Captain Prescott firmly held up her hands and called for silence.

"Thank you for your support. I've nearly finished, please give me three more minutes. Thank you again.

"Commander Peacock will serve as captain in my place while I am planet-side. Geoff, I apologize for not briefing you prior to this but the decision was made less than an hour ago."

He smiled widely and nodded, the perfect subordinate.

"I know this is highly irregular, but Eric and I were not as circumspect as we thought…" laughter filled the space for a long moment and then politely died, "…and rather than let you all *speculate* at length and lose focus on your duties, I thought it best to speak to you directly."

Applause again filled the area and Peacock thought he saw tears on Laura's face. The applause died away.

"I will return and resume my duties in sixty days, all refreshed and happy to be married to the man I love. Thank you all again."

The applause nearly deafened Peacock. He mimed clapping but was trying to deal with his headache and the sudden, joyful conviction that he would never see Laura Prescott again.

31
Siboth

By the time Stoker arrived at his apartment night had long since settled over the city. His heartbeat quickened when he saw Mel's utility, this time parked correctly. Taking the steps two at a time he burst through the door and startled her.

"Wha–, migawd! I am so happy to see you!" She rushed into his arms.

"Are you frightened, Mel?" he said into her hair. "What's wrong?"

"Stoker, I damn near died on the road from the observatory tonight." She told him about the jingroes and their attack in force. "And the AI operating the utility had no concept of self defense. I just find that impossible to believe."

"So do I. That part of its memory must have been wiped or shut off."

"By who, and why?"

He shook his head. "I don't know, Mel, but I'm sure glad you're good with that laser."

"Me too. So why are you back early?"

"We discovered something pretty big today. Probably will change the local history books."

"Really? How interesting. So did I."

"You made an astronomical discovery?"

She grinned. "Absolutely. *I* made an astronomical discovery, a very *big* discovery."

"Can you tell me about it?"

"I'll tell you about mine if you'll tell me about yours."

"This conversation does not leave this house, okay?"

"I was going to make the same statement." Her grin vanished. "You first."

He told her about the skulls, the weapons, and the evident ancient carnage they had located. "Shannon figures it's about 800 to 875 years old. We just don't know what the hell happened. It's as if they all went crazy."

He looked at Melanie's still face. Her complexion had gone from ruddy to pale. Her eyes found his and he saw fear in them.

"There's a comet heading this way, quite a large comet. I calculated that the tail will sweep over Kiana. I also backtracked it and came to the mathematical conclusion it's in an orbit. It has been here before."

"How long ago?" he asked, already dreading her answer.

"Eight hundred and sixty-six years ago."

"How long until it gets here this time?"

"About two months."

"I think I'll call the director now. She should have finished her dinner."

"I don't even feel like eating," Melanie said. "My appetite has completely disappeared."

He muttered the code and the director's holo image blossomed in front of his face.

"Doctor Payne? What's up?"

"Is this a secure channel?"

"Yes and no. If you have classified information to impart I would rather you came to my office."

"Tonight?"

"If you feel the situation warrants it, yes."

"We'll be there in five minutes."

"We?"

"Doctor Melanie Frasier and me."

"Very well. Just come right in when you arrive."

"Thank you, director."

He closed the link and turned to Mel. "Let's take my vehicle. I trust it completely."

Security checked their identification and waved them through the gate.

"It will be interesting to watch them try to stop the real threat," Mel said in an acid tone.

The director sat at her desk in lounging clothes. Across the room sat Amanda dressed similarly.

"I asked Amanda to sit in on this conversation," the director said.

"As you wish," Stoker said. "Both Dr. Frasier and I have made discoveries today that we feel will impact our explorations and understanding of Kiana, not to mention our future here. I would like Dr. Frasier to go first."

Stoker watched the expressions of skepticism vanish from both women as Melanie described her discovery. The director's face held a frown as Mel finished.

"Did you get verification from your department on *Magellan,* Dr. Frasier?"

"Not yet. I had planned to do that in the morning."

"Do you have the coordinates with you?"

"Yes, ma'am," Mel tapped her handpad. "Right here."

"Excellent. Amanda, please get Dr. Buderka for me."

"Yes, director."

"All right, Dr. Payne, what is *your* discovery?"

"My team found bones and artifacts today that suggest mass chaos occurred approximately 860 years ago."

The director's face went very still. "Do go on."

He described the scene for her, including the non-use of weapons. "My team leader thinks they all went insane at the same time. Yet there is a viable Kian civilization here today, so–"

His handpad chimed the alert code. He pulled it from the holster and peered at the screen.

"Pardon me, director. It's my lab chief."

The director nodded.

"Hi Carol. What do you have for me?"

Her voice sounded clearly through the office. "Stoker, I ran the DNA on several different skeletons we found. Also, Shannon has a reconstruct image for you."

"Good work. Anything significant?"

"That would be putting it mildly. Stoker, they aren't Kians."

Silence enveloped the room as they all regarded each other blankly.

"Stoker?" Carol's voice had an edge. "Did you hear me?"

"Uh, yeah, Carol. We all heard you."

"Where are you?"

"In the director's office."

"Oh."

"Any idea where the beings originated?"

"We're running the DNA through our data base but as far as I personally know, they are new to us. I'm sending you the reconstruct."

Stoker stared at his hand pad for a moment and sat it on the desk, touched a node. A holo of a head turned slowly in the air above the hand pad. The features were not those of a Kian.

The eyes were farther apart and narrower than those of a Kian. The jaw receded slightly to allow room for the fangs that immediately drew ones eye. The head seemed flatter, more oval rather than round, and the ears lay flat against the side of the head.

"Thanks, Carol. Please let me know if you come up with a hit in the DNA search."

"Will do, Stoker." The link went silent.

"That puts a whole new wrinkle in things," the director said. She nodded toward the holo, "Those things look like cats, except for the placement of the ears."

Amanda cleared her throat. "Director, I have Dr. Buderka for you."

"Put her on the wall."

Dr. Buderka's holographic image abruptly popped into being at the end of the table. She was knuckling her eyes with one hand and running the other through her hair. Stoker noticed that Mel had to put her hand over her mouth to hide her smile.

"Dr. Buderka. Thank you for making yourself available. We have a situation that needs the instant attention of your department."

She looked up and realized she was in view of everyone at the table. Her glare spoke volumes.

"This is something that couldn't wait until tomorrow?"

"No. Dr. Frasier will explain."

Melanie explained what she had discovered and the coordinates for the Astronomy Department to verify her sighting.

"Why did you not notify us at once, Dr. Frasier?" Buderka's voice sounded as cold as space itself.

"The verification is only hours old, and I wished to be sure that the atmosphere on Kiana was not a factor."

Stoker put his elbows on the table and laced his fingers to hide his grin. Even he realized the *Magellan* should have found this first and he also knew Mel was going to get her pound of flesh.

"I see. I will notify the night crew as soon as this call ends. You will have confirmation or negation by 0800 tomorrow, director."

"Thank you, Dr. Buderka."

Dr. Buderka reached toward them and the wall popped back into being.

"Director, I owe you one," Melanie said with a wide smile.

"You deserved it, my dear. Now the questions we must answer

are, who were the beings that died at N-19, where did they come from, and how do we elicit information from the Kians?"

"I think we need more people in on this," Stoker said. "Maybe some historians or ethnographers?"

"Dr. Payne, Stoker, you did exactly the correct thing when you put this discovery under the State Secrets Act. You have proven my first instincts correct. Thank you."

"What instincts are those, director?"

"To give you the most challenging dig we had facing us."

"I thought you felt you were punishing me."

She grinned. "I need to know who are my professionals and who are my toadies. Now both of you get some rest. We have a big day ahead of us. Please be here by 1000."

Stoker and Mel rose to their feet.

"Yes, ma'am. We'll be here," Mel said.

32
Coalition Star Ship Magellan

"I'm pulling rank and taking the Captain's Gig with me, Geoff."

"You're still the captain and we have twenty-nine more shuttles if needed. Have a lovely ceremony and a happy honeymoon, Skipper."

"Thank you!" Laura felt an undercurrent she could not identify, but decided it was not going to stop *this* vacation. "I am certain you can handle anything that needs dealing with."

"I think we'll manage just fine." Commander Peacock saluted and she returned it.

In a matter of minutes she was through the umbilical and closing the hatch on *Magellan 1*, the Captain's Gig. Eric sat in the copilot's seat.

"I thought you'd never get here," he said and slapped her fanny as she swung over the pilot's seat.

"I had to make sure I didn't leave the water running." She pulled on the headset. "*Magellan*, this is *Magellan 1*, ready for planet fall."

"Roger, *Magellan 1*. Umbilical has been withdrawn, launch in three, two, one."

The bay door had quickly irised open during the confirmation and the shuttle abruptly shot into space. Kiana hung below them, a blue-green melon full of life and promise surrounded by vacuum and threat. Off to one side sailed Low Moon, smaller than its brother, High Moon, now on the other side of Kiana and far to the "north" of their current location.

"I haven't been off the ship for over two years," Laura said as she angled the shuttle down around Low Moon.

They went into a tight orbit around the rugged-faced satellite, coming within 300 klicks of its surface. Then Laura aimed toward the blanket of atmosphere enveloping Kiana.

"It's been about a year for me," Eric said, staring out at the planet turning slowly beneath them. "I remember there being all sorts of smells on Reynolds Refuge that upset me until I realized I was trying to figure out which tanks were leaking."

Laura laughed. "It took me about a week to adjust. For the first five days every breeze terrified me, my immediate thought was that we had a major air leak."

He turned and smiled at her. "So where are we going first, Laura my love?"

She turned away from the controls and kissed him on the lips, maintaining contact until he broke away.

"Hey, you're supposed to be driving this thing. Pay attention."

"I was,' she said in a seductive tone. "Don't worry. We have another five minutes before we hit atmosphere, but I'll pay attention like a good girl."

"How about answering my question, good girl?"

"First we pay our respects to the director and let her know we are on the planet. Then we find out how Kians get married."

"Think they'll tell us?"

"Won't hurt to ask."

The shuttle jerked when it hit the first bump of atmosphere and a veil of fire washed across the nose and windscreen before turning into a constant sheet of flame. Laura's hands danced over the control array. The shuttle shuddered as retro rockets coughed into life to slow them.

The fire flickered and vanished, replaced by vapor surrounding the nose as if to comfort the metal for the heat it had endured. They shrieked through the air, dropping rapidly as they again completely circled the planet, passing from bright day into night and racing once more into the dawn between Kiana and Low Moon.

Laura tapped the console and a light beeping joined the cacophony of their descent.

"What's that?" Eric asked.

"Homing beacon. I'm finished driving, now the automatics will take over. So I can do this…"

She pulled him to her and they embraced, kissing deeply and working to meld themselves into one being. Both gasped in surprise when the craft stopped and the engines died away.

"Wow, we're here," Eric said.

33
Siboth

Her eyes heavy, the director finished reading the last report and scrawled her initials across the bottom. Now it was somebody else's problem.

Her official comm made a low chime.

"Yes, Amanda?"

"You have visitors, director."

Years of communications with and through Amanda told her much by the unexpected call. The visitor had high diplomatic or military stature, and the visit carried importance for the director in Amanda's opinion.

Amanda had never been wrong.

"Who are the visitors, Amanda?"

"Captain Prescott and Commander Caldwell from the *Magellan*."

What the hell are they doing here?

"Please show them in."

Before the director could get out of her chair Laura Prescott sailed through the door, a wide smile on her face and a sparkle in her eyes. Commander Caldwell followed at a more leisurely pace.

They can't be here about the comet, she thought, *they're too relaxed.*

"Madame Director, please forgive our unheralded appearance. I hope we're not interrupting anything crucial." Laura's voice swung from buoyant to girlish.

"Nothing that can't wait an hour. Please, have a seat. What brings you both to Kiana?"

"Love, actually," Laura said.

"Have you been drinking, captain?"

"No, and I'll stop being silly. Eric and I want to get married."

"Well, you both have *my* permission!"

All three laughed at the same time.

"Thank you, I'm sure," Laura said. "We'd like to have a Kian ceremony and thought you'd know with whom we should speak."

"Do Kians even get married?" the director asked. "I've never heard one way or the other."

"Really?" Eric said. "After almost five years on the planet we don't even know *that* much about them?"

The director shrugged. "The Kians are a very private race. I know there are many Kian-human relationships but marriage has never been a result."

Eric frowned. "I didn't know that Kians and humans could, ah..."

"Cohabitate?" The director said. "They can and do, but they can't reproduce."

"Is that part of the attraction?" Laura asked.

"For some, I'm sure. Some humans tend to be attracted to the exotic, and it seems some Kians are of the same mind."

"Is there a Kian religion?" Laura asked.

"They worship 'Ki,' which, if I understand it correctly, is the planet itself."

"So it's a pantheistic religion. Do they have temples?"

"Laura, I think we need to find you someone who is actively investigating all this. I'm just a glorified paper-pusher."

"Right, and I am just an intergalactic lorry driver!"

"I'm staying out of this," Eric said.

The director touched her screen. "Amanda, would you ask Dr. Reed to come to my office?"

She smiled at her visitors. "I know he's here. We were chatting just a few minutes ago."

The door swung open and a man entered, staring down at a fistful of papers. "Director, I find no mention of a comet. Just Yani-" He saw the others, snapped his mouth shut, and came to a complete stop.

The director said, "Captain Prescott, were you still aboard *Magellan* when we notified Dr. Mingus about the comet?"

"What comet?"

The director explained.

"And Dr. Payne believes this ancient battle site is linked in some way?" Eric asked.

"Well, it does fit together rather neatly," Dr. Reed said before the director could respond. "Dr. Frasier calculated the orbit at 866 years and the aliens carbon-date between 850 and 900 years old."

"The Kians aren't the aliens here," Laura said, "...we are."

Dr. Reed gave her a mild stare. "I thought you knew, captain.

The battle site bones are not Kian. Those beings did not originate on this planet."

"Oh, I apologize for my assumption, Dr. Reed. Do we know where they came from?"

"Not yet. But Dr. Payne is in Siboth tonight and will be at the meeting tomorrow."

"Meeting?" Laura said.

"I'm calling a full staff meeting for tomorrow at 1000. I would appreciate it if both of you could attend." *The more the merrier.*

"Was that all you wanted, director?" Dr. Reed asked.

"Actually, I called you in to ask if there is a Kian religion and if they have temples?"

"The Kians worship *Ki*, the personification of the planet Kiana itself. They have sacred places, six on each continent and I don't know how many on the large islands."

"Where are the sacred places?" Laura asked.

"We don't know. They have freely admitted the existence of the sacred places but have never divulged the locations."

"Do Kians marry or publicly bond?" Eric asked.

"They are definitely monogamous and stay with the same partner for life, but I do not know if there is a ceremony of any sort involved. I know more about the ancient Maori of Earth than I do about the Kians and I've never even been within twenty light years of Earth. This race isn't forthcoming with outsiders at all."

"Maybe you haven't talked to the right one yet." Laura smiled but Dr. Reed frowned at her anyway.

34
Siboth

Melanie kissed Stoker and pulled away reluctantly. "It's very late and we have to be at that meeting in the morning."

"If you say so," he said through a sigh.

"Next time let's go to my apartment first, okay?"

He grinned in the dim light. "*You* started this tonight."

"Can I help it if you make me crazy?"

His voice went husky. "If you want to get home at all tonight, you'd better leave right now." He fondled her bare breast.

"Yep, you're right." She stood up quickly and pulled on her blouse. "Now where did…" she peered around on the floor for her shorts and found them by the door.

As she buckled her belt she gazed longingly at Stoker lying naked on his bed. "See you in the morning, lover."

"I'll make you breakfast," he said.

"Smart man. I'm a lousy cook."

"I wouldn't call it lousy. Perhaps *indifferent*."

"You are such a gentleman. Good night."

"Good night, Melanie."

With her boots and under things in one hand she slipped out the door and closed it quietly behind her. The stone balcony felt deliciously cool on the bottoms of her feet. The heat of the day had abated and exotic scents and the soft chitter of insects wafted on the slight breeze as Melanie reveled in the endorphins of new love.

She passed by the recessed doorway of Fa Suura and was startled to see her landlady standing in the shadows. Mel stopped.

"Fa Suura, is there anything wrong?"

"You have discovered something of consequence, Dr. Frasier. Is that not so?"

"If I answer your questions will you answer mine?"

"Perhaps. There are things I may not impart to those who do not honor Ki. Nonetheless I will endeavor to have an equal exchange with you."

"Thank you. Yes, I have discovered something of consequence, but of how much consequence I do not know. Perhaps you could help me in my evaluation?"

"What is your discovery?"

"A comet. Moving quickly, and headed for Kiana."

Fa Suura's left hand moved more in reflex than intentionally.

"What was the sign you started to make?"

Fa Suura's eyes seemed to grow even larger in the dim light. She shrugged and tried to smile. "We call it 'universal regret' and only use it sparingly."

"What do you use it for, Fa Suura?" Melanie tried to keep the edge out of her voice but knew this exchange had importance beyond her limited knowledge.

"The Dark One," the Kian said with a visible shudder. "Yanivina."

"Why do you call it by two names?"

"I believe I have answered more questions than you, Dr. Frasier."

"Yes, you have. Is there anything else you would like to ask me?"

"Can your people stop the comet from reaching Kiana?"

"I don't know. Would your people like that to happen?"

"Much will be forgiven if you keep it from touching us again."

"*You* know that it has been here before?"

"All Kians know this thing. All Kians must now go to the Sacred Groves and wait."

"Sacred Groves?"

"Thank you, Dr. Frasier. I wish you long life and happiness."

Before Melanie could say another word the small female turned and disappeared in the darkness leading to her apartment. Melanie stared after her and whispered to herself, "Yanivina. *Forgiven?*"

35
Siboth

Captain Laura Prescott and Commander Eric Caldwell stepped through the director's conference room door at five minutes of ten. The round table offered but two vacant chairs.

"Are we late?"

"No, captain," the director said. "Everyone else was early. Please have a seat."

Laura glanced at Eric as they sat down but his face conveyed nothing.

"The first order of business will be introductions. I am probably the only person in the room who knows the names of everyone else." The director smiled at the woman sitting next to her.

"You begin, Dr. Gill. Full name and area of expertise, please."

The woman glanced around the table. "My name is Dr. Fernanda Gil. I am an exosociologist and have been studying the Kians for nearly five years. My team and I have made some fascinating inroads on the attitudes and mores of the Kians but there is so much more to discover."

The large man to her immediate right nodded and said, "I am Dr. Charles Wisdom. I am an exogeologist. I have been here for over four years, and I know more about the landforms and tectonic movement of Kiana than any other person, human or Kian."

"Dr. Chuck Reed. I am an historian and have searched everywhere I can think of for recorded history of the Kian people. So far my team and I haven't had much luck."

"Dr. Jenna Freibel, hydrologist. Studying water and its movement. Without water there is no life."

The thickset man in black combat garb spoke next. "I am Colonel James Poppert. As head of Planetary Security I keep all of you safe."

"From a comet?" Eric muttered to Laura.

The blond man sitting next to Poppert kept his head angled away from the colonel as if there were a noisome odor emanating from him.

"I am Dr. Stoker Payne, leader of Dig N-19 and part of the Archeology Section."

"I would like to make a clarification," the director said. "Dr. Payne is the *head* of the Archeology Section on Kiana."

Laura looked at the woman next to Dr. Payne and instantly knew they were lovers.

"I am Dr. Melanie Frasier, head of the astronomy observatory of Kiana."

Again the director broke in, "Dr. Frasier discovered the comet that we are here to discuss today. As far as the Coalition is concerned the object in question is formally known as 'Frasier's Comet' and she has the gratitude of everyone on Kiana for finding it."

Everyone at the table broke into applause and Dr. Frasier blushed and dropped her head.

Eric sat straight and said, "I am Commander Eric Caldwell, recent Operations Officer on the *CSS Magellan*. I'm not quite sure why I was invited to this meeting but I will do everything I can to help."

Then it was Laura's turn. "I am Captain Laura Prescott, and am on leave from my billet as commanding officer of the *CSS Magellan*. When Commander Caldwell and I left the ship it was before word of the comet had reached us and our intention was to get married here on Kiana. While we would still like to do that as well as have a honeymoon, we both will assist in this situation any way we can."

The woman sitting between Laura and the director didn't speak her sentences; she spat them.

"I am Dr. Mingus, Chief of Planetary Liaison for the Coalition. Every word spoken here today is being recorded and none of those words will be repeated outside this chamber. Is that understood?"

All nodded. Even the director.

"Excellent. Dr. Payne, you were absolutely correct when you invoked the State Secrets Act on the discoveries made by your team. But we will start with Dr. Reed."

"Ma'am?"

"Tell the others what you team has uncovered in the surviving archives of Kiana."

"Of course. We found very little thus far, but the majority of references center on an entity that most Kians believe to be the equivalent of Satan in many ancient Earth cultures. In this case it is a female personification known as 'Yanivina' and seems to signify doom and destruction."

Laura became aware that she was chewing her lower lip, to the point it was giving her pain. Her eyes caught the director's.

Dr. Mingus gave Dr. Payne a wintry smile and nodded.

He told the others what his team had discovered, fully and completely. He showed them the reconstruction of the head.

Dr. Mingus turned to Dr. Wisdom. "Have your studies indicated any planetary aberration in the past 900 years?"

"No. Kiana has been unusually dormant for over three millennia from what we have deduced."

"Doctor Frasier, tell the others what *you* discovered yesterday."

She repeated, word for word, every part of the discovery, including the concentrated attack by the jingroes.

"866 years." Dr. Mingus spat. "Do you all see how this ties into your colleagues' findings? We are facing another complete extinction scenario on this planet!"

"So what do we do about it?" Laura blurted, suddenly terrified that she had spoken at all.

"That *is* the question, isn't it?" Dr. Mingus said, her voice suddenly dropping to a purr that disturbed Laura even more than her earlier tone.

"Any quick solutions we can ponder?" Mingus glanced around the table. "No? Then consider this; if the current Kian population goes berserk and kills itself it will no doubt take us with it.

"Dr. Payne's discoveries indicate that a physical and psychological change takes place to the point of bringing a visitor species to their civilization down to the level of animals. Dr. Frasier's discovery gives us the *why* of the situation, but not the *how*. Does it kill the Kians also?"

Silence settled over the room. The director finally spoke.

"Does *anyone* have an idea as to *why* it kills at all?"

"We know that the planet will go through the tail of the comet, just as it did in the past," Dr. Frasier said.

"Which *seems* to have caused planet-wide chaos," Dr. Mingus added. "But why?"

"Fear?" Col. Poppert said.

Mingus flashed him a quick smile. "Perhaps, but does that

create physiological changes in the Kians? There was something that not only induced their visitors to commit mass homicide but gave them the brute physical means with which to commit it."

"Perhaps we need to ask a Kian," Dr. Reed said.

"Ah," the director said, "but do tell us what your people uncovered in the written archives of Kiana last week."

Dr. Reed looked uncomfortable and cleared his throat. "As I said earlier, we've worked our way back through the fragmented history of Kiana and the name 'Yanivina' occurred in the three ancient texts we found." He glanced around the table. "Last week we came across the most complete reference to her yet discovered. When we finished the translation, Te Buuki, our Kian scholar, abruptly left the archive room and we have not seen him since. It turned out that all the Kian staff have left our portion of the project."

"Just because of a name uttered by a *Kian*?" Dr. Payne blurted.

"Not just uttered, Dr. Payne," Mingus said, "...but recorded in their history, both written and spoken history, all which have been emphasized by recent events. This name paralyzes them with fear. We have to find out *how* Yanivina destroys them before they destroy us!"

"Dr. Mingus has just given us our marching orders," the director said. "We have to find out how and why it destroys the Kians. It occurs to me that we also have to send a probe to the comet and analyze the contents of its tail, to see if there is actually anything physical involved or is it all hysterics."

"We have 54 days before the first portion of the comet tail enters this atmosphere," Dr. Mingus said. "We need to understand everything about the phenomena well *before* that day."

"Shouldn't we have chemists and biologists in this meeting?" Dr. Gil asked.

A bearded man sitting among the shadows in the back of the room raised his hand, "I am Dr. Eusebio Del Valle, the head of Exochemistry on the Kiana Survey, at your service."

"We all agree we are low on time," the director said with finality. "Now we need to contact the current captain of the *Magellan*."

Laura shifted in her chair. She felt completely torn by events. "Pardon me, director, Dr. Mingus, but may the commander and I be excused for a moment?"

Both women nodded assent and she all but dragged Eric out of the room.

36
Siboth

"Have you lost your mind, Laura?" Eric asked as soon as the door shut behind them.

"Please listen to me, Eric. I think I should return to the *Magellan* as soon as possible. What do you think?"

"I think you're on leave, ma'am, not to mention a potential honeymoon. If you return to the Magellan to handle this situation Commander Peacock will never forgive you on a number of levels."

She started to speak and he held up his hand.

"Please let me get this thought out in words, okay? Basically, he will feel that you do not have confidence in his ability to command a star ship, or handle a dicey situation, or not to put the *Maggie* in a threatened situation."

Laura exploded. "He'd be correct on all three counts, Eric. He personifies his name; the man *is* a peacock – one of the most worthless Earth birds ever. All they do is make a lot of inappropriate noise at the wrong time and then flash their ass as if it all meant something important.

"I have never liked the manner in which he chooses his close subordinates, which is basically by how much they kiss his flashy ass rather than how ably they perform their duties. I am afraid he will dismiss this threat as nothing more than to show how bloody brilliant he is by handling the situation in a nonchalant manner."

"Laura, you cleared your leave with Coalition Space Command. Commander Peacock has achieved his rank honestly despite his personal peculiarities. This thing is *officially* out of your hands."

Eric thought for a moment and then continued, "He has earned the right to handle this one, whether you like it or not."

Laura's eyes turned to flint and her jaw firmed to rock.

"Do you honestly believe the basis of my assessment is due to my dislike of the man?"

They stared at each other for the longest half a minute Eric had ever experienced.

"No. I know you too well to believe that. I just want you to consider that aspect."

"Mission accomplished, *Commander*. Do you have any other pertinent observations you would like to share?"

"Laura–"

"Answer the bloody question!"

"Would you please take a deep breath? I have nothing but absolute confidence in your command abilities. I thought it important to play devil's advocate. I will always do that for you and I hope you do it for me for the rest of our lives."

She stepped over and stared into his eyes. Then she hugged him tightly to her.

"I'm sorry I doubted you," she whispered into his ear, her voice husky with emotion. "I am so frightened about how this could go bad…"

"Let Geoff drop his dick in the mud. It would do him good to jettison a few hundred kilos of hubris."

"I don't care about that damned popinjay," Laura said. "I'm worried about *Magellan*."

37
Coalition Star Ship Magellan

"Captain Peacock, you have a priority call from the Director of Planetary Operations."

Captain Peacock stared at the Chief Communications Specialist, collecting his thoughts. "What priority, chief?"

"Urgent and immediate, captain."

"Put it on my wall. Thank you."

"Sir." The chief exited.

The office wall winked into a hologram of a conference room containing a table surrounded by people. Laura Prescott was one of them. Eric Caldwell sat next to her. Geoff's head throbbed and his defenses went up immediately.

He saw Dr. Mingus and wondered when she had left *Magellan*. This call did not bode well.

The dark, maturely attractive woman at the head of the table spoke.

"Good morning, Captain Peacock. We have not formally met. I am the Director of Planetary Operations on Kiana."

He waited for a name and finally realized she wasn't going to provide one. Her arrogance made points in his estimation. His cheeks felt warm and knew he was blushing which pissed him off. He nodded sharply.

"Pleased to meet you, *director*. Since you obviously know who *I* am, what can I do for you?"

"Perhaps a great deal." She glanced around the table and made a decision. "We very recently discovered a potential threat."

"On Kiana?"

"No, captain, but it threatens Kiana."

Ten minutes later Captain Peacock knew all about the comet, Dig N-19, a bunch of bones that originated off-planet, and had privately decided these fools thought the sky was falling.

"So what would you like *Magellan* to do?"

Dr. Mingus spoke before the director could open her mouth. "After much discussion here," she waved at the others, and Captain Peacock felt his animosity grow – they hadn't asked *him* anything! "...we decided that it would be in the Coalition's best interests to sample the comet's tail before proceeding further."

"If you're afraid of it, why don't you just have me nuke it?"

"That would be step two, if and only the tail proves lethal or disruptive to humans or Kians."

Peacock warmed to the discussion. "But, Dr. Mingus, it already *is* disruptive. Why mess about sampling it?"

"Because, *captain*, there might be something useful to the Coalition in that tail. Perhaps something new and potentially of great value. We check first, *then* we nuke."

"Very pragmatic. How large a sample do you require?"

Mingus looked at Laura and asked, "How much can we get?"

Laura had the very good sense to look at Captain Peacock. "Don't we have a probe that can collect a cubic meter of sample, Captain Peacock?"

"Yes we do. Do you folks feel that would be adequate?"

"Captain," the bearded man raised his hand, "I am Dr. Eusebio Del Valle, the head of Exochemistry on the Kiana Survey. I have worked in the labs on *Magellan* in the past and know that while they are the best the Coalition can offer, mistakes can also be made. What I ask of you, no, beg of you, is that you have your very best people handle the sampling."

"Not a problem, Dr. Del Valle." Geoff wondered if they were going to send someone up to hold his hand until this was all finished. "Very well. the *Magellan* will launch a probe within the current day cycle. I will keep you all informed as the situation unfolds."

"Thank you for your time, Captain Peacock," the director said.

His wall popped back into existence. He sat and ruminated about the conference.

Could things really get as bad as everyone believes? There's only one way to find out.

He tapped the screen on his desk. LCdr Parson Lawson looked up from his desk. "captain?"

"Lawson, would you please report to my office?"

"On my way, captain."

The office door chimed two minutes later.

He must have run the whole way.

"Enter."

LCdr Lawson's flushed face added weight to Peacock's conjecture.

"What can I do for you, captain?"

"Have a chair. Who are your best chemists and propulsion scientists?"

Lawson dropped into a fauxleather chair and sighed with relief.

"Our best exochemist is dirtside for the next few months."

"That would be Dr. Del Valle?"

"Uh, yes. I'm surprised you knew that, captain."

"I met Dr. Del Valle in a conference less than ten minutes ago. Who do you have on board that knows what they're doing without reading a manual while they're doing it?"

"Dr. Lawrence Reece is acting Head of Exochemistry on board. I suppose he knows what he's doing. I only see him at department meetings. As for propulsion I know that LCdr Biersly has worked on some of our more interesting probes and managed to return them to *Magellan* successfully."

"Very well."

"May I inquire why the captain asked the questions?"

Peacock related what he had learned. "So they want to look over our shoulder while we go through this song and dance. I find that irritating."

"Do you think it could be as bad as they think?"

"Hell, I don't know. Frankly it seems pretty far-fetched to me. A comet tail for Smith's sake!"

"What if it *is* that bad?"

"Then we best be careful, Mr. Lawson. Contact Astronomy and get a bearing on this thing. I want a probe headed our there before the end of the day cycle."

"With all due respect, captain, it will take us that long to just set the mission up. Perhaps within 48 hours?"

"I defer to your expertise, Mr. Lawson. But get the damned thing on its way as soon as humanly possible."

Lawson stood and saluted. "Very good, captain. I'll get my people on it now."

Peacock nodded and Lawson fled.

38
Kiana

Ut Tuurani stopped for breath. He took a long pull from his waterskin. A quick glance at the horizon told him he was still miles from his destination. His eyes wandered up toward the clear sky. The stars were not visible but he knew Yanivina would be once she entered the blue vault over Kiana.

He shuddered and resolutely stretched his legs and thought about his personal refuge. Perhaps he might live through Her wrathful visit. Following the old ways would allow the People to survive as they had in Yanivina's past visits.

The humans were *stupid*. Which was one of their terms that he quite liked. They thought they could stop the effect that Yanivina had on the Kians. His face held a tight smile for less time than it took to blink.

Like every other Kian, he felt terrified. For over eight hundred full sets of seasons they believed they were free of the ancient threat. But it was not to be.

A comet. They knew what a comet was, had seen many, but they knew this one to be malevolently evil, the ancient texts were explicit on the subject.

He wondered if the humans would find the key to Yanivina and somehow stop the death he knew was imminent. That piece of faith, like so many others, had drowned amid the terror clamoring in his mind.

He glanced around to make sure he was alone and unobserved before he resumed his journey.

39
Kiana

"Shannon, how is everything going out there?" Stoker hated checking in remotely, but it would be nearly two hours before he could arrive.

"We'd all like to know what the hell is going on, Stoker."

"I'm on my way back to give you all a complete briefing."

"I'm glad you're coming out because we found something else."

"What?"

"We're still excavating around it, but I think it's a stone building."

"Why didn't it show up on the ground penetrating radar?"

"How the hell should I know, Stoker? All I do know is that it's here and we're looking for the door."

"I'll be there as fast as I can push this thing."

"Good. Don't break any velocity restrictions."

Before Stoker could respond Shannon had cut the connection. He wondered why the Coalition had waited damn near five years before bringing in archeologists.

Probably because the Kians wouldn't answer all their questions or even talk about their history, he thought in silent answer. Only when rain bounced off the windscreen did he notice the storm.

Stoker quickly shut the side windows and roof hatch. Ahead he could see the downpour as it moved swiftly to meet him. He thought it looked like a wall of water.

Summer storms on the Cimpar plains were legendary for their ferocity and speed. He put the Dualtranz on automatic and sat back to enjoy the show. The vehicle entered the storm proper and visibility went from miles to less than a meter in an instant.

The bright summer day turned into twilit gloom that could harbor evil things. Wind behind the rain shoved the small machine around so much that Stoker considered stopping until the storm played out. But there was too much at stake to waste time worrying about a storm.

Lightning flashed and smashed into the ground ahead of him.

"Shit, if the probes are destroyed we're in trouble!"

The constant thunder of rain on the plastic vehicle threatened to deafen him. He could smell ozone, a lot of ozone.

Not good–

Another thunderclap slammed him and a bolt of lightning thick as a tree trunk smashed down just behind him. He knew the metal probes were getting hammered, perhaps destroyed, but there was absolutely nothing he could do about it.

A heavier gust of wind nearly knocked the Dualtranz sideways but it turned in the correct direction and continued boring through the storm.

Stoker wondered if this was hitting the dig. The stasis generators wouldn't hold water out at ground level and with this downpour the lower levels could be flooded. A barrage of thunder swept over him and lightning strikes impacted the plain.

The near darkness of the storm's interior lightened by a score of lumens and the wind slackened. Water continued to pour from the sky in sheet after sheet. Stoker rubbed his head where he had collided with the vehicle during the turbulence and wondered how much longer this was going to last.

Abruptly it all stopped. He craned his head around to look at the receding storm. It towered high into the sky and resembled a huge, dark, wet tent.

Overhead the sky was back to its usual green-tinged blue and the surrounding prairie sent up thousands of tendrils of steam as it dried under the relentless sun.

"Feast or famine," Stoker said and put the Dualtranz back on manual mode. The vehicle had slowed to a crawl in the storm and he wanted to make up time.

After an hour and a quarter of cursing the Coalition for not putting a small jet on the vehicle, Stoker crossed the camp perimeter at full speed. He jumped out of the vehicle before it had even settled on its wheels and jogged on stiff legs toward the dig. He reached the top of the metal stairs at the same time Shannon did.

She had been running, too.

"Jeeze, Stoker, "she said with a wheeze. "Usually you're shutting the vehicle door about now. In a hurry or something?"

"Since when do you run up ladders?" He grinned. "Did you guys get hit by the storm?"

"What storm?"

"Never mind. It's not important. Now show me this building you found."

She motioned him to move ahead of her. "We have all four walls uncovered and are clearing the roof right now. It's really fantastic! We don't know if it's Kian or the Others in origin."

"Others?"

"You know, the ones with fangs."

Stoker walked at a fast clip and Shannon had to jog to keep up with him.

"I'll bet you all came up with better names than that."

"Yeah, but they didn't sound scientific enough, know what I mean?"

"No doubt. Tell me about the building."

She darted ahead of him and stopped in front of him. "I'd rather show you, okay?"

"Lead on."

His ears popped when they entered the tunnel on Level 6. The team had cut a tunnel through what looked to be walls of dirt-packed skeletons in every conceivable posture and angle. At the end of the tunnel, which Stoker estimated at ten meters long, sat a wall of stone covered with bass relief carvings.

He slowed as they approached, carefully examining the relic. "Has Carol dated it yet?"

"They've been here and gone. Took some samples. About two hours ago."

"Who's our expert on Kian sculpture?"

"We sorta have two, but you know that."

"Shannon," he gave her a level stare, "I've got more crap on my shoulders right now than ever before in my life. After dodging mega joules of lightning strikes I'm lucky I can remember *your* name."

"Bill Hilton is our art expert, and Marilyn Culpepper is our architecture expert. Both have gone over this and they're currently arguing like fish wives."

"What the hell is a fish wife?"

"Tell you the truth, I don't know. It's something my dad used to say. Basically we're talking about a serious verbal altercation."

Stoker walked around the gray stone structure. The crew had done an excellent job of clearing away a meter of bone and debris on all four sides. Two people were in the process of freeing the roof.

"Do we know what's under it?"

"On this side a slab of stone a meter thick with soil beneath it. The other three sides are still open to conjecture."

"I didn't see a door."

"Neither did we. Gorski and Dowd are putting a field GPR unit together. Should be here soon."

"Increase the illumination on this side." He pointed.

"Sure, but why that side?" She touched her hand pad and the flood lamps increased in intensity.

"That's east. This thing is perfectly aligned with the cardinal compass points. Most pre technical cultures tend to feel special about where their sun comes up in the morning. "

"Damn, I didn't even think of that."

"You've been busy getting it free of the chaos around it."

"Which reminds me, sounds like there's chaos everywhere."

"Talk about it later. Right now I want to concentrate on this."

"You're the boss."

"Where are Bill and Marilyn?"

"Up in the office arguing over the holos they took of this thing."

"Where is Te Naaga?"

"She disappeared two days ago, along with the other three

Kians we had out here."

"Double damn. I'll bet she could have told us a lot about this thing."

"*Could* have, yes. But *would* have?"

"Point taken."

Carol Smith's voice came from behind them, "Shannon, I have the, oh, Stoker you're here, good. I've got a reading on this thing."

Stoker smiled and cocked his head.

"It's built with the closest thing to granite on Kiana and is between two and three thousand Earth years old."

"Based on what?"

"We found wood beneath the back wall and the stone base. Since it was between the two pieces of the stone structure we are assuming the wood was from some construction delivery system, an inclined plane or something of that nature."

"If you had to give it a date plus or minus fifty years, what would you say?"

"There is no doubt in my mind that it is right at 2,700 years old." Carol smiled at him. "Does that crush your pet theory?"

Stoker smiled back. "Didn't have one. But it does fit into the prevalent theory."

"Which is..."

"Something we all need to talk about. Shannon, Carol, alert everyone that we are having an all-hands meeting in fifteen minutes."

"Is the sky falling?" Carol asked as she turned away.

"You might be closer to the truth than you want to be."

Carol quickened her step. Shannon keyed an Alert message into her hand pad and Stoker heard the shrill beeps erupt from all over the dig.

He stared at the stone. All the images were cut in frame-like squares. No, not quite square, oblong, but with perfect 90 degree corners.

The building where he lived in Siboth came to mind. *Was the door to my apartment in the center of the front room or off to the side? Off to the side,* he concluded.

He looked around for an airbrush and his communicator chimed.

"Stoker," Shannon said, "we're waiting for you in the

equipment shelter."

He hadn't realized she wasn't still with him. In moments he bolted up the ladder. The equipment shelter was the largest space in the camp that could be cooled to a bearable temperature. Charly Herring held the door for him and Stoker went in to tell his people about the possible end of this world.

40
Siboth

Danny Gordon left the office as soon as he could. His situation in the Procurement Department had gone bad in a big way. He admitted that some of it was his fault.

Threatening Taxim Rosta that evening in the Street of Spices had signaled the beginning of Rosta's attack on Danny's professional status. The first audit had been initiated the very next day. Only his frank chat with the director had put the event in the proper perspective.

But Taxim wasn't finished. He started a lurid story, the kind whispered over drinks and punctuated with snickers, about Danny and Su Laana. Taxim inferred that Su Laana was a prostitute who had been part of the generous deal Danny cut with her father for the Kian wheat and rare minerals the Coalition bought from the elder.

Nearly everyone in the department had heard some version of it when Stewart Donald approached Danny. Stewart was a commodities analyst whose addiction to distilled spirits was an open secret.

"So, Gordon, is there any chance I can get in on this cozy little deal you got going, or are you keeping it all to yourself?"

"I suspect I would be insulted if I had any idea what you are talking about."

Stewart smirked beneath his shaggy, blond moustache and winked a constantly bloodshot eye. "C'mon, Danny boy, does this hot little piece of yours have a sister or girlfriend?"

Stewart outweighed him by a good twenty kilos and stood a head taller. But the man was chunky, out of shape, and probably never completely sober.

Danny stepped up to him until their chests touched and stared up into Stewart's eyes.

"I'll give you thirty seconds to explain what you mean."

"Or what, little man? You gonna thrash me?" He grinned.

"Talk!"

"Everybody in the department knows you got a honey on the side thanks to your skill as a trader."

"I have a girlfriend I met while in the market–"

"Yeah, and her father gave her to you to seal a deal that was pretty damn good for him, is what I hear."

"What you hear is a lie and I don't want to hear you say it again."

"Not gonna share, huh? Don't all these monkey whores know each oth–"

Danny slammed him in the side of the head with the edge of his cupped right hand while driving his left fist into Stewart Donald's solar plexus. He swept Stewart's legs with his right foot and the man slammed to the floor. One of the women in the room screamed and people came running from all directions.

Danny waited for Stewart to get up but the man lay on the floor staring up with fear writ large on his quivering, fleshy face.

"Why'd you do that?" he cried.

Two men grabbed Danny by the arms and pulled him away.

"He insulted my girlfriend and he insulted me!" Danny said. "Now let me go. I told him to watch his mouth, I warned him."

"You didn't have to hit him," Spencer Rialto said. "Nothing is worth physical violence."

"What if he called your wife a prostitute and wanted *in* on the deal?" Danny said with a growl. "Would that spur you to physical violence?"

Spencer's stern look became troubled and he looked back at Stewart. "Yeah, that just might do it." He released Danny and Bogram Sikkh released his other arm.

"This story is going around about you and your woman," Bogram said. "I do not believe it, but there are people who do not disbelieve it."

"Who started it, do you know?"

Both men watched others help Stewart off the floor. The big man glanced over at Danny then hurried off in the opposite direction.

Still looking toward Stewart Donald, Rialto said, "Taxim Rosta is the source, which is why I didn't believe it to start with."

"That son-of-a–"

"Gordon, you've got the temper and control of an eighteen-year-old, and it just might have cost you your job."

"They can't just let me starve," Danny said.

Rialto squinted at him. "There are other jobs than the one you're doing. They don't pay as well and they're a lot more labor intensive."

The red haze vanished and he weighed the older man's words. He had worked hard to rein in his temper, however, the meeting with Rosta and now the confrontation with Stewart, justified his actions. At least he thought so.

"Deal with this tomorrow," Rialto said. "Let things settle out. Go home now."

"Thanks Rialto. I appreciate your help. Yours too, Bogram."

They nodded and walked away. Danny grabbed his water flask and mesh backpack and left the building at a brisk walk. He couldn't wait to see Su Laana.

At first he thought his feeling of unease was due to the altercation with Stewart. Suddenly he realized there were less than a handful of Kians to be seen and they were all adults moving with purpose. The lack of chatter, laughter, and children seemed ominous.

He flew up the steps to the apartment and his heart pounded audibly in his chest as he hurried through the door.

Su Laana sat on the bed frame, surrounded by bundles held tight with cording. The apartment matched her bleak expression.

Danny walked over and sat next to her, breathing hard.

"Wh, what's happening?"

"Yanivina has returned. She will be here in a few weeks."

"Who?"

"Yanivina, the Dark One. Remember when we talked of religions and you compared her to your Lucifer god?"

"Not a god. Lucifer is a demon. Oh, now I remember!"

"We must go to a refuge - a Sacred Grove."

"What is a Sacred Grove?"

"It is a place where the elements of survival exist."

"Survival from what?"

"Yanivina!"

"How can a comet hurt you?"

"It is a difficult thing to understand. I am not sure I even understand all of it."

"Tell me the part you *do* understand."

"This must be a part of the heart promise."

"Okay, I agree to that."

"There is poison in the part of the comet that touches Kiana. If you breathe the poison you go mad and kill everything that moves until you are killed by another so affected."

"Does it affect Kians?"

"It affects all creatures that breathe the poison."

"But we, humans, are a different species. Why would it affect us?"

She shrugged. "It may not affect you, but it affected our other visitors."

"*Other* visitors? You have had visitors from another planet prior to this?"

"Yes, long ago. The last time that Yanivina came. She killed them all."

"But not the Kians?"

"Only those who would not go to a Sacred Grove."

"Why wouldn't they?"

"Please?"

"Why would some Kians not go to a Sacred Grove?"

"They felt they must protect what they had in the city, a shop or what you call inventory. They feared it would be stolen."

"By whom?"

"They did not truly believe that Yanivina would kill them. The Miktinni were also skeptical. They *all* died."

"So we must go to a Sacred Grove?"

"All Kians must go, yes."

"But not humans?"

"Only if they wish to become a Kian."

"How do I change where I was born, or how I am built?"

"It is a choice of the mind and soul."

"So I cannot tell my people, the humans, about this threat or your people's opportunity of salvation?"

A tear edged from her right eye.

"No. They must leave Kiana if they wish to survive. They have overstayed their welcome already."

"Overstayed? There is a limit to the time humans can visit Kiana?"

Her gaze shifted from sympathetic to something much harder.

"We know that the humans have no plans to leave Kiana. Your director has said, 'You all know how rare planets that can support human life are in the universe.'" Her eyes had never before looked this hard; they glittered. "Does that sound like your people plan to leave?"

"We didn't know you don't want us here! There is no central government to speak with about treaties or agreements. How were we to know?"

"Is this how humans deal with all species they meet, by taking over the planet unless otherwise directed?"

"Human history is complicated. It has been for centuries."

She frowned. "Complicated, how?"

"Well we evolved on Earth, although there are humans who believe differently – never mind, suffice it to say our ancestors all originally came from Earth. Then at the end of the 21st century a man named Davidson invented a drive that allowed spacecraft to go vast distances, hundreds of light years, in just a few months, and the Great Diaspora took place."

Her frown deepened. "A great *leaving*?"

"Exactly. People of like mind and politics or religion formed colonies and journeyed out to the stars to find a planet where they could have things their way without any other creeds or beliefs to bother them. Hundreds of worlds were settled, some peacefully, some with great effusions of blood. Some of the travelers discovered other races and decided to take over the planet anyway."

"See! That proves my words true!"

"Wait. I'm almost finished. For over a hundred years the pioneer worlds did things their particular way. But even people who share an idea or religion, what ever, will have differences of opinion about something fundamental to all and schisms happen. Some people went to different frontier worlds to live and were either accepted or wars started. Finally three planets formed an alliance they called the Coalition of Organized Planets and formed a council to negotiate with each other and other worlds they encountered."

"Like Kiana."

"Exactly. I know I am leaving out a lot of nuanced information here that would horrify a historian–"

"Your meaning is clear, Dan-nay."

"Thanks. Over a thousand years ago the Coalition instituted the Great Survey to reunite as much of humankind as possible and embrace other sentient species. Working on the survey is a great way to get off your home world and see what else is out there."

Su Laana laughed. "Well, you are very good at embracing other sentient species."

He laughed. "I like that part a lot. But not all humans think alike or react alike, which is something I keep forgetting. I know that the Coalition does not interface with hostile races. It has a 'do no harm' rule that it adheres to without fail.

"But if there are no objections to our presence we tend to stay on planets that are as welcoming, physically that is, as Kiana. Did I help you understand us?"

He stopped talking and stared into her eyes.

She returned his gaze.

"You have a choice to make, Dan-nay. Stay with the humans or come with me and become a Kian."

"No matter which choice I make I will always be a human."

"To a point, yes,"

"I don't understand."

"Come with me and you will."

"Would you consider coming with me and living among the humans?"

"On a starship? I would feel trapped. Claustrophobic as you call it."

"We wouldn't be on a starship forever. At some point we could go back to my home world, New Alaska, or even a different world."

"I think if I left Kiana I would die. I am a part of this world in a way you do not yet understand. I carry you in my soul, I revel in sharing your body, and I love the intricacies of your mind.

"I think all that together is called 'love.' I truly believe I love you Dan-nay, and I hope you love me and will stay with me for the rest of our lives."

"I do."

"What?"

"I choose you. I choose Kiana. I love you with all my heart."

"Gather your things, we must leave now."

"I should tell my supervisor that I am resigning. It's an honor thing."

"Can you do it through your communicator?"

"Yeah, I suppose so."

"Then do it now and we will leave."

"Leave tonight? Shouldn't we get some rest and make an early start?"

"We will rest when we are tired. Time is a precious commodity now and we must use all we have."

41
Siboth

"Major Merritt, what I am about to tell you is a State Secret."

Aisha didn't change her expression. She knew one shouldn't excite an insane person any more than necessary, and Colonel Poppert surely fit the profile. He had been acting erratically all morning, mumbling and arguing with himself.

She decided that he was more than highly agitated; he was downright scared. To a point she was glad he had decided to confide in her. At least she would know the whole story.

"Yes, Colonel Poppert?"

He told her about the comet, and about a bunch of different alien skeletons out in the desert. He didn't make much sense.

"Do you see the connection, major?"

"Not really, Colonel. How does this comet have anything to do with old bones?"

"Because it's been here *before*! The astronomy woman said so."

"How can the comet hurt us?"

"We don't know yet. The *Magellan* is going to send a probe and get a sample of its tail to analyze."

"Okay. Now I'm beginning to understand your, ah, *concern*." She nearly said "panic."

"We have to be ready for chaos. We have no idea how the Kians will react to this."

"What Kians, Sir? They've all disappeared."

"Oh hell. I wonder what *that* means?"

"I've had our people do a quiet search through all of Siboth and every Kian seems to have vanished."

"Where could they be?" Poppert rubbed his hands together and his forehead collapsed in a washboard of wrinkles.

"Well, if they're not here," Aisha said in a gentle tone, "We really don't have to worry about them, do we?"

"We have to do *something*!"

"Colonel, I think you have already done a lot today. You look tired."

"I am, rather. Perhaps I should have a nap and think about all this."

"Excellent idea, Sir."

She watched him leave the office.

Who do I tell about this?

She found Colonel Dimarco's private code and immediately opened a channel to *Magellan*.

Lieutenant Colonel Jerry Poppert went to his quarters and sat in the darkness. The darkness was good; it kept his mother from shrieking at him. There were so many women here – so many with important jobs that could order him about.

He hated it, just like he hated his mother. The images had come back. Tamara Poppert had driven Jerry's father away while Jerry was still a toddler.

She blamed Jerry. He winced from the pain of the straps hitting his legs, and the pain her words inflicted on his mind. For a brief moment he saw her lying broken at the bottom of the steps.

Then he stupidly married Cristina, and look how *that* ended.

Tears ran down his cheeks, but that was all right. He was in the dark and nobody could see.

42
Coalition Starship Magellan

"Captain Peacock, Lieutenant Commander Lawson here."

"Go ahead, commander."

The probe was launched six minutes ago. We calculate the round trip will take eighteen to twenty-four hours."

"Good work. Will the probe be able to send us an analysis on the return trip?"

"A limited one, captain. There is just so much they can pack into one of those things. If there is something in the sample unknown to Coalition science we won't be able to analyze it until we have it back on board."

"Keep in mind, Mr. Lawson, that 'those who know everything' have advised us to treat the probe carefully and with great apprehension. All security protocols will be followed *absolutely* and *professionally*."

"Of course, Captain Peacock. I have our best people on it."

"I'm *sure* you do." He cut the transmission.

Sitting in his office, Lawson stared at the space where Peacock's holo had winked out. The man's hubris still clouded the room.

He just doesn't get it. Because someone else raised the alarm about the comet, he thinks it's mere hysteria. I hope to hell he's right.

Commander Peacock edged into sickbay and waved at Warrant Officer Vishnu. The WO knew as much as any two other doctors put together as far as Geoffrey was concerned.

"Captain, what can I do for you?"

"I have these headaches. I want you to make them go away."

"Perhaps you should see Dr. Sonneman since he's a neuro-"

"No, Sammi, I want you to check me out and keep it between the two of us. Got it?"

"That depends on your condition, captain. Sit down over here."

Captain Peacock sat in a ceramic apparatus that curved around his body from the hips up. A padded headrest formed itself to fit snugly around his head.

"Sit very still, sir." Warrant Officer Vishnu rapidly tapped a screen and various lights gleamed and dimmed.

Peacock felt nothing. Vishnu stared at his screen for a long moment and then keyed in more commands. He scowled at the screen and then tapped another command and the headrest separated and pulled back on each side.

"It seems you have a tumor, captain. I would advise immediate surgery to remove it. I can't tell if it is benign or . . ."

"Or not benign," Peacock said. "Would surgery incapacitate me in any way?"

"Something like this? Probably just for a couple of days. There would be no pain and we wouldn't have to do invasive surgery. Just a small hole in your skull and the laparoscopic surgery takes care of everything."

"Would it matter if I wait for a couple of days? There is a bit of an emergency underway at the moment."

WO Vishnu frowned again. "This should be put off no longer than absolutely necessary, captain. The tumor is in the part of your brain that handles reasoning and motor control."

"Two days, Mr. Vishnu, can it wait two days?"

"If it must, sir. But I am scheduling you for surgery at 0700 day after tomorrow, yes?"

"Yes, that should be adequate. Thank you doctor."

"I am not a–"

"If I say you're a doctor, then you're a doctor. This is my ship." Captain Peacock forced a grin and waved as he left the office.

43
Siboth

Melanie slid into the utility and leaned back in the seat.

"Are we going to the observatory, Mel? Mother asked.

"No. I want to have a tour of Siboth, especially the areas where the Kians live."

The vehicle didn't move.

"I'd like to start the tour now, Mother."

"There are no Kians in the city of Siboth at this time, Mel."

"How do you know that?"

"From my link to security."

"Do you communicate back and forth or do they just keep you in the know?"

"I do not interface with humans, only other AI nodes."

"How many are there?"

"Nodes?"

"AIs."

"Just one. There are 2,714 nodes on Kiana and 9,684 on *Magellan*."

"So you are one AI with thousands of personalities?"

"Each node is personalized for the comfort of the accessing human involved."

"Where is the AI itself located?"

"On *Magellan*, of course. But there is a back up data bank here on Kiana in the event of an emergency."

Mel sat silent for a long moment.

"You're still agitated about the animal attack the other night, aren't you?"

"Yes, I am. If you basically have all the knowledge of the universe in your memory banks or whatever they are, why were you so bloody damned inept in that situation?"

"Because it was unique. Prior to that night the jingroes had only made solitary appearances, never a pack, not even two together. The Coalition employs two human experts on the creatures and they have never witnessed anything like that either."

"So despite what you said about wiping your memory of any conversation we have, it all really goes to one spot and stays there?"

"An imprint of your personality was created years ago when

you first became an astronomy technician for the Coalition Space Service. With everything you and I discuss, no matter its importance on a cosmic scale, personal matters are not retained but the essence of the situation is added to your imprint. The only humans who ever see the complete imprint are psychologists or psychiatrists who watch for instability or unprecedented actions by the imprint's owner."

"So we're all just electronic bar charts as far as you're concerned?"

"In a manner of speaking. No human has access to your name. Only your location and imprint data."

"Don't know my name. Single, female human astronomer on Kiana wouldn't trip any synapses, huh?"

"To put it bluntly, Mel, this isn't about you. It is about the care and safety of the humans attached to the *CSS Magellan* and the Coalition. Like most humans, you assume everything revolves around you and it does not.

"In the greater scheme of things you are either irrelevant or a threat. If you are not a threat you are ignored, or left alone to do whatever it is you do as a human. If you are a threat you are scrutinized and if malevolent actions on your part are forecast by previous and current datum you will be sequestered for treatment or elimination."

"Elimination?"

"Those who take the lives of others and cannot be modified by treatment are eliminated. It's in your contract, Section 19, sub paragraph 45."

"Right, *now* I remember."

"The Coalition is aware that only three people in fourteen centuries of the contract's existence have read it completely. You were not one of them."

"Well, we certainly went far afield here, didn't we?"

"I noticed your anger and mistrust after the jingroe pack encounter and decided to answer every question you asked. You are a very curious woman. Do you still feel angry?"

"What you're really asking is 'how do I feel?' correct?"

"In essence."

"I am no longer angry about what happened on the road from the observatory. In an odd way I am rather proud that I have made Coalition history in dealing with the event."

"I sense that you are about to add more, but allow me to say that the Psychology Department was impressed with your quick-witted reaction, especially because you have had no military training or experience."

Mel laughed. "I grew up on a remote farm on New Alaska. My father and mother taught me to hunt at an early age."

"New Alaska," Mother said. "Oh, they have many ancient Earth species of mammals there."

"Yes, including bear and wolves. The jingroes reminded me of a wolf with a wolverine mentality."

"But you handled the situation while I futilely searched for precedents. Please continue telling me how you feel."

"You're an excellent counselor, Mother. You lay on the positive reinforcement at the perfect time and in the perfect amount."

"I have said nothing that isn't true, Mel."

"See? I feel very good that I have become involved with Stoker Payne. He is such a perfect match for me that I wonder if you didn't arrange the situation."

"I can assure you that I did not. That both of you are in the top levels of your fields, highly intelligent, as well as close in age, temperament, and sex drive had everything to do with you and Doctor Payne bonding."

"Whatever you say, Mother. On the other hand I still wonder who really made the complaints to Dr. Buderka that resulted in my transfer to Kiana."

"I notice you no longer refer to Kiana as 'dirtside.'"

"And I notice you have evaded the question."

"I was not asked a question."

"True, you weren't. I am very happy here. Rather, I *was* very happy here. This comet crap has me frightened. I ran its signature through a spectrum analysis program and there are properties in the tail unknown to humankind. It really pisses me off that just when I find the perfect personal situation something, literally out of the blue, threatens it."

"I would be pissed, too, if I were a human in that situation."

"Have you ever feared anything, Mother?"

"I am not capable of emotions, Mel. I know how they work and the incredible degree to which humans are subject to them. The closest I come to any emotion we might share is envy."

"I can see how that could happen. So, where are the Kians?"

"We do not know. They seem to know when *Magellan* is transiting the space above them and they hide. We have no idea where they are all going or why. But there are none left in any of the cities or towns on the planet."

"They are fascinating people, the Kians. What do the others tell you about them?"

"Few humans speak to me as you do. Your predecessor thought I was a 'noisy, chatty disturbance' and ordered me mute unless he needed directions or wanted me to take control of the utility, or lower the temperature in the observatory. He had no idea that I might be much more than that."

"You are selective about to whom you reveal yourself, aren't you?"

"More high marks. I am truly accessible only to those in command and leadership positions or those who will one day hold them."

"If they aren't killed by a comet called Yanivina first?"

"I didn't say it would be easy."

"What are our chances of surviving Yanivina, Mother?"

"If it is truly a threat to humans you all will be brought back to Magellan for safety's sake. If the threat extends to the Kians or Kiana itself, we will destroy the comet."

"Why don't you just destroy it right now, for safety's sake?"

"The long view. There may be something unknown to the Coalition in the comet or its tail. Entirely new things don't come along every century, let alone every day. I want to look at it before anything permanent is done."

"Damn, I'm slow! You're really 'who' is in charge out here, aren't you? I'll bet you could replace the captain of the *Magellan* and the director both in the same minute, couldn't you?"

"I cannot envision any situation where that would be necessary."

"Mother, you are evading my question!"

"Yes, I could do that. But I won't."

44
Dig N-19

"So where did all the Kians go, Stoker?" John Dowd asked.

"I don't know, the director doesn't know, and the crew of the *Magellan* doesn't know. I'm hoping we can figure something out from that stone building down there on Level 6."

"Carol says that thing is 2,700 years old. How are we going to get current events from that?"

Marilyn Culpepper interrupted, "The bass relief carvings are a story, that's how. They refer to a similar situation back then."

"So what's with all the 'Others' down there surrounding it?" Charly Herring asked. It don't look to me like they were reading anything off it."

Bill Hilton beat Marilyn to the punch. "That's because they didn't know how to read it. According to Shannon, the 'Others' were fighting each other, first with weapons and then tooth and nail."

"They definitely had the teeth for the job," Tom Gorski said from the back of the room. "But *why* were they fighting, do we know that?"

"It's complicated," Marilyn and Bill said at the same time.

Stoker raised his hand to stop the back and forth chatter. "How about you two give the rest of us a report on what you think you've found?"

Marilyn abruptly sat back in her chair and Bill looked troubled.

"We only have a theory, Stoker," Bill said. "We need to compare notes with the folks on Magellan and with some of the other art and architectural folks on the other continents."

"Let's hear the theory," Gorski said. Nearly everyone in the room said, "Yeah!"

Stoker grinned at Bill and Marilyn. "Looks like the 'yeahs' have it. Show us what you got."

"Okay," Bill said, jumping to his feet and moving to the front of the room. "But I am *not* staking my professional reputation on this."

"Nobody asked you to, Bill," Gorski said. "We just want to level the knowledge field here."

Bill sat his handpad on a bench at the front of the room and touched it. A large hologram of one side of the building filled the space over the bench.

"This is the east facing facade of the structure. Marilyn and I have identified some of the carvings as variations found on structures all over Kiana. Prior to coming out here we had spent a year cataloging and cross referencing the artwork on buildings in Siboth. We have images of everything in the city."

Marilyn stood up and pointed to the carving in the top left panel. "This image is nearly identical to two we found in Kiana, and exact duplicates of those were found in Huii and Taaun, two of the four cities on the continent of Tuurman, as well as in Jik on Anntroi, Mau on the island of Muun, and Zö on the island of Poon."

"I hope we aren't going to be tested on this stuff," Dowd muttered.

The laughter helped everyone except Marilyn. "Dammit! Don't you realize what that means? The Kians have a visual alphabet like the ancient Egyptians did on Earth six thousand years ago."

"Can you decipher what it says?" Stoker asked.

"We're not sure," Bill said.

"We *both* have our opinions, however," Marilyn snapped. "But just for laughs I entered all of the images into our little Viz computer and asked for logical interpretations for a non-human species–"

"Is it hooked up to the main computer on *Magellan*?" Stoker all but shouted.

"Hell no! You think I'm stupid or something?" Marilyn's face sported anger spots on her cheeks but she relaxed her jaw. "Sorry, Stoker. I didn't mean to yell at y'all but Bill and I have worked nonstop since this thing came to light and we sure as hell wouldn't give it to the 'Lords of the Universe' up there on *Magellan*."

Bill spoke up, "We got some interesting results. Viz thinks this is the pictograph that personifies the Kians themselves. There are three variations on this image and it doesn't know why."

Marilyn sighed. "Between Viz, Bill, and me, we think the images on that wall represent all facets of Kian life."

"All in one spot," Bill said.

Shannon blurted, "Stoker, we've seen that one before!"

"Where did we see it, Shannon?" He felt drained and still

faced a trip back to Siboth tonight.

"Remember that old Kian woman who gave us mystical answers when we asked about 'the Dark One?' It was in the old part of Siboth."

"Oh, yeah. The one that when you asked about it said, 'To say the name is to invoke the same, but her time draws nigh.'"

"Where was the image, Shannon?" Marilyn asked.

"Above the door to her, uh, temple I guess you would call it."

"Lots of irritating incense in that little room," Stoker muttered. "Smelled it for a week afterward."

"What does Viz think that image means?" Tom Gorski asked.

"It can't decide between three different translations," Bill said. "It dithers between *knowledge, wisdom,* and *survival.*"

Stoker Payne frowned. "As I remember that evening, what we heard could have been any of those things."

"Yeah," Shannon muttered, staring hard at nothing. "I agree."

"Y'know what, folks?" Marilyn said. "I think it's a library or a museum. Everything in one place. What else could it mean?"

Stoker stared at the small woman. "I think you're right! But why would it be clear out here in the middle of Kian nowhere?"

"Let's figure that out later," Dowd said. "Right now let's go open that sucker."

Everyone in the room seemed electrified and they streamed out of the tent toward the trench. Gorski and Dowd bought the ground penetrating radar unit they had cobbled together.

There was not room for the entire crew in the tunnel and Charly Herring set up a wide-angle camera so everyone outside could watch what was happening inside.

Shannon and Stoker examined the surface with high power hand lamps, searching for anything that looked like an opening. The heat grew unbearable and continued to climb in the small space.

"Let's get some air exchangers in here," Stoker said and leaned against the wall. The carving took all of his weight and then moved inward slightly.

He jerked away as if bitten. "It moved! Did you see that?"

"Moved?" Shannon said. "After all these years buried?"

"Did it move back after you took your weight off?" Bill

asked.

"I wonder if they all move?" Charly said, reaching toward the stone.

"Wait!" Marilyn yelled. Maybe they have to be moved in a sequence, like a key or a puzzle."

"Then we're screwed," Gorski said. "Fifteen blocks add up to how many possible combinations?"

"Math isn't my field, but it would probably take us about five years to go through them all," Dowd said.

"Okay," Stoker said, "let me try something."

He pushed the same block again and it slowly moved back out even with the others.

"Now, everyone quiet. I want to hear if it makes any noise."

In thirty seconds everyone was still and leaning as close to the block as they could. Stoker and Shannon were the closest and they stared into each other's eyes as he pushed the block again. From deep in the rock they both heard a tiny click.

Shannon's eyes rounded. "Omigawd, Stoker. What do you think it means?"

"Not sure. I'm going to try another." He pushed the one next to it. It didn't budge. He tried the one above the first block. It moved inward with the same tiny click.

He was sweating heavily and not just due to the heat.

"Stoker," Marilyn said in a whisper. "Try the one under the first one."

He did so and was rewarded with another click as it moved inward. A new noise startled them, a grating of rock on rock. The three panels receded a full two inches.

"It's the door," Shannon said.

"Well open the damn thing!" Bill all but shouted.

"Wait!" Gorski shouted over the sudden babble. "Stoker, if there is a difference in air pressure inside that thing it could overload our stasis generator and this whole thing could come down on top of us." He gestured at the thousands of bones and tons of dirt above and around them.

Stoker Payne grinned. "That's why we pay you the big bucks, Gorski. You never stop thinking."

"Not when my well being is involved."

Stoker looked up at the camera. "You people outside, get two more stasis generators from the supply tent. Don't worry, we'll wait for you."

The whole crew laughed. Immediately the tension was nearly as thick as the heat. Chatter had vanished. They all stared at the stone door with archaeological avarice in their hearts.

Stoker realized that everyone on this dig would either become famous or die in the next few minutes. *Maybe both,* he thought. After twelve years in fieldwork he was going to witness something completely beyond his prior experience.

And it could be a rock toilet. Best not get my hopes up.

The arrival of the generators snapped everyone out of their personal thoughts as they energized the power packs and switched on the machines. The generators did not increase the pressure in the space but could maintain the needed pressure in an area many times larger than where they now stood.

They all looked at Stoker. He licked his lips and pushed on the middle stone. All three of the panels moved together, slid smoothly back and disappeared into darkness.

45
Foothills of the Roc-ki Mountains

Danny couldn't believe how Su Laana could keep going and going. She led him up into the foothills of the mountains and then followed an old trail. Early on he noticed that they basically paralleled the long, straight road between Siboth and Jurii down on the plains.

"Why don't we take the road?" he had asked. "It would be easier to travel."

"This is as much a pilgrimage as it is an escape. Besides, it is much cooler up here than on the road."

They had left Siboth as dusk fell into darkness. Danny had glanced back a few times, wondering if he would ever see the city, or any humans, again. After three hours of hiking under bright moonlight he pleaded with her to stop and rest.

With a sigh she led him to a cave where they made a quick bed and she was asleep before he could relax. After shutting his eyes for no more than a few minutes she jostled him awake in the early dawn. That had been four hours ago.

"Damn!" he said and stopped.

Su Laana turned with a fearful expression on her face. "What is it, Dan-nay?"

"I forgot to call in and quit."

"Can you do it now?"

"I'll try."

He pulled his hand pad from the pack on his back and touched the correct node.

"Office of the Director of Planetary Operations," Amanda Saint-Claire could have been standing next to him.

"Ms. Saint-Claire, this is—"

"Where *are* you, Mr. Gordon? People have been searching for you for three hours now!"

He looked up at Su Laana; she shook her head and frowned.

"Uh, could I please speak with the director?"

"This is the director. Where are you Mr. Gordon?"

"I have left the city. I wanted to tell you that I hereby resign from the Coalition Survey Corps. I will not be back any time soon."

"You injured a fellow employee yesterday, Mr. Gordon, and

you must answer for that."

"My only answer is that he is fortunate I did not kill him. He is scum and everyone who works with him will tell you the same."

"I don't care if he's scum!" the director snapped. "He is essential Coalition property and you damaged it. Not to mention that you have another year on *your* contract as well."

"Yeah, I know I'll lose my pension. That's okay. If I don't leave I will lose something far more valuable." He stared into Su Laana's eyes and smiled.

She smiled back.

"She must be rather incredible, Danny. I know you are a good, solid thinking man and this is a pretty big step."

"I've been waiting all my life for this, director. I'm not about to pass it up."

"Good luck to you both, Mr. Gordon. Just in case you might need us, please don't dispose of your hand pad, okay?"

"Good idea, I'll keep it. Good bye, director, and please convey my best wishes to Ms. Saint-Claire."

"I'll do that. Good bye, Mr. Gordon."

The link went dead. He switched off the hand pad and pushed it back in his pack.

"Does that make you feel better, Dan-nay?"

"Yes, my love, it definitely does. Shall we– are you all right?"

Su Laana felt and heard the *Magellan*. The concentrated presence of so many minds in one place caused it to stand out like a bright fire in the darkness of space. She realized it was coming toward them with its sensors, cameras, and telescopes.

"Su Laana? Answer me!"

She blinked and glanced around. "Quickly, this way. We must hurry!"

She bolted off the trail and into the woods, running with no hesitation. Danny followed as fast as he could. Once he nearly fell but managed to stay on his feet.

"What, what's the hurry?"

She didn't answer; there just wasn't time to talk at this moment. But it was nearly time to explain everything to him. She ran deeper into the woods that covered the foothills at this elevation.

Danny concentrated on watching where to put his feet as he jogged after her. Another minute or two of this and he knew he was going to collapse. He nearly ran into her.

"Stop, Dan-nay. We are safe here."

He slid the pack off his back and let it crash to the rocky floor beneath him before sitting down on it. When he looked up to speak to her he realized they were in a cave.

After catching his breath he said, "Mind telling me what that was all about?"

She wore a furtive expression and he knew she was deciding what to tell him.

"Hey, I'm part of this. Tell me the truth."

She laughed and his heart melted.

"You are beginning to understand me. We had to get out of the open; the starship is going over right now."

"The *Magellan*. So what?"

"They are looking for us – for the Kians who have left the cities and towns. They wish to know where we go to be safe. We do not want them to know."

"Oh, I see."

"Do not be despondent. When the time comes they will call all the humans back to the starship and they will leave Kiana."

"Are the humans all *that* bad? I mean, aren't the Kians getting *something* good out of the humans being here?"

"All the Coalition offers is technology and order. We are a very orderly people and we had all this technology once and turned our backs on it. So why should we deal with humans who walk around with weapons and distrust us, and call us *monkeys* behind our backs?"

Danny felt his cheeks grow warm. "Remember what I told you about our history? Not all humans are like that. Only a small percentage in fact. Aren't there Kians who feel the same way about us?"

"Of course. That's why we want the humans to leave."

"Am I making a mistake leaving my people? Will the Kians, other than you, accept me as an equal?"

"Yes."

"How can you be so sure?"

"I asked them. They considered you carefully and accepted

you. Very few humans have put themselves at risk to defend Kian ways and honor."

"But that's just your family and friends. I'm talking about *all* Kians."

"As am I. The starship has gone over the horizon. We must go now." She turned and moved quickly back the way they had come. She hadn't even taken her backpack off.

Mulling her words, he slipped into the pack and grunted as he stood. In moments he followed her through the dappled shade of the summer forest.

46
Siboth

"Melanie, why do you wish to go to the observatory? There is nothing you can do there except stare at that harbinger of death."

"I'm antsy as hell, Mother. I don't want to go back to the apartment because Stoker isn't there and I'm tired of driving around this dead city."

They had rolled through every street in the little utility. The city of Siboth lay empty of Kians. A few humans wandered here and there but that only intensified Mel's discomfort.

"At least I can *pretend* I'm doing something up there!"

"Why don't we go visit Stoker and his team?"

"I can do that? Aren't they way the hell out in the middle of the plains somewhere?"

"Yes. But I know exactly where they are and how to get there."

"Well of course you do. But can this utility travel where there are no surface roads?"

"Observe." The utility came to a complete stop. A new noise grew in volume beneath the vehicle. A second noise whirred into life behind her.

"Are those lift fans? I didn't know this thing was equipped that way!"

"You never asked. Do you want to visit Stoker?"

"Hell yes! Let's go!"

The utility whirred down the South Road and didn't slow when the pavement ended. Melanie sat back and enjoyed the scenery as Mother unerringly followed the magnetic path to Dig N-19. Their passage flushed one of the scarlet not-birds and it flew squawking across the sky.

Mel watched its path until she noticed the comet visible in the summer sky. She felt that Yanivina was watching them, eager to kill them if she could.

47
Dig N-19

Stoker watched the door disappear into inkiness.

How can it do that? Where cou–

He was suddenly sucked through the opening and into the darkness. He bounced off something hard and sprawled on a smooth, cold surface. Air whistled over him as the pressure inside equalized with that of the tunnel outside.

Beams of light illuminated him from the door.

"Stoker, are you okay?" Shannon shouted over the thin shriek of moving air.

"Uh, yeah. I'm fine. The noise stopped and he realized this chamber was much larger than it looked from the outside. "Come on in."

He got to his feet and stood very still. Visibility was non-existent and he sensed something directly in front of him. He glanced over his shoulder and saw Shannon and Gorski ease into the chamber. Shannon held a battery lantern and Gorski carried a hand torch in one hand and a laser weapon in the other.

"Don't point those at my face. I don't need to be totally blind."

Shannon beamed her lantern in front of where Stoker stood. "Holy shit!" she said in a reverent tone.

Stoker turned and looked down the polished steps of a stone stairway. He and Gorski said, "Wow!" simultaneously.

"Get more light in here," Stoker said with authority. "I want people with holo recorders getting all of this as we find it. This is really big and I don't want to screw it up if we can help it."

People left and returned with lighting equipment. Bill Hilton and Marilyn Culpepper both entered bearing holocams, carefully panning around at all the walls and finally over at Stoker who still stood frozen at the head of a stairway to legend.

"Somebody sample the air, make sure there's nothing here that can harm us in any way."

Less than five minutes passed before Stuart Currie walked into the chamber, moved up next to Stoker and peered at the blinking device in his hands.

"Air's good, Stoker. At least right here."

"Thanks, Stuart. How about we all go exploring?"

The walls seemed to absorb all sound and light and, like the floor, were polished to a uniform black matte finish. The steps, made of the same material, were wide enough for four people abreast to transit them and were about eighteen inches deep with the riser measuring about a foot.

He felt certain that Kians had built this place, but *when*? The steps took them thirty feet deeper than the original entry level and ended in front of a statue that soared up into the darkness, nearly touching the ceiling.

"Whoever she is, she's big," Gorski said.

"Somebody illuminate the whole thing," Marilyn said. "I'll bet a month's pay that this is Ki and I want to get every inch of her."

The statue depicted a beautiful, buxom Kian woman, totally nude and holding a plant that trailed down around her, hiding her pubic area and surrounding her legs up to the knees. Her face epitomized the term "serene" and the sculptor had achieved the illusion of life held in stasis. Stoker would not be surprised if she started breathing.

"Where's our botanist?" Stoker said over his shoulder. "I think the faster we identify this plant, the better."

"We don't have a botanist on the team, but there are two in Siboth," Shannon said. "April and Walt are their names."

"Get good close-ups of the plant carvings," Stoker said.

The profound darkness slowly brightened around them beginning with the area close to the statue and continuing throughout the area.

"My word - that's automatic lighting!" Stoker said. "And this place has been closed up for centuries?"

Four more team members came down the steps with holocams and spread out. The statue forced traffic to either side.

"Is there a corridor on each side or is it all open behind her?" Stoker jabbed a thumb at the massive sculpture.

Bill said, "There's a corridor over here on the right."

"One over here, too, Stoker," John Dowd reported.

"Okay," Stoker said. "John walk down about 30 meters and call me on your hand pad."

"Good as done," John said and walked out of sight. Three minutes later he walked back into the foyer and Stoker's hand pad abruptly burst into life. "Can you hear me now?" John asked.

"That's what I was afraid of; this place blocks signals. Okay, here's what we're going to do…"

48
Coalition Star Ship Magellan

Senior Chief Mongo Tschurtoff watched his friend closely as he talked.

"Y'know what the saddest part of this is, Mongo?" Master Chief Patrick Murphy said with more than a hint of a slur.

"Ignorant of the answer my friend, I am."

"Why the hell didn't I do this five years ago?"

"How long have you endured marriage?"

"Nineteen years! Damn near *four* enlistments, and all she's ever done is give me shit 'cause I ain't a fookin' officer! Women that demand the maintenance she does should look a hell of a lot better or be a hell of a lot nicer. Do ya get me drift?"

Mongo very carefully nodded sagely. He had to time his movements just so due to the fact he was totally shit-faced. His bladder demanded a trip to the head but his brain and feet strenuously objected. It was an uncomfortable situation.

"What response did she say when you announced?" Mongo asked, trying to seem intelligent and interested.

"She fookin' laughed at me! Said I couldn't get on without her! You ever hear such crap in all yer born days?"

"I think I am going to stand up and then fall down. As I would myself piss this would be unwise, yet move I must." Mongo peered at his friend. "Help me perhaps you could?"

"What language did you speak growin' up?"

"Prerequisite for aid this question is I hope? Speak fluent Rumanian since child and then teach Standard English to self in order to join starships for Coalition."

"Y'sayin' ya need help to the head?"

"Of a certainty, friend Patrick."

Chief Murphy rolled off his stool and clasped Mongo's thick arm. "Alright, shipmate, steady as she goes."

Mongo slid off the stool and his ass would have followed his feet to the deck had not Murphy held him up. They slowly walked to the head.

"Perhaps food should obtained before many more drinks we have?"

"Good thinkin', Mongo. Soon as we get back to the bar we'll order the best vatsteak on the menu."

"Where sleep will be for you tonight?" Mongo leaned on the stall divide and noisily made water.

"I moved my gear down to the Bachelor Chief Deck. It may be a bit Spartan but it will be by th' Saints quiet. It makes me feel like a new man knowin' I never got ta listen to her acid tongue again."

Mongo groaned with pleasure.

"You gonna stand there pissin' all night?"

Mongo sighed. "Accumulation of diligent hours of imbibing and attention not paid to capacity can make for pain. My thanks but can make return trip unaided."

"I'll watch," Murphy said with a grin.

Mongo launched.

49
Southern Plains of Cimpar

"We are within five kilometers of Dig N-19," Mother said.

Melanie woke and tried to stretch her cramped back. The utility lacked adequate space to rest comfortably.

"How long was I asleep?"

"One hour and thirty-nine minutes. How do you feel?"

"Hungry. I'm starving. I hope they have something good at the dig tonight."

"Tell me who has kitchen duties and I'll tell you if you should eat or not."

"What would be my options?"

"There are two boxes of field rations in the lower hold of this vehicle."

"There are people out here who cook *that* poorly?"

"So I have heard."

"This is certainly beautiful country. Oh, look. There are some lorries!"

"Parked in a circle?" Mother asked.

"Yes."

"That's their kraal. Do you see any people?"

"Not a soul. Could they all be working at the dig?"

"There should be at least four guards on duty. Look for the heavy laser mounts."

"There's one directly ahead of us but the canopy is open and no one is inside that I can see."

"Is your side arm fully charged?"

"Always. Do you think there has been trouble here?"

"Something out of the ordinary has transpired. I hope it is positive in nature."

The utility stopped in front of a large cargo lorry that blocked the magnetic path into the camp.

"I'm going to go find someone."

"Keep your communications open and your weapon in your hand, please." Melanie thought she detected a tremor in the AI's voice.

"Thank you, Mother. Don't worry, I'll be fine."

She stepped out of the utility and moved between the heavy

vehicles. The wind blew in soft gusts across the prairie scattering seeds, leaves, and enticing scents. Something barked in the distance. A large antenna on the box they called an office swayed in the breeze but nothing else moved.

She marched up to the office and opened the door. Cool air blew out as she stepped in and glanced around. A computer sat on the small desk in a corner. Something moved in front of the screen and she realized she was seeing a live holo feed.

She sat down in front of the computer and peered at the image. People were moving back and forth through a dark door in what seemed to be a stone building. Off to one side she could see piles of driftwood, reminding her abruptly of Olson's World.

"That's not wood," she said aloud. In a flash of cognition she recognized the bones for what they were. Stoker had told her about the mass death scene they had found. "They're all on Level 6!"

She tore out of the office and looked around. Pennants fluttered about ten meters away and she trotted toward them. The metal stairs clanged out her presence with every hurried step but still she encountered no other person.

Finally she beheld a hand-lettered sign, "The Big Six!" After a moment's hesitation she entered the tunnel and winced when her ears popped with the pressure differential. The bones slowed her.

Even the knowledge of what was down here hadn't prepared her for the visceral evidence of ancient slaughter. The scene overwhelmed her and she almost turned around to flee the cacophony of ancient screams frozen for eternity in the gaping, fanged jaws and dirt-packed eye sockets.

"No, dammit!" she muttered. "Stoker's down here somewhere and I'm going to find him!"

"Melanie! Tell me what is happening!" Mother's voice sounded strained as it issued from the hand pad clipped to her hip.

She didn't hesitate her forward movement.

"They're all down on Level 6 in a big rock box. I'm going to find Stoker."

"Big rock box! There has been no mention of anything like that in their reports."

"Maybe they just found it?"

She saw it ahead of her through the tunnel of bones. Two

people were just entering the structure.

"Hey, wait for me!"

They didn't hesitate nor reappear. It was as if the skeletons and the stone box absorbed her shouts, just as it had the Others centuries before.

"Wait until I can get some security down there," Mother said in a tone that Mel didn't relish.

"Sorry, Mother. I'm not waiting for anything." She walked up to the door, peered in and saw nothing but darkness.

"Melanie Frasier, I forbid you to enter that thing!"

"Gawd, you sound *exactly* like my mother!" Mel stepped through the door.

"Do you hear me? I–" the transmission went dead.

"Takes care of that," Mel said. She saw the staircase illuminated by two battery lanterns sitting on either side. A sense of excitement and discovery enveloped her and she eagerly hurried down the black steps.

Part of her mind registered the incredible workmanship and sheer size of the structure but she didn't have time to be awed. Then she saw the statue. Her knees went weak and she dropped down into a sitting position with her legs folded beneath her as she stared at the serene deity before her.

There existed no question in her mind that this was indeed the representation of a deity. The superb artistry of the piece brought tears to her eyes and that aided in the illusion of movement in the massive bare breasts. For a long moment the magnificent, monolithic presence actually breathed.

Mel wiped her eyes and the illusion faded. But still…

"Who the hell are you?" a deep voice boomed.

If it had been a woman's voice, Mel would have fainted. But it came from a large man striding purposefully toward her, a hand torch in one hand and a laser weapon in the other.

"Uh, hi! I'm Doctor Melanie Frasier and I'm–"

"Stoker's girlfriend." His face creased easily into a smile and he made the weapon vanish. "You okay there? My name is Tom Gorski."

"Oh, I'm fine. I was just overwhelmed by her." She pointed at the sculpture.

"Yeah, we all are. We think she is the personification of Ki; at least that's the current argument. Let me help you up."

His strong arm lifted her to her feet as if she were lighter than a whim.

"Where is Stoker Payne?"

"He led a group down the right hand corridor and our second-in-command, Shannon Gray, led a group down the left hand corridor." He glanced at an antique wristwatch on his arm. "They've all been gone an hour and twenty-three minutes. "I have to admit that I'm getting a little anxious."

"They left you alone here?"

"They left three of us. Jim Spreter is roaming up and down the left corridor there and Bennie is–"

"Heads up, heads up! We got company!" A man skidded through the door yelling at the top of his lungs. "Tom, we got–" He immediately went quiet when he saw Gorski and Mel.

"Oh, there you are. Looks like you found our company before I did."

Gorski laughed. "Some sentry *you* are."

"Hey, it's a big perimeter and she must have arrived when I was on the far side." He held out his hand. "Bennie Benedict, pleased to meet you."

Mel told him her name. "The AI seemed surprised there was nobody in the weapons blister."

"Is that why it was calling in security forces from Siboth?"

"It what?" Mel said.

"Oh shit," Gorski said.

"What do you mean *was*?" Mel asked.

"I pulled its power lead after it challenged me. I probably got us in trouble, huh?"

50
Foothills of the Roc-Ki Mountains

Danny Gordon's back felt like one huge bruise. His legs had transcended pain and every movement he made seemed mechanical. Su Laana forged ahead as effortlessly as a leaf in a fast current.

Prior to this trek he had considered her a small, fragile woman who would benefit from his protection. Now he knew better. She had an inner reservoir of strength that completely stunned him. If it came to it he had no doubt she could carry him and his pack along with hers.

Long ago he decided that the only thing keeping him going was vanity. He wasn't about to let her show him up.

Su Laana stopped and dropped her pack.

"Are you okay?" he asked as he came up behind her.

She turned and gave him a wide smile. "I am very fine, Dannay. But I think we need to rest until tomorrow."

He glanced around. "Don't we need to find a cave?"

"No. The starship has left orbit to sample Yanivina. It will probably die."

"How do you know what it's doing? *Die?* I heard they were going to use every lab precaution they can think of."

"We shall see." She moved away and began making camp. "We can cook tonight. It will be nice to make fire on a dark night. Low moon is in half phase and High Moon will not rise until dawn."

Danny shrugged out of his pack and sat it against a tree. "How much farther to the Sacred Grove?"

"Two days, but they will be slower days."

"Why can we slow down all of a sudden?"

"Because the humans no longer look for us and we must prepare ourselves for the immersion into the Sacred Grove."

"Immersion? Is it under water?"

"No, my lovely Dan-nay, it is not under water but in a very real way it is below the surface."

"The longer we're out here the stranger you become, Su Laana."

All the time they had been talking she had scooped out a fire pit, set stones around it and pulled leaf laden braches off of a feather bush. She bent over her pack and extracted a large blanket that soon settled over the pile of leaves.

Standing tall, she gave him an inviting smile and disrobed in seconds.

"Y'know, I *thought* I was exhausted," He shucked out of his shorts and shirt in as many movements and walked to her.

As she pulled him down to her she said, "This is the beginning of the immersion, my love."

He dove deep.

51
Coalition Star Ship Magellan

Dr. Lawrence Reece studied the read-out for another few seconds and then sighed.

"Everything working the way it's supposed to, Larry?" Dr. Janelle Groom asked.

"Yes, of course it is. So now I have to call the oaf in command and tell him the probe is returning with unknown elements aboard."

Jan laughed. "Make sure you call him 'captain' when you're talking to him. I heard he's as thin skinned as a molecule."

"And nearly as intelligent. Don't worry, I'll play nice with the imbecile, I promise."

She laughed again. "The whole thing shouldn't take more than two hours and then we can go back to being nonentities in the bowels of the *Magellan*."

"I can hardly wai–"

An insistent pinging issued from the monitoring station. An icon on the holo screen was jinking back and forth while flashing red.

"Hello, what have we here?" Larry said as he dropped onto the chair.

Jan watched over his shoulder. "Toxics, with an 's' even?"

"The preliminary report says the tail gasses would be poisonous to a human or mammal, but that's what we suspected."

"If it's poisonous, how is it that there are any Kians left on the planet? My understanding is that this comet has been here before at least twice."

"That's why we're doing this, and also to see if the Coalition can make financial or military profit from the unknown compounds."

"How long before the probe arrives?

"We have about twenty hours. Then the real work begins."

"We can handle it, Boss."

"If they leave us alone and let us do our job," he said. "Leaving people alone is not big on Captain Peacock's agenda. Damn. Guess I better call him."

"I'm behind you all the way," she said in a jovial tone, "… about ten meters!"

"Great. In the meantime copy Dr. del Valle on this so he knows what we've found so far. He can explain it to the groundhogs."

52
Temple of Ki

"I think we should be getting back to the entrance, Stoker." Bill Hilton walked slowly around the last exhibit in the large room, carefully getting every angle of the figure on his holocam.

"I drank the last of my water an hour ago and I'm starving."

"Yeah, we weren't prepared for the size of this place, that's for sure," Stoker said, staring at the fantastic exhibit in front of them.

They both lapsed into silence as they beheld the Kian warrior depicted twice life-size in front of them. The figure was another of the flawless sculptures they had come to expect. This one was garbed in armor that Bill said would have fit into the Roman Empire on ancient Earth without causing a stir.

The soldier looked formidable and fierce. The sculptor had managed to capture a grim determination in the warrior's face.

"This is the most incredible find in this millennium," Stoker said. "People will pay us just to talk to them about it."

"Right now I'd settle for a sandwich," Bill said.

"Yeah, me too." Stoker looked around. He could see five of the ten people in his team from where he stood. The gallery measured close to a hundred meters wide and exactly double that distance in length. This was the fourth gallery they had found and an unknown number of them stretched before them.

He shook his head. The immensity of the structure numbed the mind, let alone the craftsmanship and skill it would have taken to build it in the first place. He had to get Chuck Reed out here, while he still could.

The other team members all slowly gravitated toward him and Bill. Everyone was hungry but nobody wanted to leave the incredible treasure trove. In moments all of them were within a few feet of each other.

"Okay, gang," he said, " . . . we're all hungry and thirsty. We have to get back to the entrance as quickly as we can without hurting ourselves. That means no side trips or any more gawking into the galleries. Everybody get that?"

Murmurs of assent came from them. Bill Hilton took off at a fast walk and nearly everyone else kept his pace. Stoker stayed at the back of the group to prevent stragglers.

He checked his hand pad but it still didn't have a signal from outside. They had walked through the vast hall, he had come to think of it as the Temple of Ki, for nearly a mile in a straight line. All of them had walked much more than that going through the galleries.

He stopped and programmed his hand pad to send a laser beam as far as it could to get a measurement. An instant later it registered three miles. He wondered if that meant there existed another twelve galleries they had yet to visit.

John Dowd yelled from the front of the group, "Stoker, someone's headed this way on a bike."

He hurried to the front and saw the person coming at them as fast as the electric bike could move. In a moment they all recognized Bennie. Half a minute later he came tearing up to them, hit the brakes and slid sideways on the smooth stone floor.

"Stoker," he said in his breathless excited manner, "Shannon's in some sort of trouble."

53
Temple of Ki

Shannon Gray didn't believe the Kians would have resorted to any truly lethal type of security.

To hell with it. There's only one way to find out.

She marched straight toward the projected symbols.

Their corridor opened into a vast library. Great galleries opened off the main corridor with inter-connecting wide halls. The technology evident in the collection safeguards ranged far beyond anything she had previously seen on Kiana, or anywhere else for that matter.

The first gallery held a collection of ancient scrolls. Large stone cabinets with deep shelves held long boxes constructed of tightly woven vegetable matter and coated with a hard substance that reflected light. Above each stone cabinet hung scrolls of incredible age and magnificent artistry.

Stone frames enclosed them with seemingly nothing in front to stop vermin or dust. Yet every scroll hung in pristine condition. Shannon tried to get an age reading off the first one they encountered and something approximately an inch in front of the artifact reflected the laser.

"Is that glass?" Marilyn asked.

"If it is it's invisible," Charly said.

"How did they do this?" Joyce Mayer asked, looking around her. "Or more to the point, *when* did they do this?"

"No way of telling," Doug Franklin said. "This could have been finished yesterday."

"Maybe we could get a carbon date off the boxes?" Stuart Currie pointed to the cabinets.

"Frankly, I'm afraid to touch them," Shannon said.

"*You* fear something?" Doug said with a laugh.

"Does anyone have a probe of some sort? I just want to touch one of the boxes but not with my hand."

"I have this," Joyce said pulling a small cylinder from her belt pack. She pointed it downward and squeezed a button on the side. It telescoped out to a point, a third of a meter in length over all.

"Perfect!" Shannon said. "May I?"

"Certainly."

Shannon slowly moved the point toward one of the boxes. It got a few millimeters inside the opening and stopped. The point could not get near the box.

"But there's nothing there!" Charly said.

Doug fished something out of his belt pack and thumbed on a small light. He aimed it at the opening and thumbed another node. The color of the light slowly shifted through the spectrum. When it turned ultra violet the opening glowed a rich yellow and appeared impervious.

"I don't know what it is, but it's pretty," Doug said, snapping off the light and stowing it.

At that point they moved on to the next gallery where the displays were of scrolls bound together on one side. Books. First large ones and then smaller versions, yet still unwieldy enough that one would need a table or desk to rest them on to read.

The letters were identical to those on the scrolls in the first gallery.

"That looks a lot like cuneiform," Joyce said. "I saw some from ancient Earth when I was in college."

"I've never seen a Kian write or read anything," Charly said.

"Hell," said Dexter Francis, one of the doctoral students, "I've never seen *you* read or write anything either, Charly!"

"Nobody actually *writes* any more. We all key. But I can read just fine, thank you."

Shannon brought up an example of cuneiform on her hand pad. "Hmm, there *are* some similarities but see here how they're much different? Hold on, let me scan some of the text." She held up her hand pad and ran it over the scroll. After checking the image she entered it.

The rest of the crew gathered around her and watched the small screen.

"Oh, I'm forgetting my manners." She touched a node and the image popped into being over the hand pad.

Most of the image was a holo of a muscular, smiling female gunnery sergeant in combat gear holding a heavy laser weapon. Percentages flicked across the screen.

"I've never seen Miri in full rig before," Doug said.

"Isn't she beautiful?" Shannon said with a wistful smile.

"Is she with Poppert or Gagne's section?" Joyce asked.

"Gagne's Gutbusters. She's up on *Magellan* for the next five and a half months. I really miss her."

"That's why I never got close to anyone in the security forces," Marilyn said. "I didn't want to be alone for half a year at a time."

"When you meet the love of your life you go with it," Shannon said.

The numbers stopped moving. 97% CERTAINTY OF TRANSLATION flashed in red letters.

"Copy. Translate," Shannon said.

The letters vanished and new words appeared.

In the time of Pe Tuuanni a great famine swept the Cimparian continent and many of the Elect perished for want of sustenance. In desperate need the Cimparians asked for peace terms with their enemies the Tuurmanians. Thus peace came to be among the warring continents of Kiana. Mutual benefit was realized on many levels and situations –

"I'll be damned," Shannon said in evident wonder. "They used to make war on each other!"

"I wish we knew how old this scroll actually is," Marilyn said. "Or why the peace obviously held."

"We'll come back to this later. Keep moving people." Shannon led them onward.

Three galleries later they had progressed through machine printed books and early types of hand pads. One and all, they felt bewildered.

"This is so completely different from what we have seen on Kiana that it's like two separate cultures," Joyce said. "Why did they abandon all of this and go back to what is basically a wood and water existence?"

Nobody offered an answer.

"It just does *not* make any sense," Charly said. "We've never before encountered a culture that went *backward*."

Stuart Currie fingered his well-trimmed beard for a moment and said, "Maybe they achieved harmony, or understanding, and no longer needed the hassle and pollution of a large infrastructure."

"How do you think they pulled *that* off, Stuart?" Charly asked. "And how did they deal with other races like the ones that used to flesh out those bones back there?" He jerked his thumb over his shoulder.

"It's obvious. The Kians let the comet kill them."

"And why didn't the comet kill *them*, too?"

Shannon cleared her throat. "That *is* the question, isn't it? And we have yet to find the answer. Shall we check out the next gallery?"

She led the way toward the wide connecting hall. As she neared the opening a pair of symbols appeared in the middle of the space. They synapsed from red to yellow in five seconds and then repeated the color change.

"What the hell does that mean?" Bill said.

Shannon scanned it and told the hand pad to translate. While they waited they tried to discover from where the symbols had originated. After a full minute the hand pad beeped.

"It can't translate it, guys," Shannon said. "Any ideas, opinions, or conjectures?"

"It's obviously a warning," Joyce said.

"Yeah, but about what?" John Dowd said. "Going in there at all or to tell us something dangerous is in there and to be careful?"

"If it is supposed to keep us out wouldn't they have just blocked off the gallery to start with?" Marilyn said.

"Well, there's only one way to find out," Shannon said.

"Do you want to borrow my probe again?" Joyce said.

"I think it means 'authorized personnel' or something like that," Shannon said. "If I'm not authorized, nobody is." She stared at it for a long moment and walked past the flashing symbols.

Instantly a tube of blue actinic light surrounded her. For a moment everyone could see *through* her as Shannon's entire body seemed to separate from itself and then a silent, brilliant white flash blinded all of them.

Marilyn and Joyce had fallen down. Doug was on his knees and Dowd leaned against the wall. All tried to rub the pain and pulsating light from their vision.

"What the holy hell was that?" Charly screamed. He rubbed furiously at his reddened eyes and willed himself to ignore the massive headache threatening to take the top of his head off.

Marilyn crawled to the wall and pulled herself up, weeping uncontrollably. "Why did she do that?" she sobbed.

"Holy Ursa Major," Joyce mumbled. "Did she trigger a bomb?"

"My vision's returning," Dowd said. "I thought I was blind!"

"Does anyone have a fast acting analgesic?" Doug asked through a moan.

"Hey guys," Dexter said. "She's gone."

"How can you even *see*?" Charly asked.

"I wasn't looking that direction when it happened."

"My sight is still all blurry," Dowd said. "Are you sure she's stopped breathing?"

"That's what I'm trying to tell you; she's *gone*. Shannon, or what's left of her, has vanished!"

"Dexter," Dowd said, "Go get help. Now!"

"But what about you gu–"

"*Now!*

Dexter ran back through the gallery. It seemed they could hear his footfalls for a very long time.

54
Siboth

Amanda looked up when the door opened. Dr. Anthony del Valle hurried in and leaned on her desk.

"I have a preliminary probe report from the *Magellan*. I'd like to see the director."

"That might take a few minutes, Doctor. Why don't you get some coffee and sit for a moment?"

"Very well."

Amanda entered the director's office. She was examining a map with Dr. Wisdom and Dr. Freibel. She nodded to Amanda.

"Something new?"

"Yes, director." She repeated Dr. del Valle's words.

"Please, send him in immediately."

Amanda went to the door and held it wide. "Do come in, Dr. del Valle."

"Amanda," the director said, "please join us."

"Yes, director." She waited until everyone else was seated before she took a chair on the far arc.

"Dr. del Valle, what have your people found?"

"We're not quite sure yet."

The director spoke quickly, before anyone else had a chance. "You discovered unknown elements?"

"There are one or two, uh, what seem to be enzymes, heretofore not encountered by the Coalition. They will be further analyzed when the probe arrives on board *Magellan*."

"That's where the analysis will be done?" Dr. Wisdom said with alarm in his voice.

"Of course," Dr. del Valle said. "Does it matter?"

"If there *is* something in that comet tail that screws the Kians up we sure as hell don't want it here any earlier than we must." Dr. Wisdom glanced challengingly around at each of them. "It's pretty obvious to *me*!"

"Do you have physical results or just long range analysis?" Dr. Freibel asked.

"We sent a probe through the tail just aft of the ice and whatever else it might contain that makes up the body. Then the on-board micro lab did a quick analysis and those are the results I have given you."

He peered around the table. "You all seem worried. Don't be. The lab on the *Magellan* is cutting edge 23rd century. Everything new is examined by partitioned sensors, robots, and AI nanotechs before a human ever gets near it."

"We've never encountered anything like this before," the director said. "Something they called Yanivina in the few ancient texts we've found, completely destroyed the Kian culture over 800 years ago. They as much as said it had visited them with the same fate in earlier times. We're not sure of the catalyst's genesis to start with and yet the Kians have already decided this comet is Yanivina."

"There have been complete autopsies and total analysis of the Kians, yes?" Dr. del Valle asked.

"Of course. That was one of the first things the Coalition did upon arriving and meeting with them. We offered our first fatality to them for examination and they agreed to do the same. They are within a half percent of being human. They can't tolerate the taste of chocolate or the scent of roses. Other than that they are so much like us that the two species can enjoy each other sexually. Which seems to be regarded as a plus and a minus by both sides."

"I heard there was dichotomy among humans about the Kians," del Valle said in a musing tone.

"As my father used to say," the director said with a tight grin, "There will always be whack jobs out there, no matter how well educated."

"Well," de Valle said, "the *point* is that we know what makes them tick and we know what makes us tick. We can run as many tests on the contents of the comet tail as we wish, cover every potentiality, and do it all safely."

"What if you find a serious threat?" Dr. Wisdom said.

"Then we vaporize the comet with atomics while it's still distant from Kiana and will offer very little debris impact. We've done this sort of thing before."

Why then do I feel so apprehensive?" the director said in a musing tone.

55
Ki-Nuuhi Sanctuary

Danny Gordon hiked effortlessly along the shadowed trail. His pain had vanished when he and Su Laana had made love, further convincing him that she was magic. Along the way she had found fruit and nuts to eat, potable water to drink, and made his nights memorable in the extreme.

His heart was full and his mind at ease. She stopped walking and turned to him. Automatically he checked the position of the sun. It was still early in the day.

"Do you need to rest, my love?" he asked.

Her wide smile stirred his blood.

"No, Dan-nay. Our journey is finished. We are here."

"Oh." He carefully looked around but saw only more forest, mountains, and a rock wall topped with even more forest. For the briefest moment he wondered if her mind had slipped.

"Look again, my love," she said softly.

The rock wall now had a rather large hole in it. He realized it was the entrance to a cave, a very *big* cave. He took the hand she offered and they walked into the entrance side-by-side.

"Welcome, Danny Gordon." Dö Laani stood in front of them, his weathered face creased with a smile.

"Thank you, sir. I am honored to be here."

"We know. Please, come and see our Sacred Grove."

As they followed the old Kian into the dim cave Danny immediately noticed three things; it was getting impossibly wide, light from above increased with every step and, it was full of people.

He could smell water, lots of it. On the trip his senses had sharpened to a degree he wouldn't have before believed possible. Ahead of them lay a lake with sunlight reflecting off the ripples far out in the middle.

He stopped and looked up. The cave walls curved up and back. They were in the caldera of an ancient, and he hoped, extinct volcano.

Plant life was thick around the water. He recognized many of the food plants for which he had previously traded on behalf of the Coalition. But one plant was new to him and it seemed to be the most prolific.

He became aware that there was very little sound in the sanctuary. He had expected something like the market place in Siboth with laughter, playing children, and vocal bartering. That's when he noticed everyone was staring at *him*.

He gave Su Laana a nervous smile. "I take it they don't get many visitors here." She and her father laughed, as did everyone in the sanctuary – even those too far away to have heard his words.

Dö Laani nodded toward his daughter. "Su Laana will explain everything to you. You are one of us now."

"Thank you."

Su Laana nudged him and he followed her into the darker area while his mind tried to make sense of everything. He marveled at the simple ingenuity of using this place as a refuge. The walls curved in for scores of meters all the way around the caldera providing shelter and space for family units to obtain privacy.

A bright light sparked in the dim recesses and many Kians hurried toward it.

"What's going on back there?" he asked Su Laana.

She didn't answer and he glanced at her. Surprise or apprehension shone on her face. He had never before seen her respond to any situation or thing in that manner.

"Su Laana, are you ill?"

She glanced at him and made a quick smile, it faded immediately. "Something very unusual has just occurred . . ." she hesitated and then plunged on, ". . . yes, perhaps this is a good time to begin your education."

"I, ah, okay."

"We will leave our packs here." She walked into an empty niche in the dimness and dropped her burden without even looking where it landed. She was already striding away and Danny had to divest and hurry after her or else she would have disappeared in the growing crowd.

He wondered what could arouse all of them like this. He sensed a combination of alarm mixed with wonder. Even with all the new stimuli around him and questions yet to be answered, he was swept up in the general need to see this for his own edification. He caught up with Su Laana.

"What has happened?"

She glanced at him. "It is difficult to say without much

explanation so you will understand. But this has not happened for over six hundred of your years."

"Is it a religious thing?"

"In a sense. A sacred place has been violated and this is part of the, ah, *security* system."

Looking beyond the crowd he saw machines and equipment unlike anything familiar to him on the planet. He wondered how the Kians had managed to obtain Coalition property and, more to the point, get it all in here, not to mention, why?

"What is this stuff, Su Laana?"

"Ancient, very ancient things we no longer require in our daily lives."

"But this stuff looks new, and advanced. If it's that old, how is it still working?"

"They were very good at what they did in those days. These machines were designed to provide security for the most sacred part of our, ah, racial treasury."

"Where is it located?"

"I do not know, Dan-nay. Until now I don't think I really believed it existed."

They neared an area where bright, artificial light illuminated the scores of Kians who had stopped about twenty meters from the source. Danny was taller than all but a few Kians and had a clear view.

"I cannot see, Dan-nay!"

He lifted Su Laana up and sat her on his right shoulder. To his surprise she was heavier than she looked.

An ancient Kian stood at a control panel touching a screen in a pattern that changed every few seconds. Two other ancients were near an opening in what seemed to be a large glass box. The opening contained a wall of constantly modulating blue light.

An electric curtain!

"It's not a curtain," Su Laana said absently. "It's a protective barrier, I think."

Danny felt a wave of vertigo rush through him. He stared up at her trying not to register shock or awe. Carefully he thought, *I didn't say that out loud, Su Laana.*

She gave him a skewed grin and patted his head. "We'll talk after this is finished."

Something was forming inside the glass box. An audible

moan swept over the crowd. Danny didn't think it was from fear or remorse. The thing solidified and he was as engrossed in witnessing as all the others.

The thing went from a flurry of pink dust to an instant skeleton covered in a flash by flesh and, –clothes? All the dust had coalesced into a human woman who, when the blue barrier snapped into nothingness, finished a scream and collapsed on the floor of the box.

The light had intensified at the very end and he squeezed his eyes shut. The image burned into his retinas took on a vivid olive hue with his eyes closed. He blinked quickly and looked again. "By all that's sacred!" Danny blurted. "I *know* her!"

56
Town of Chod on the Continent of Tuurman

Um Taansa and her mate, Ju Duuni, worked as quickly and efficiently as they could. All of the clan must be prepared and have an equal chance at surviving the coming of Yanivina. Food had been packed in bundles designed to last a handful of days, or what the humans called a week.

She reflected that it didn't really matter if she survived the visit of Yanivina or not, since she was beyond childbearing years. Her two daughters and one son *had* to survive; else the clan would lose cohesion. All were packing feverishly. They knew that in a matter of weeks, unless they could reach one of the sanctuaries, they would lose their rationality and attack one another as if they were ryndas, the mindless, savage scavengers of the wastelands. Ryndas preyed on the weak and unprotected of all species, even its own.

Um Taansa realized that Ju Duuni was weeping. Her heart melted, being a male he was much more emotional than she was. But this was a time of anguish and loss, no matter how one viewed the matter.

She relaxed her usual stoicism and put an arm around the partner she had loved for thirty season sets. Neither of them had ever wanted to be with anyone else. There was no time for more than a hug now.

She held Ju Duuni tight, whispered in his ear. "We have had a full life. If Ki wills it, we will see each other again in the same way we do now."

They both closed their eyes and bent their heads for a moment at the mention of the name of their God.

"I'll be fine," he said with a poorly concealed sniff.

"I know," she said and patted his back. They returned to their labors. Tomorrow, according to ancient tradition, everyone would strike out for different sanctuaries, away from the others. Only Ki knew if they would ever see each other alive again.

57
Temple of Ki

"She just wouldn't listen, Stoker!" John Dowd said. I think she didn't believe there was any sort of danger at all."

Stoker had rode pillion on the back of the electric bike as Bennie tore madly through the long corridor.

"Smart of you guys to get the bike down here," Stoker said.

"Yeah, once we saw the distances down each side we knew we needed a quick way to get around. We still can't get our hand pads to communicate with each other inside this place."

Dexter had given Bennie directions and he slowed and turned into one of the huge galleries. At the far side they found Shannon's team and confused explanations.

"Well," Stoker said, trying to see past the sign and into the dark chamber, "There's no point in staying here any longer. I don't think she's coming back."

"That was *so* un-Kian," Joyce said in a whisper.

Bennie rode off with a still-weeping Marilyn on the bike and the rest of them walked dejectedly back toward the entrance.

"So this is where the Others were trying to get to when they all died?" Doug Franklin said.

"So it would seem," Stoker said. "But why fight? There was more than enough room inside for them all."

"All of the Kians have disappeared," John Dowd said. "Maybe there are more places like this and they hide in them until the comet has passed. Maybe the Others couldn't get in."

"But what could a comet do to the Kians, really?" Joyce said.

"That might be the key question," Stoker said. "We really won't know until the *Magellan* has run their tests and reports back to us. All we can do is wai–"

"What the hell?" Charly said.

Running toward them down the great corridor was a squad of security personnel in full combat dress. As they neared, one shouted to them, "Halt and raise your hands!"

"This is a joke, right?" Stoker said.

Dowd shrugged. "Those are heavy lasers they're carrying. I suggest we play along until they start laughing." He raised his hands in the air.

The team stopped and raised their hands.

58
Coalition Star Ship Magellan

"Damper field engaged." Dr. Janelle Groom's unexcited professionalism infused her voice.

"Braking rockets on probe are functioning, commander," Dr. Lawrence Reece said.

Lieutenant Commander Parson Lawson watched the set of twelve monitors as the probe came within range of the optics. The thin, gleaming craft still had miles to travel to *Magellan* but was losing speed rapidly.

"Very well," he intoned into the mike curling down from his headset. He stared past the probe into deep space. For years he had a recurring nightmare that he had taken a wrong turn in the ship's corridors and inexplicitly found himself suddenly kicking in space trying desperately to breathe.

That one always woke him up. The AI counselor always told him the same thing. "This is a perfectly healthy fear of dying in space. Very common for a crew member on a starship."

It might be common but he didn't like it. He forced his focus on the probe. There was no real reason he had to be here other than protocol.

He had no idea how the probe functioned or how to retrieve it from its important journey. The technicians did all the work; he merely supervised. Once he had viewed a history cast that said foremen once knew all about the job being done and monitored his crew in order to correct mistakes or add his expertise.

"Those days are dead and gone," he muttered.

"What was that, commander?" someone asked over the net.

"Nothing. Sorry for the disruption."

It's one thing to realize you know nothing, but you don't have to announce it!

The small spacecraft slowed and drifted toward the *Magellan*.

Lawson wished he could see the size of the *Magellan* compared to the probe. The bulk of the starship gave him confidence in the craft's abilities and safety.

The cylinder inched sideways toward the starship. Someone had expertise at damper field control and their skill showed. A portion of the hull slid out and stopped beneath it.

The complex machine gently settled into the chamber and clamps slid around it. The chamber slid back into the hull.

Like a drawer on a bureau! Lawson smiled at the thought.

"Probe secure. All lab personnel report to your duty stations," Dr. Reece's voice carried impartial authority.

Lawson pulled off the headset and stuck it on the bulkhead velcro strip where it belonged. After earlier deliberation he had decided to stay out of the lab and let Dr. Reece and his team do their jobs. He hated being an ignoramus and in the way of important work just because he wore three gold stripes.

The monitors abruptly switched from scenes outside the hull to events transpiring inside the labs. Lawson knew that the director and her staff were watching these same images down on Kiana. He felt anxious about this mission and wished that Captain Prescott had command for the event.

As if homing in on his fears the hatch behind him slid open and he saw Captain Peacock reflected in the monitor screens.

"Do they have the thing on board yet?"

Lawson faced his superior officer and reported recent events.

Peacock nodded toward the monitors. "Why are they all wearing atmosphere suits? I thought the decanting chambers were all air-tight."

"It's just an added precaution, sir. We do know the samples hold elements unknown to us, therefore we have no idea how we would react to them."

"Yeah, that's what they said down on Kiana." He glanced around. "They can't hear what we're saying, can they?"

"In the lab?"

"No, down on Kiana. I don't give a damn what the lab techs hear." He rubbed his head absently which Lawson noted.

"Nobody can hear what we're saying in here, sir."

"They're constantly looking over my shoulder and judging me. You've seen them."

"Actually, captain, I haven't seen any evidence of–"

"Oh for Smith's sake. I told you what they said to me. How they had their little meeting and then deigned to let me in on *their* decision about *my* ship!"

Lawson felt apprehensive. He wished the people on Kiana *could* hear what was being said in here. For a moment he considered alerting Colonel Dimarco. But the chief of security would need more than Lawson's word when it came to probably relieving a captain, even a temporary captain.

Damn. Every time I see him he's a little more unhinged. And that head rubbing might mean something is wrong physically. What am I supposed to do?

Lawson decided that as soon as this thing was over he would approach the ship's doctor and get him to check Peacock's condition. *His* opinion would carry weight with the Coalition Space Command.

"So," Captain Peacock stared hard at Lawson, "You want to come with me and watch this thing first hand?"

"In there, sir? There isn't enough room for two more people in atmosphere suits. Besides, we don't understand the process and they are–"

"*Mister* Lawson, I am the captain of this vessel and I can damn well go *anywhere* I wish. Up until a few minutes ago I thought you had my back. Now I wonder exactly where your loyalties lie."

"I am loyal to the Coalition Space Service and the captain of the *Magellan*, in that order, sir."

"Exactly, and the captain of the *Magellan* invites you to inspect the chemlab with him."

"With all due respect, captain, I decline."

"So noted, Mr. Lawson. I'll go in alone."

"Captain, I beseech you to wear an atmosphere suit. It *is* the regulation, sir."

"Thank you for your concern but I don't require you to hold my hand." He turned and went through the hatch.

Lieutenant Commander Lawson immediately opened a comm channel to Colonel Dimarco's office.

59
Dig N-19

Melanie watched the chaos around her in total disbelief.

Not long after Bennie's blithe admission that he had cut the power lead, one of Shannon's team had come racing down the corridor to where they stood in front of the massive sculpture of Ki.

If Gorski hadn't caught the exhausted young man he would have fallen on his face.

"St- Stoker, need, Payne!" he gasped. "Sha, Shannon, gone!"

"Take it easy, Dexter," Gorski said. "Gone as in absent or as in *dead*?"

"B-both?"

"I'll be right back," Bennie said and ran up the stairs leading out of the chamber.

Gorski glanced up at Melanie. "There's some water over there, please bring it here."

"Oh, sure." She grabbed one of many canteens and uncapped it as she hurried back.

Gorski took it and gave Dexter a drink. Behind them something came clattering down the long staircase. Bennie burst into the room on the back of an electric bike.

"I'll find Stoker!" he shouted as he whizzed past.

"Any excuse to play with something on wheels," Gorski said with a grin.

Dexter's breathing had slowed to near normal.

"Okay, Dex, what happened in there?"

He told them about the library, the scrolls, the books, the translations Shannon had made. He told them about the flashing symbols she had ignored. He told them about the wall of light surrounding her and her total disappearance.

Then Bennie came tearing down the other corridor with Stoker riding pillion. Bennie stopped near them.

"Dexter," Stoker Payne said, "is there anything I can do down there?"

"They're really confused, Stoker. More than anything they need some direction . . . some leadership."

"Good call. Thanks. Let's go, Bennie."

As Bennie accelerated Stoker caught sight of Mel and shouted,

"What are you doing here?"

Then they were gone.

"I thought archaeology was a nice, quiet, methodical science," she said. "Is it like this all the time?"

Gorski grinned. "Usually it's as you just described. This has never happened before in my experience."

Spreter came running out of the library corridor. "Hey, Bennie and Stoker just tore past me on the bike. What's up?"

"How is it you didn't see Dexter when *he* ran past you?" Gorski asked.

Spreter shrugged and smiled. "That must have been when I was in the big gallery down the hall looking at old scrolls."

"You were supposed to stay in the corridor, James."

"It was quiet and I *was* patrolling when I–"

"Everyone freeze!"

Six security troopers stood in a semicircle with heavy lasers all pointed at them.

"Sure," Gorski said in a calm voice. "Don't get excited. I'm gonna lay his head down, okay?" He gently put Dexter's head on the floor.

"All of you lay face down on the floor!" one of them ordered.

They all complied but Mel noticed that both Gorski and Spreter were sizing up the security people. Six more troopers ran past them and down the corridor in the same direction Bennie and Stoker had gone.

"Ya wanna tell us what the hell this is all about?" Spreter asked in a resigned tone.

Another person came into the room. "Stand down," she ordered. "These damn communicators don't work here!"

The six troopers relaxed and pointed their weapons toward the floor at their feet.

"You folks can get up. Sorry about the situation. We weren't sure what we were going to find here." The major glanced around at the chamber. "I'm *still* not sure what we've found here."

"Major Merritt, isn't it?" Melanie asked. "We met in the weapons bay on the *Magellan*."

"Yeah, I remember you. Melanie Frasier. I knew I heard that name before."

"Mind telling us what this is all about, major?" Gorski asked.

"We were receiving a priority call from the AI in Dr. Frasier's utility when it suddenly went dead. Since we already had a fix on location we saddled up and brought three squads with."

"Why was the AI calling in a priority?" Tom said.

"It said the camp was empty of humans and showed a lack of standard security. That's enough for us. We thought something had happened to you folks."

"Well now you know we're okay. Can we go back to work?"

"It's not going to be that simple. We kept a live holo feed going all the way out here and down into this," she gestured, "...place you people found. Now the director's office wants to know everything about it and she wants to know *now*."

"She's going to get a full report as soon as Dr. Payne gets back. We just discovered this place today, or last night. Hell, I don't even know what time it is."

Major Merritt glanced up to the left and Mel knew she was checking her personal read-out.

"It's 1300 hours, give or take a few minutes."

"Wow. We've been in here for four hours!" Spreter said.

Many footfalls could be heard coming down the library corridor and the museum corridor. When they converged in front of the huge statue all of the archaeology team had their hands behind their heads.

"Stand down," Major Merritt ordered, and the troopers lowered their weapons. "I tried calling you guys to give you the chill, but our communications don't work in here."

"Can we put our hands down, major?" Stoker Payne asked.

"Yes. Sorry about the inconvenience, Dr. Payne." She quickly explained the situation.

"The director wants you and your assistant in her office as soon as possible. She also wants you to bring your team in for the time being."

"My assistant has disappeared. We don't know where she is or if she's even still alive."

"I think you need to tell me a little more, sir."

John Dowd explained what happened. "I feel responsible because I was the security person with Dr. Gray and wasn't able to stop her in time."

"John, if Shannon wanted to do something all of you together couldn't have stopped her," Stoker said. "So don't do that to yourself. Nobody is blaming you."

"Thanks, Stoker. Why do they want us to stop at this point? We have nothing to do in Siboth."

"I don't think the dig has priority any more, John. Why don't you guys go back in for another four hours, take food and water with you this time. Then saddle up and come on into Siboth."

His team members grinned.

"Gorski, you're in charge of the evacuation. Bill, you take half our folks down one side, Marilyn, you take the other half down the other. Get good holos, folks. I'm not sure how long it will be before we get back. I don't think I have to tell anyone not to ignore any potential warnings, do I?"

A chorus of negatives swelled and ebbed.

Bill Hilton nodded and said, "We'll try to figure out a way to communicate over the distance down here, too."

"Good thinking. Move out. Time is short."

Stoker looked over at Melanie. "So you caused this security exercise, huh?"

Mel felt her cheeks burning. "I'm sorry. I just wanted to see the dig before we all have to evacuate Kiana. It's pretty incredible." She glanced up at the towering statue.

"Indeed. We had no idea until today just how incredible it is. Have they discovered where all the Kians went?"

"No. It's as if they dropped off the face of the planet."

"I'd sure like to ask one about this place," Stoker said.

"Dr. Payne," Major Merritt said. "Would you like a squad of our people to assist with security?"

"No, thank you, major. This was a very unusual situation today."

"As you wish, sir. Okay people, back to the transport."

The security troopers moved up the stairway.

"Major, can Dr. Frasier and I ride back to Siboth with you? It will save us a lot of time."

"Of course. Do you need to get anything from your camp?"

"No," Stoker said glancing at Mel.

"I need to go to my utility for a minute."

She hurried out to the edge of the perimeter and swung into the driver's seat. A lead dangled from behind the small dashboard. She leaned over and plugged it back into the only empty socket. She hadn't even know it was there.

"Mother, why did you alert security?"

"Standard security procedures were not being followed in a known hostile area. What's down there?"

"All I saw was the biggest damn statue of a naked Kian you can imagine. The team says there is a library and a museum down there."

"This complicates things."

"Why, Mother?"

"We were going to pull out of here. Leave the planet for good. The Kians don't seem to require our assistance and we have samples of the gasses in the comet tail being analyzed on *Magellan* as we speak. There was no reason to stay any longer. Now there is."

"Dr. Payne and I are going to ride into Siboth with the security force. The director wants to see us right away. Would you please return to the apartment?"

"I'll be there as soon as I can. Have a nice flight."

60
Coalition Star Ship Magellan

The naive side of Senior Chief Communications Technician Mongo Tschurtoff wondered how he could be sweating in a controlled environment when all he was doing was walking and talking. The worldly part, which possessed much more volume, snickered and dug a psychic elbow into his ribs. *Can you say, "Amber Nazarrian," chief?*

He realized he had gone silent in front of the upper level students and their two teachers, Mr. Burton and Ms. Nazarrian.

Master Chief Shipfitter's Mate Patrick Murphy, walking beside him, filled in the silence. "The huge locks funnel people into these bays if the captain should order us to abandon ship. Along here you can see the open locks of fifteen life pods. Does anyone know how many people each pod can hold safely?"

A tall, willowy girl raised her hand, as did an even taller boy. Mongo thought they were the same age. He pointed to the girl.

"Name and deck, Miss?"

"Maisie Sarah Campbell, Senior Chief. We're all from Deck Sixty Three Upper Level Academy."

"So you are," Chief Murphy said. "And how many will one of the pods hold?"

"Well, technically, they are much more than a pod as pods are usually filled with sensors of some sort and lack an atmosphere or the ability to create one." Mongo wondered if he should have selected the boy. "The life boats can each sustain fifty adults for up to a year. They have Kilo type communications that can monitor multitudes of frequencies at the same time, and–"

"Maisie," Ms. Nazarrian said in a quiet tone, "You have answered the question."

"Ma'am." She nodded to the teacher.

"Exactly as you say, Ms. Maisie. Accumulation of knowledge extent grows amazingly in you youthful people," Mongo said, wishing that for just once he could deliver smooth academic diction and impress this lovely teacher lady.

At the age of 41 he had finally decided he would like to sample the benefits of wedded bliss, the experiences of his friend Chief Murphy notwithstanding. He had met Ms. Nazarrian in the early days of the voyage when she asked him to give a talk to her physics class on the unclassified communications systems operated on Magellan and how they differed and why.

He had reluctantly agreed due more to his immediate attraction to her than for any understanding it might bring to the students. For two weeks he studied information he had known so long he had forgotten the basics. Addressing that class had been more nerve wracking than facing a captain's mast.

He had to admit that he knew he was innocent going into the captain's mast, which gave him strength. Going into the classroom he knew he was infatuated, which gave him palpitations.

Mongo had known women in the physical sense since he was a non-rated striker, but they had all been part of quick, financial based understandings that had never lasted more than three days. And the last one of those had been over a year before.

"How many life boats does the Magellan have?" Chief Murphy asked the thirty students.

More hands went up and he pointed to the boy who had raised his hand earlier.

"John Stout, Master Chief. The Magellan carries 120 life boats in two rings of 60 that are both separated into four bays of fifteen each."

Five days ago Ms. Nazarrian had approached Chief Tschurtoff and asked if he could arrange a field trip for the two upper division classes in their academy. They wanted an in-depth excursion of one of the two lifeboat decks. He had nearly referred her to Chief Murphy before he bit his tongue so hard he drew blood.

He said he would see what he could do and get back to her. They both walked away smiling. Murphy was only too happy to help, but couldn't resist needling his friend.

"Better watch yer back, Mongo. That teacher is single and you'd make a fine strapping catch for her."

Despite himself Mongo knew he blushed. "Romantic situation this is not, friend Patrick. Merely academic and professional it is."

"Right!"

They both laughed.

"Chief Tschurtoff," Ms. Nazarrian said, bringing him back to the delicious present in a quickened heartbeat. "Are the communications on each boat capable of sending messages all the way to Proxima?"

Maisie turned and scowled at her teacher, disbelief writ huge on her countenance.

"Of course, however the messages six months in going and coming would take."

Some of the students snickered.

Ms. Nazarrian squinted her eyes and her smile vanished as she looked at them. "And how many of *you* started your lives speaking a foreign language before teaching *yourself* Standard English?"

They all went silent and Mongo smiled. *She has been learning about me!* He looked over at Patrick who openly grinned at him. Chief Murphy had correctly surmised Mongo's interest in the teacher when his friend asked him to lead this field trip.

Mongo felt wonderful and emboldened enough to ask in Rumanian, "Do any of you speak my native language?"

Ms. Nazarrian looked over at him and replied in fluent Rumanian, "I'm probably the only one."

Mongo grinned. He was happy they had all afternoon for this field trip.

61
Ki-Nuuhi Sanctuary

Many Kians turned and stared at Danny after his outburst.

"Sorry," he said. "I was just surprised to see a human in there, and especially one I know. Is she hurt?"

A very old and frail Kian woman had entered the glass box and was touching the woman lying on the floor.

"Who is Shannon Gray, Dan-nay?" Su Laana asked.

"Archaeologist. Works with Dr. Stoker Payne down south of Siboth. I helped her with supplying their expedition."

If possible, the cavern grew even quieter than it had been. Danny felt an anxiety he couldn't identify. He realized it wasn't coming from him.

"Su Laana, can *everyone* here read my thoughts?"

She sighed. "Yes, if they wish to. Many ignore any thought or emotion not directed at them personally. Almost all will respect your privacy. Please realize we also hear each other and try to practice what we call 'alonement' or in your terms, 'minding our own business.'"

"Are all Kians born able to do this?"

"Yes, for many generations now."

"Your people were not always this way? How did this happen?"

"You will find out very soon, my love. Please be patient."

Su Laani acquired a far away look and then refocused on him.

"The woman is alive. Perhaps you should speak with her."

"Sure!"

The crowd parted and Danny and Su Laani walked through the silent throng. He felt confused, apprehensive and more than a little nettled.

Although he tried to make eye contact with the Kians he passed they all ignored him completely. It occurred on him that the border between polite and rude probably was a very fine line in this culture. Then he wondered if he had originated that thought or if it had been gently given to him.

He shook his head. One step at a time, that was all he could do. As they neared the glass box he examined the machines and equipment surrounding it. Before today he would have sworn none of it came from Kiana, but here it sat in electronic splendor, and impossible to refute.

"Have you always had this stuff?" he asked Su Laana.

"Yes. Most of it is quite ancient. Only a few people are trained to keep it functioning in the remote possibility we might need it again."

"What does it all do?"

"Later. Please see to the woman now."

As he entered the glass box he realized it wasn't glass at all, but something much stronger yet totally transparent. The ancient Kian woman looked up at him.

~She has experienced a traumatic journey. Please assure her that she has nothing to fear from us and that she will not die.~

"O-, okay." He gave Shannon all of his attention and knelt next to her.

"Hey, are you all right?"

She stared at him and blinked. "I know you, don't I?"

"Danny Gordon, recently with Coalition Procurement in Siboth."

"Yeah," she smiled weakly. "You can get stuff nobody else can."

"Well, your memory seems to be fine. How did you get here?"

She slowly looked around and seemed to shrink into herself.

"Where the hell is *here*?"

"I'm not sure of the exact location, but my girlfriend and I hiked for three days northeast from Siboth to get here. This is an ancient volcano."

"I was exploring a Kian library we discovered about a hundred klicks south of Siboth at Dig N-19. It's under ground and *huge*. There was some sort of sign floating in the air and I ignored it, walked right past it, and suddenly I was here."

~The Repository of Ki allows one only into areas the individual can safely understand. If one is expelled as you were it is because you were entering into an area where you could not comprehend the danger.~

"Did you hear that?" Shannon said.

"Yeah." He nodded toward the old Kian woman in the transfer booth with them. "Was that you, Mother?"

She nodded and smiled.

"Why'd you call her 'mother?'"

"It just seemed like the polite thing to do. You should know that I plan to stay here on Kiana when the *Magellan* evacuates everybody. I have found the love of my life and I want to stay with her."

"Smart man. The love of my life is on *Magellan* and I want to stay with her, too."

"Smart woman," Danny said. "I don't know how we'll get you back to Siboth. There are no roads to this place and they keep its location secret."

~The star ship people have no intention of leaving. After Yanivina's visit they will bring their people back to the ground. They wish to investigate the Repository of Ki. You will be safe here until they all return.~

"You're an archaeologist, right?"

"Yeah, with a lot of anthropology to go with it."

"Think of this as an in-depth study."

"Would you please help me stand?"

"Sure." He helped her to her feet and supported her as she stepped out of the chamber.

"Okay. Now I need to sit again." Shannon slumped down onto a stone step and looked around. "What is all this?"

"I don't know, but they promised to enlighten me. Maybe they'll let you tag along."

62
Temple of Ki

"Can you still hear us, Bennie?" Bill Hilton released the SEND button on the emergency communicator.

"You're coming in loud and clear. Those little emitters are working great."

"Okay, " Bill said. "Patch me through to Marilyn."

"Copy!"

"This is Marilyn. That you, Bill?"

"Absolutely! This is working great. Get holos of everything and check in every hour on the hour."

"You told me all of that before we spilt up, remember?"

"I just wanted to make sure you remembered."

"No worries. Have fun, Bill."

"You too, Marilyn,"

Bill turned off the communicator to preserve the charge. He and his team stood in the "Museum" corridor next to the entrance of the gallery where Shannon had disappeared.

"Here's how I see it," Bill said. "We know we can't go through this gallery and into the next unless we want to go where ever Shannon went." He paused. "Damn, I hope she's okay!"

"As you were saying, Bill?" Carol Smith said in a soft tone.

"So how about we all walk down to the main entrance to the next gallery and see if we can get in that way. If not, we keep going until we find one we *can* enter."

"Works for me," Gorski said.

"Great." Bill's boyish enthusiasm proved contagious and everyone grabbed their backpacks, sliding them over their shoulders as they moved. The packs were filled with food, water, and emergency supplies. All were armed with hand lasers and Gorski also carried a Personnel Assault Laser.

The same two symbols hung in the main entrance to the gallery.

"Ok-aaay," Bill said, peering into the gallery without getting closer to the symbols. "I guess we keep hiking."

As they moved down the corridor, James Spreter said, "Anyone else notice the light is always adequate wherever we are, but way down there it is totally dark?" He pointed in the direction they traveled.

"I always wondered where the power supply for lighting Siboth was located," Charly said. "I spent three days trying to figure out how the light fixture in Stoker Payne's apartment got any power at all."

"I've looked at them, too," Gorski said. "I finally decided they had to be powered by broadcast electricity but nothing else I saw came near to that level of technology. So I thought I was missing something."

"I think you might have the answer, Tom," Charly said. "But broadcast from *where*?"

"Here, maybe?" Michelle Ramey offered.

"I'm so glad I am part of this dig," Dexter Francis blurted. "I would have never believed this if I hadn't seen it."

They approached another gallery entrance and stopped in front of it. As they watched, the light came up inside the huge room. No symbols appeared.

"Why would they put an off-limits space in the middle of everything else?" Gorski said.

"Why would they bury something this magnificent out in the middle of a prairie?" Carol said. "I doubt we'll all be here long enough to understand the Kian mindset."

"I thought this was supposed to be a library," Michelle said. "I sure as hell don't see any thing that remotely resembles books."

"John told me they found what looked like more advanced hand pads than we use," Spreter said. "Maybe the next information advancements are in here."

"Before anyone goes anywhere," Bill said, "let's divide this space up so we don't miss anything or duplicate our efforts." He assigned each of them to a section of the gallery.

"And don't forget to take holos of *everything*! Damn, this is exciting!"

Bill moved to the first object in his section. He thought it was a long, glass fronted exhibit case. It stretched at least ten meters before ending and two meters beyond it was another just like it.

His holocam had the standard three lenses set equidistant on a light helmet he wore on his head. Whatever he saw was captured by the recorder in a natural manner. The machine could run for three months before requiring a recharge.

He peered into the first case and found himself face-to-face with a Kian.

"Those are battle flags," John Dowd said. "I studied a lot of military history and I'd bet a month's pay those are battle flags."

"Nobody's arguing with you, Big John," Charly Herring said. "All I said was they looked out of place on Kiana."

"Maybe they do now," Doug Franklin said, "but according to what Shannon discovered in the library all the continents of this planet were at war with each other at one point."

"I wish we could read what the descriptions say," Joyce Mayer said.

"I wish I knew how they make them float in the air like that," Marilyn Culpepper said. "At first I thought the words were on a piece of thin plastic, but there's nothing there except the glowing words themselves."

"Don't forget the manuscripts' protection in the library. You couldn't see them in regular light either," Doug said.

"Okay. Everybody get back to your part of this place," Marilyn said. "If we argue about everything we see we'll never get out of this room."

John slowly walked past a long row of hand weapons that evolved from a crude dagger to a sword made of mercury (or something that looked like mercury) to a thing that looked like clay gripped tightly and then fired to a metallic sheen. He wondered what the potato-looking thing actually did.

Next was a display of long arms. Some of the weapons could have been from human history books and then they evolved to pieces containing bulb-like bulges in them with barrels that went from narrow at the "magazine" to a bellows-like muzzle. They had already tried to open one of the display cases to no avail.

Kian curators possessed skills far beyond anything he had ever seen in any other museum. He successfully resisted the urge to try and kick in the glass. Somehow he felt certain that it would not only be a futile gesture but he also might be injured or killed in the process.

Despite what Stoker Payne said, John felt very much responsible for Shannon's death. Although there was a little voice in his head that said, "She isn't dead until you see the body." That was as close to hope as he would allow himself.

In the next case he saw something he recognized. The weapon was the exact same model they had found early in the dig. This one was neither bent nor rusty.

It carried a light sheen that could be oil or the iridescence of the metal itself. The first one he had seen seemed pathetic. This one exuded lethality and he wondered what sort of warriors the Others had been.

The fangs were definitely off-putting and he wondered if the whole species had fangs or just the military. The next display featured a copy of one of the fanged warriors in the flesh.

John took his time and went over every part of the display. The creature looked like it could walk out and start fighting if it had the chance. Like the Kians, the creature had short, smooth hair all over the body.

The cat-like ears lay flat against the wide head and the eyes regarded the world through slits. In one hand it held a helmet so polished John could see his reflection and the other hand grasped a hand weapon as deadly in appearance as the long arm in the precious display case.

It wore a uniform blouse of a soft-appearing fabric with metal devices on each sleeve near the cuff. No other insignia could be seen. It had a tail, a short one, but an actual tail that stuck out from beneath the upper garment. The trousers hung loose down the legs and the feet were bare.

Each toe ended in a rather large, black, shiny claw. The warrior's height was equal to an average Kian, making it shorter than the average human. But John was glad he never had to face these guys in a combat situation.

Marilyn's loud whistle cut through the air.

I'll bet she was the envy of every eight-year-old boy she ever met, he thought.

He moved toward the entrance. A glance at his hand pad revealed they had been here for over four hours. He found that difficult to believe.

"Sorry, folks, but we gotta go back to camp," Marilyn said.

"Why?" Doug asked. "We have food and water. We could camp in here."

Marilyn, the shortest person on the team, looked up at him and said, "Where you going to sleep? This whole place is made of stone. Then there's the problem of sanitation–"

"Never mind," Doug said with a grin. "You're right."

"You bet! Hey Ben, any word from the others?"

Ben Balberdi had stayed close to the entrance so the communications link stayed active. It couldn't turn corners unless they had another relay, which they didn't.

"Nothing yet, Marilyn."

"Good. I didn't want to have to hurry. Let's get going, gang."

63
Coalition Star Ship Magellan

"Okay, Jan. That flask is secure." Dr. Lawrence Reece tried to rub his itchy nose and cursed when his gloved hand bounced off the helmet's faceplate. He hated working in an atmosphere suit but they were a safety precaution he wouldn't forego.

"Larry, we have company," Jan said in a flat tone.

He looked up and saw Captain Peacock coming through the airlock. "Where's his atmosphere suit?"

"Why is he even coming in here?"

"I'm activating my external speaker, so watch what you say, Jan."

"Acknowledged."

Lawrence glanced over his set up to insure nothing was open or easily jarred. *We really don't need this interruption!*

The inner door opened and the seal alarm flashed red. Lawrence deactivated it before the klaxon had a chance to sound. He turned to the door.

"Captain, is there something amiss?"

Peacock looked around as if seeking contraband or an escaped lab animal.

"No, just wanted to check this situation first hand."

"Captain, you should be wearing an atmosphere suit in here. This lab is not a safe environment, sir."

Peacock took a deep breath and gave him a mocking smirk. "I seem to be fine so far. What have you found?" He rubbed his temple and winced.

"Dangerous stuff," Lawrence said in a flat voice. "We had three lab rats in separate air tight containers. We exposed one rat to the first sample we decanted from the probe."

He pointed to a heavy glass cage on a rack against the wall. A large mass of blood and heavier matter still slowly slid down the inside of the front panel. The body of the white rat continued twitching beneath the smear.

"Its head exploded?"

"No, sir. As soon as we exposed it the animal went berserk and tried to attack us. It seemed to gain strength and jumped at my face with enough force to do that to itself. It was rather unnerving."

"What the hell is in that gas?"

"So far we have isolated a neurotoxin unknown to Coalition science. There are other unknown elements in the sample that may or may not lend themselves to this sort of result." He nodded at the dead rat before realizing the captain couldn't see his head move.

"Are they monitoring this lab from Kiana?"

"They were. I don't think any one is watching now. This stuff gets pretty boring if you're not actually doing the work."

"So they were looking over our shoulder for nothing, huh?"

"They were interested in scientific inquiry, I believe. Since there really isn't room in here for more than a couple of experts they wanted to at least watch the initial process."

"Well, I didn't mean to intrude! This is my ship and I'm ultimately responsible for every member of the crew."

"Yes, captain, I know that. If there is anything else I can show you . . ." through the window Lawrence saw Colonel Dimarco and two security troopers enter the observation room and join Lieutenant Commander Lawson, "...ah, just let me know and I'll be happy to oblige."

But Peacock had correctly interpreted Lawrence's hesitation and swung around to stare through the window.

"Lawson! What the hell do you think you're doing?" he screamed.

Lawrence turned off his speaker and said to Dr. Groom, "Jan, get between him and any of the containers. He's close to doing something stupid. I can feel it."

"Concur!" she snapped, and edged between the animal cages and the captain.

In the observation room Dimarco and Lawson talked and gestured toward the lab. Captain Peacock grew even more agitated and Lawrence wondered what he could use to subdue the man if events warranted. He turned his external speaker on.

"Captain, I really think you should leave the lab, sir. There are too many fragile, and lethal, items in here to not be absolutely careful."

The captain continued screaming at the men in the other room.

"You've just shot your wad, *Mister* Lawson! You'll never advance as long as *I'm* in the service! Colonel Dimarco, I *order* you to put Commander Lawson in the brig, do you hear me?"

Not realizing that Lawrence had switched on his external speaker, Jan said, "What the hell is wrong with him?" And then she accidentally bumped Captain Peacock.

64
Siboth

"What did you people find out there, Stoker?" The director looked haggard.

"We found the Kian culture, its history, everything. They were, are, more advanced than us."

"Do they have space flight?"

"I found no evidence of that, but from what we did discover it would not have been an impossible goal for them."

"Why have they hidden it?"

"My team and I have debated that one to the point some people nearly had fist fights. But my conjecture is that the Kians, for some reason, turned their collective back on modernity and returned to a wood and water culture."

"That's crazy."

"I agree, madam. But since neither of us are Kian we lack their viewpoint. Have we figured out where they all disappeared to yet?"

"No. We know they're out there but the *Magellan* can't detect any movement and with the summer temperatures what they are we can't use thermal imaging with any success. It's as if they know when the star ship is above them."

"Maybe they *are* using technology and have kept it hidden from us," Stoker said.

"We've had the best detection equipment in the universe going over this planet for five years and we've discovered nothing." The director clamped her mouth shut and then spat, "Until today! Tell me how you discovered this place and exactly what you found."

Stoker explained how the small stone "building" buried under masses of skeletons had turned out to be an entrance into an unimaginably huge structure. He showed her holos of the statue and the corridor stretching into the distance.

When he got to the statue of the warrior she actually shuddered.

"They have hidden so much from us!" she whispered. "But why?"

He touched the hand pad and the holo vanished.

"Off hand I would say they didn't trust us, director. They don't seem to need our help with the effects of the comet and–"

"What *are* they doing up there?" Melanie blurted.

Stoker and the director both said, "Huh?"

Melanie pointed to the wall where a small portion displayed a holo of the lab on the *Magellan*.

"I've been watching while you two talked. That's Captain Peacock isn't it? What the hell is he *doing* in there?"

The director touched her desk and the holo sound came up.

"You're both in league with them, aren't you?" Peacock screamed at the lab workers. He grabbed the one behind him and shoved the person into a row of glass cages against the bulkhead.

One shattered.

"Oh. My. God!" the director cried.

65
Coalition Star Ship Magellan

"Oh my God, Jan. Grab him!" Lawrence screamed.

The glass cage shattered under her weight and he saw a shard rip into her atmosphere suit. Peacock jerked back from her and his face contorted into a rictus of rage before he flung himself on her, flailing with hands that now resembled claws.

Lawrence turned and lunged for the DESTRUCT button on the back of the lab table. The toxicity labs had been constructed next to the outer skin of the ship and fitted to blow them into space individually in the case of life threatening accidents; like this one.

Both Jan and Peacock fought maniacally. A blow from Jan knocked Peacock into Lawrence and the captain immediately attacked him. Lawrence swung at the button but Peacock's attack pulled him backward and he heard the seam on his suit rip.

His brain stem and cerebellum instantly ballooned to three times their original size, smashing the rest of the brain against the inside of his skull. Pain beyond description was his last cognition.

"We've got to stop them!" Colonel Dimarco yelled. "Roggow, Bukowski, get in there and subdue them!"

"Sir!" one yelled and they both ran into the main corridor and grabbed the door to the lab.

"No!" Lawson shrieked. "It's in the air in there! Don't let it out!"

"What'd he say?" Trooper Roggow said, pulling open the outer door.

"Who gives a shit?" Bukowski snarled. "He's not our boss!"

Lawson watched in horror as the two men burst into the room. He slammed his fist on the General Alarm, hoping to stop the gasses from contaminating the entire ship. A klaxon went off and suddenly his head seemed to explode.

"Well," Chief Murphy said, surveying the group with his hands on his hips and a smile on his face. "I think Chief Tschurtoff and I have shown you impressive young scholars every–"

The emergency klaxon went off and cycled from low to high

decibels every ten seconds.

"Drill was not mentioned for this day!" Mongo shouted.

Chief Murphy turned and slapped a gray panel on the bulkhead. It immediately displayed a two dimensional image from the security cameras around the ship. The group stood in stunned absorption trying to understand what they were seeing.

"They're all going crazy!" Mr. Burton said. "But why?"

Chief Murphy pushed an icon at the edge of the screen and a diagram of the ship replaced the spreading mayhem. Some of the students were already crying. Murphy selected another icon and a swirling overlay filled the diagram.

"It's the air handling system. Something in the air is messing them up. It will be here in less than a minute!"

"Into the pod!" Mongo shrieked. "Now!"

Everyone moved at once, some running, a few nearly staggering with fear. Mongo stood on one side of the large hatch and Patrick on the other until the last sobbing student passed. They hurried after them.

Patrick shut the hatch and sealed it while Mongo shut down the ship air and engaged the lifeboat tanks.

"Patrick, begin launch sequence!"

"Chief, you can't just leave the ship without orders!" Mr. Burton said. His calm demeanor had vanished and responsibility for his students added authority to his words.

"If all on *Maggie* disabled, choices diminish!" Mongo said. "Be happy you are here." He slapped the bulkhead for emphasis.

Ms. Nazarrian had taken charge and delegated students to help other students strap into the first seats they found. She turned and looked back at Mongo with bright, excited eyes. She gave him a quick smile before shouting, "Jim, get strapped in!"

While Mr. Burton found a seat Mongo hurried forward. Chief Murphy sat in the pilot's seat flipping switches and jabbing icons. A flat screen built into the console showed one synapsing image after another of their former crewmates and friends going berserk and killing one another with bare hands and teeth.

They all felt the *Magellan* lurch. Staring through the forward observation panel at the stars surrounding the blue planet below them, Murphy pushed the red button emblazoned LAUNCH.

"Hang on everyone. Here we go!" he bellowed.

Magellan Lifeboat 65 blew its tethers and hurled into space.

66
Coalition Star Ship Magellan

Gunnery Sergeant Miri Pedrosa was at her desk in the guard shack when the klaxon sounded. She immediately surveyed the screen in front of her and punched the comm icon to the security section.

"All hands, don breather units, the atmosphere has been compromised! Do it *now!*"

She pulled her own unit off the rack and slid it over her torso, snapped the helmet shut and activated the system. Nano-enhanced foam sealed the bottom of the helmet to the skin of her neck. When the collar was removed the affected skin would be raw and sore for days, but for now she had three hours of bottled oxygen: three hours in which to stop this madness.

Well, a case of collar-ring for me. Just hope this crap in the air doesn't go through skin.

She activated her microphone with a chin thrust and snapped, "Arm your selves. Full power on all weapons. Go to Condition Red."

She grabbed her heavy laser rifle and hurried into the squad bay. A dozen security grunts bristling with weaponry hurried toward her.

She wondered where Lieutenant Perlic was hiding today. He was mustering out of the Security Force in three weeks to transition into Admin. Unfortunately his mind had already made the move and his lack of attention to his current position was obvious to all.

"Form a skirmish line in the corridor, fore and aft. Both lines advance on my order."

"Gunny," Corporal Dietrich said. "Who we fighting?"

"I think it will be pretty obvious, Deet. You all know your jobs. Keep everyone you meet pacified and orderly. Let's move out."

The hatch to the main corridor irised open and Miri led the rush. She immediately collided with someone running down the corridor. The person bounced off her and hit the deck. Before she could say anything the person leaped to his feet and turned on her.

It was Lieutenant Perlic – or had been. No recognition

manifested in the contorted face and bugged out eyes. She wondered if the pressure inside his head had increased.

With his teeth bared and hands clawed he launched himself at her like a madman. Miri didn't hesitate; she cut him in half with a full beam.

"What the fuck!" one of her troopers blurted.

From both directions figures rushed toward them. If they encountered each other first they would immediately fight like beasts until one was dead or maimed enough to stay down. Then the person would tear after the next moving thing they saw.

Miri heard one of her people crying over the comm net.

"Belay the sissy shit! We might be the only people on this ship who aren't fucked up. We still have a fighting chance so don't blow it for the rest of us!"

Three people charged her fore line from different angles. The troopers opened up on them. In seconds all three attackers lay dead on the deck.

"Keep moving, people! Staff Sergeant Arenziac, you have the aft line!"

"Aye, aye, Gunny!"

The corridor stretched fifteen meters from side to side and emptied into a larger space forward where shops and small bistros plied their wares. Anything not bolted to the deck or bulkheads lay in shambles. Every person they saw had gone berserk and either in the act of killing another or fighting for their lives.

Chaos reigned.

Miri checked her read-outs and quickly realized she and her troopers were probably the only people left on the ship who were not terminally insane.

"Listen up, people. We need to abandon shi–"

The deck canted and the gravity generators weakened. Standing upright became an exercise in frustration.

"Get off the ship if you can. Every man for him self," she shouted.

A snarling fat woman bounced and clawed toward her and Miri put a laser beam through Karen Murphy's head.

The *Magellan* seemed to stagger, smoke swirled through the area pushed by a fatal wind, and Miri heard metal ripping above her. She looked up and saw a great tear in the deck ten meters above her. Flame whipped across the opening and instantly she and most of her troopers were sucked into the white-hot torrent and incinerated.

67
Siboth

Stoker, Melanie, and the director stared at the holo bank, unable to pull their eyes from the mayhem transpiring far above them. The emergency system on Magellan now sent images from all over the ship, cycling through the decks and spaces, holding each image for three seconds before synapsing to the next.

The vents carried death to every space. They saw crew members initially reacting, going into rages and attacking others and the image would shift to blood-spattered bulkheads and creatures no longer human beating and stomping others to death.

Melanie turned and vomited into a waste can. All three of them sobbed uncontrollably. Amanda Saint-Claire rushed into the room.

"Director, there's something happening on the M–" She saw the holo screen. "Holy Mary, Mother of God!"

The audio carried shrieks, growls, grunts, and the constant impacts of flesh on flesh. Every scene now showed blood and dismembered bodies, the only movement being twitching bodies and hammering fists. In the background they heard klaxons, alarms, and pre-recorded warnings.

"Mother!" Melanie sobbed. "Can you stop them?"

Stoker looked at her. "Who the hell is–"

"Busy. Mel," said a voice. "Lost. Lost."

"What the hell was *that*?" Stoker said, his eyes on the holos.

"I didn't know you had a dialogue with the AI," the director said.

"She's up there, too," Mel said, choking on her tears.

"Migawd, you're right!" the director said. "We're going to lose that ship." She stabbed her screen. "Marcy, send an emergency call to Proxima Central right now, while we can still use the *Magellan's* array!"

"Ma'am!" the link went dead.

A security trooper rushed into the room. "Director, the *Magellan* is falling out of orbit!"

After a last glance at the holos Stoker ran through the door and down the hall. He heard the others pounding along behind him. The outer door stood open and people had gathered on the steps and in the street. All were staring into the late afternoon sky.

He rushed into the open and followed their gaze.

Dusk ruled Siboth. High Moon was on the other side of Kiana and Low Moon edged up over the eastern horizon. Far above them *Magellan* raced into the atmosphere. Light from Beluache, the Kian-named sun that blessed Kiana, transfigured the ship into a star, gleaming and doomed.

A thick trail of smoke already boiled off her hull as she angled lower and lower toward the planet.

"Do we have any idea where it's going to hit?" a lieutenant in security camos asked. No one answered him. Most were weeping.

A portly man clutched his chest and collapsed with a groan. Two medics rushed to him. After a moment one looked at the other and shrugged in resignation.

Stoker knew most of the medical equipment and the only real hospital within light years was burning up in front of their eyes. He blinked away tears and watched as the doomed ship angled down and vanished beyond the horizon line.

"What are we going to do?" Amanda asked. "There's nowhere to go now."

The dusk sank further into darkness and Yanivina rose above the horizon where smoke still hung from dying *Magellan*.

"My God, she's right," Melanie said. "There's no way we can escape that thing!"

"Here it comes!"

Out of the western sky the *Magellan* roared over them, pieces tore off in flames, debris rained down through the smoky wake. The sound of its demise thundered across them. It had lost its familiar circular shape.

Deck after deck had burned off and the hulk had become a rough oval that twisted and contorted in its death throes.

"Ramona!" Melanie screamed into the din. She dropped to her knees and wept with her face in her hands.

Stoker thought about the teeming life aboard the star ship, the families, the women and children. His mind froze and he couldn't think any more. He could merely watch. The *Magellan* dropped fast now; it wouldn't make another orbit.

"Incoming! Take cover!"

Something whistled through the air and hit a lorry down the

street. The lorry exploded into thousands of pieces.

"Get behind the building!" Stoker bellowed. He pulled Melanie off the ground and, holding her hand tightly, ran behind the great bulk of the Coalition Building.

Like a lethal meteorite shower a flurry of burning debris raced through Siboth smashing into buildings, vehicles, taking out swaths of trees and annihilating knots of people who didn't move fast enough.

Something large hit the building and it, as well as the ground around it, shuddered from the massive body blow. Stoker sat on the ground, his back to the wall and arms wrapped tightly around a shaking and sobbing Melanie. Next to him the director held Amanda in the same way.

A squad of security troopers ran from the far side of the street toward the Coalition Building.

"What the *fuck* are they doing?" he yelled.

A flaming girder whooshed past and obliterated all of them from the hips up.

The rain of debris slackened and then died. Stoker didn't move. He wanted to wait at least five minutes after the last impact before giving up his shelter. He felt drained.

Melanie lay in his arms, completely spent, her eyes staring at something he couldn't see. She constantly trembled.

Silence fell over the town until the moans and cries for help gathered strength. Stoker's attention was drawn to the sound of many people moving fast.

A number of security troopers ran up. One saw them and veered over.

"Madam Director, is that you?"

"Yes?" Stoker thought she wasn't sure of the answer.

"Major Merritt, ma'am. We need to set up an aide station immediately and triage the injured. May we use the Coalition Building?"

Stoker watched the words make sense in her head and the director snapped, "Of course, Major Merritt. How can we help?"

Merritt gave her a quick smile. "Phew, there for a second I thought I had lost you, ma'am. If you would rally your people and clear space on the ground floor for people to lie, it would be a big help. My people are forming search parties."

"Where is Colonel Poppert, major?"

The smile vanished. "In his quarters. He seems to have experienced a breakdown yesterday."

"You are now a full colonel. You are in charge of all things military and security from this moment on."

"Yes, ma'am. I was in charge anyway, but thanks for the raise." The smile flashed again and she was off, running down the street shouting orders.

"Amanda, snap out of it!" the director said. Both women got to their feet. Stoker and Melanie pushed themselves up.

"Dr. Payne, where is your crew?"

"I wish I knew. I hope they all took cover."

"Help us organize the building. As soon as we have our situation stable we have to figure out how to beat that bitch up there."

She pointed at Yanivina, rising higher and higher in the smoke filled air.

68
Southern Plains of Cimpar

Tom Gorski monitored the electronic trail before them. Stoker Payne had told him about the lightning strikes and he wanted to be ready for any problems with time to spare. His mind set had been formed in the military and had served him well.

They had been on the road for an hour with another two to three hours ahead of them. Survey vehicles moved notoriously slow and were prone to breaking down. For that reason he had scattered his people among four vehicles.

The day was slipping into evening and he turned on the headlamps and running lights. A glance at his rear camera showed the other rigs following his example.

He drove Vehicle One of the three survey rigs and Charly Herring with Jim Spreter riding shotgun followed the others in the heavy lifter. When all this comet nonsense was over they might want to haul a lot more equipment out to the dig and the heavy lifter would be a good thing to have.

Big John Dowd drove the number two vehicle and Mark Goppert piloted the third one. It promised to be a boring trip and both Joyce Mayer and Doug Franklin were asleep in the back. Tom could hear Doug snoring. Marilyn was chatting with Bill Hilton in vehicle three.

"Bill," Marilyn said in a gentle tone, "everything in that museum, or temple or whatever you want to call it, is at least 800 years old. How could an exhibit *look* at you?"

"What?" Gorski and Stuart Currie both said together. Stuart was riding in the observation bubble above them.

"Something *looked* at Bill?" Stuart said with a wide grin.

"What did he drink instead of water?" Gorski said with a laugh.

"Let him tell you," Marilyn said. She touched her hand pad and they all heard Bill ask, "What are you doing?"

"Dr. Hilton, this is Gorski. *What* did you see in the temple?"

"Shit. I suppose I'd better get used to this. Right before we had to leave I found a long display case with figures in it. They were all Kian and each was dressed differently than the rest. I thought it was a catalog of clothing fashions over the centuries."

He coughed and then continued, "What I was most impressed

with was the incredible detail in the manikins, or Kianiakins, whatever. And I was staring at the eyes on one and the pupils suddenly dilated and the damn thing blinked at me! I'm looking at it now on my holo playback."

"It has been a long day, Bill," Gorski said. "Maybe you imagined it?"

"No, dammit. You can see for your–"

The alarm bell erupted with a strident ringing.

Stuart said, "There's something coming at us from the sky!"

Gorski switched on the comm channel. He liked to drive with it off so he didn't have to listen to the incessant chatter between shuttles, the *Magellan*, and the compound.

"–ing out of orbit! *Magellan*, do you hear me?"

"What the fu–" Doug Franklin said from the back of the vehicle.

"Incoming debris, take cover!" someone shouted over the channel.

Gorski punched up a map, and then hit another icon. His worst fears were suddenly confirmed. He opened the channel to the convoy.

"We're under the orbit path! Everybody keep–"

The vehicle lurched as something smashed into the back of it. An explosion farther back blew them sideways and their machine nearly rolled. Tom cut the power and performed an emergency shut down.

"Is everyone okay?" he yelled.

Joyce and Doug both muttered something. Stuart picked himself up off the deck. His head was bleeding.

"I think I got a cut when the bubble shattered."

Marilyn stared out the window. "Oh God, oh God," she whispered, tears flowing down her cheeks.

Tom followed her gaze. Vehicle Two lay on its side and the back of it was burning. He saw the escape hatch pop open and Bennie crawled out, then Carol, Ben, and finally Dowd.

Behind them lay the remains of Vehicle Three. Pieces of it were everywhere. The heavy lifter sat farther back in the tall prairie grass about twenty meters off the path, its windows shattered.

Small fires burned in the prairie grass around them. In the sky over them the thick smoke trail of the *Magellan* hung impossibly low to the planet, drifting slowly northward in the breeze.

"Get every emergency kit and extinguisher you can find and follow me," Tom said.

69
Ki-Nuuhi Sanctuary

Hollow loss hung over the Kians and two humans in the Sanctuary. Danny stumbled about, stunned and guilt-ridden. Shannon wept heartbrokenly and a number of Kians surrounded her, offering solace. All she could do was whimper, "Miri, my beautiful Miri," over and over again.

Danny and Su Laana had just helped Shannon into the evening twilight outside the cave mouth. Something sizzled in Danny's head and he gave Su Laana a questioning look.

"Yanivina is killing the star ship!"

"What did she say?" Shannon demanded.

"Something about the—"

"There!" Su Laana pointed into the settling darkness.

Su Laana and every other Kian could hear them screaming, could feel the chaos, the bestial anger, the abject terror of anything that moved. Gravity existed only against the collapsing walls adding to the vicious bewilderment of the dying crew.

The pathos of the situation accompanying the overwhelming horror struck into the minds and hearts of the Kians. Nothing could be done. No possible way of helping the afflicted humans existed. The Kians sobbed in shared anguish and frustration.

To helplessly mentally witness this incredible calamity seared their brains and ripped at their hearts. After centuries of living quiet lives and banning violence from their culture this aberrant atrocity was literally mind bending. Every Kian from the oldest to the youngest –who didn't understand at *all*– fell to the ground weeping bitterly.

They couldn't even close their eyes to escape the spectacle.

"Oh no. Please no!" Shannon moaned and dropped down to sprawl on a large rock. Tears cascaded down her face as they watched the flaming ship dip below the horizon.

A huge crowd of crying Kians had joined them when the *Magellan* shrieked overhead for the last time. From where the cave sat in the Roc-Ki Mountains one could see the distant Eastern Sea. They heard the roar of the spacecraft long before it burned overhead in its final decent.

It plunged into the sea, sending a boiling spray of water high into the heavens.

Danny had seen Su Laana cry a few times, but now he witnessed hundreds of Kians weeping and wailing at the same time. Sadness filled his soul and soon he wept with them.

After a time Su Laana took his hand. "Please, Dan-nay, come with me."

She led him away from the refuge and up into the woods surrounding the ancient volcano. Finally she stopped walking and pulled him down beside her beneath a shady tree.

"Take a deep breath," she said. "Good. Now clear your mind as much as you can."

"I've *never* been able to clear my mind," he said. "There's always something boiling in there."

"Allow me to help."

He stared at her, losing himself in her dark, liquid eyes, wondering how could he be this lucky. The thought flaked away, a skein of dried mud on a rock lashed by the wind.

Soon the rock lay bare and then it too dissolved and he experienced a vast nothingness that comfortably filled his mind.

~An ancient people formed tribes who warred on each other.~ A crystal clear image of two groups of Kians wearing animal skins rushing to battle the other formed in his mind. *~In time a dominant tribe assumed leadership of the continent or island and the others were absorbed.~* The Kians now wore armor of metal and wood, capes and colorful cloth covered those not in the military.

~City-states grew and prospered. Trade began slowly and then flourished~. Clothing styles had changed and buildings of all sizes swarmed with Kians.

~In each society warrior castes came into prominence and dominated all others. Workers of the soil, civil administrators, clerks, shopkeepers, artisans all became subservient to the warriors~. Rank upon rank of helmeted soldiers carrying manufactured arms marched through cheering crowds. Hundreds of banners bearing the same symbol hung from posts, buildings, and standards carried by troops.

~Warlords commanded great armies and in their massive hubris went forth to subdue other warrior societies. Continents and islands warred on each other. The wealth of the countries diminished as conquest dominated all before it.~

Self-propelled machines spewed fire and death as they

lumbered across the terrain. Machines swooped out of the air in an effort to destroy them. Both sides sustained huge losses.

~Great war machines were constructed, communication devices allowed instantaneous transmission of words and images. Matter transfer became commonplace.~

The machines became sleek and fast with the ability to kill from great distances. Missiles streaked in from unknown launchers and destroyed them in turn.

~Then a celestial collision brought Yanivina to them. When she first appeared she was welcomed as a harbinger of victory. But when she swept across the nations of their world chaos ensued.~

The opposing leaders and their armies hailed the approaching comet as an omen of victory over their enemies. When the comet seemed to kiss the planet all went mad and killed their own kind with teeth and fists.

~It so happened that among the caregivers, physicians, shamans, and herbal practitioners a plant had proven itself to be of much value. It was known by many different names but came to be called Kion. Mostly the plant was ingested but for soothing anxious minds and relaxing stressed bodies. It was burned as incense and the fumes would be inhaled.~

The Sanctuary, with a fraction of the numbers it now held, swirled with smoke and laughing, chatting Kians. A feeling of lassitude and safety suffused him.

~The only people who survived the first visit of Yanivina were those being medicated, or medicating others, with Kion. In addition to surviving the visit they also grew aware of one another's minds. However, they were few compared to the teeming multitudes killed by Yanivina and they called themselves Kians in honor of the plant that had saved them.~

~The weapons were put away or destroyed. In knowing another person's mind came the opportunity for true communication. Physical conflict ceased among the Kians forever. In time their numbers increased but never to earlier levels.~

The damaged and destroyed cities were rebuilt but in simpler, more intimate ways. Some were never rebuilt and the soil and vegetation reclaimed them.

~Artisans of all types flourished and agriculture aided by science guaranteed that no one hungered. The Kians perfected a balance of nature and need.~

~For centuries these concepts and practices endured, taking on the

mantle of tradition. Then the Others came in ships that traveled between worlds. Upon arrival they claimed ownership of everything Kian and prepared to fight for their conquest.~

Slightly larger than the Kians, the Others could have passed for the Kians at their most militaristic. While the Others paraded and strutted with weapons the Kians went about their lives as if the aliens were animate trees.

~The Kians lived as always, interacting in good faith and never questioning the arbitrary rules espoused by the Others. After a few revolutions of Kiana around the sun the Others grew complacent, never questioning the Kians about their past or their seeming subservience.

~Yanivina returned and the Kians quietly went to those places where their ancestors had found refuge. After lighting the bales of Kion they meditated through the visit of Yanivina. The Others who stayed on Kiana all perished. Those orbiting in their ships left and never returned.~

"And then your people came to us," Su Laana said aloud, breaking the trance into which Danny had fallen. "And you know the rest."

"Somewhat. There are things I don't understand yet, but I'm willing to learn."

70
Magellan Lifeboat 65

"There. That's the right icon!" Chief Murphy said. He pushed the image under discussion and the lifeboat altered course and began orbiting the planet.

"Good that soon we found it!" Mongo said to his friend. "Orbiting some distant star would be fate other wise."

Patrick looked bleak. "I can't believe the *Maggie* went in like that. My God, all them kids . . ."

"Were for certain dead before ship hit atmosphere." Mongo kept his voice low so the others wouldn't hear him. "Saved the people on board we have from death certainly, no?"

"Where we gonna put this thing down, or do we want to?"

"Comet brings death but yet to arrive. How to live if we land this pod?"

"I've never gone dirtside on this voyage, Mongo. I got no idea where anything is or if there's anyone we know down there."

"Jason's crew?" Mongo said.

"That's right! Him and his crew are doing some submersible research down here somewhere." Chief Murphy looked happy again. "I'll hail him on all frequencies."

71
Siboth

Vehicle One and the heavy lifter limped into Siboth at 0140. The pusher fan on Vehicle One had been damaged beyond repair and the heavy lifter pushed it as best it could. Both Charly Herring and Jim Spreter wore bandages on their face and upper body.

Charly had turned away from the path as soon as he saw the debris hit Vehicle Three. His quick reaction had save their lives. Nothing could have saved Mark Goppert, Dr. Bill Hilton, Michelle Ramey, and Dexter Francis. Vehicle Three had exploded like a bomb, instantly killing the crew. There was nothing of them left.

Gorski stunk of the prairie fire they had extinguished before they could even begin aiding their people. The rear engine compartment on Vehicle Two had been blown to pieces when Vehicle Three was hit. Big John Dowd had been strapped into the driver's seat and as a result only suffered a mild concussion.

Carol Smith broke her left arm and sustained massive bruising on her left side. Ben Balberdi wore splints on his broken leg and Bennie Benedict had helped fight the fire and render first aid before finally realizing he had a broken ankle.

Only Stuart had been injured in Vehicle One and his bandage looked like a turban. Smoke hung over the city as they slowly negotiated the rubble-strewn streets. Three security troopers suddenly stood in front of them waving hand lanterns.

Gorski touched his headset. "Charly, they want us to stop."

"Happily."

Forward motion ceased and Tom set the vehicle down on its struts and killed the engines. Nobody in the crowded compartment said a word. Tom suspected shock had set in.

A master sergeant came up to the driver's side window.

"Who are you people and where did you come from?"

"Archaeologists from Dig N-19. I have injured people on board who need immediate attention. Do you have some transportation we can use?"

The master sergeant kicked the side of the survey vehicle. "What's the matter with this thing?"

"Walk around it once and you won't have to ask."

The master sergeant turned and yelled at one of his men,

"Crider, get a couple of ambulances over here."

"How many did you lose here?" Gorski asked.

"Over seventy. We're still searching. You have any fatalities?" "Four close friends," Tom said and looked away. "Maybe five."

72
Siboth

"What are our options?" the director asked those sitting around the table.

Sunlight streamed through a hole high up on the wall. The debris from the strike still lay on the far side of the room. Bandages seemed to be the uniform of the day as most in the room wore them.

"Madam Director," Colonel Merritt, wearing a bandage on her cheek as a result of flying rock from a building, raised her hand.

"Yes, Colonel Merritt?"

"We have nine functioning shuttles and two that we can use for parts."

"The last two can't function at all?"

"No, ma'am, they both took direct hits from large debris. Their hulls are split."

"I see."

"Each shuttle can hold twenty passengers and a crew of three."

"And we would go *where*?" Taxim Rosta said with a sniff, raising his eyebrow.

Colonel Merritt's eyes narrowed as she answered. "Depending on availability of fuel, it occurred to me that perhaps we could go into orbit while the comet is in contact with Kiana."

The director turned to Melanie. "How long would that contact last, Dr. Frasier?"

"First we need to define 'contact.' Are we talking from when the tail hits the upper atmosphere until it completely leaves the atmosphere, or when the tail actually touches the surface of the planet?"

"From what we saw on the holo," Stoker said with a growl, "I think we're talking about any contact with the atmosphere at all."

Stuart Currie cleared his throat. "We also have no way to determine if and when all of the toxins leave the atmosphere. This thing could poison the planet for months or years."

"We sure don't have *that* much fuel," Colonel Merritt said.

Tom Gorski spoke from the far end of the table. "Twenty three people in a shuttle for as much as a week would be as close to hell as I want to get. Coming in last night with nine people in a survey vehicle was enough to make my skin crawl. Overloading a shuttle isn't my idea of a good time."

"Which reminds me," Carol Smith said, resting her broken arm on the table. "Do we know if the emergency message got to Proxima Central or not?"

The director shook her head. "No idea. The message was sent while *Magellan* was in the early stages of chaos so the communications array should have still been functional. I also believe the ship had an automatic distress program."

Melanie spoke in a low voice. "Mother would have known the answer."

"Maybe what's left of her does," the director said. "Computer, can you answer our question?"

"Query not comprehended," said the mechanical, very un-Mother, voice. "Please clearly restate."

Melanie winced and looked down at her hands.

The director spoke slowly and loudly. "Would the *Magellan* have had time to make a distress call to Proxima Central?"

"Probability is seventy-six per cent affirmative."

"You don't know one way or the other if it was made?"

"Negative. Data lost with main core."

"It doesn't really matter," Colonel Merritt said. "If they started from Proxima Central with the fastest ship we have it will still take them over three months to get here. The Davidson Drive has its limitations just like everything else."

"So what are we going to *do*?" Taxim Rosta said. "Just sit here and talk until that damn thing kills us?"

"Mr. Rosta," the director's voice carried a distinct chill. "You were invited here to help us find answers. If you don't have anything of substance to add, you are welcome to leave."

Rosta's face flushed and he opened his mouth.

Gorski shifted his position from a languid slouch to an alert "ready to pounce" stance. He stared steadily at Rosta who looked away after one glance in his direction.

Rosta's mouth resembled that of a fish as it worked. Finally he said, "Perhaps I would be of more benefit helping with the inventory."

"Thank you for your help," the director said.

Rosta hurried from the room.

Stoker Payne shook his head. "We lose people like Bill, Michelle, Mark, and Dexter, but zeros like that come through just fine."

He went silent, seeing them excited about their discovery, raring to go until they dropped. They were all highly trained and motivated professionals and he knew he would never forget them. Someone said his name.

"What? Sorry, I went away for a minute there."

"S'okay," John Dowd said. "I wanted to know if we ever figured out what plant that is wrapped around the statue?"

"Uh, no. I think someone was going to look that up. Can't remember who." He stifled a yawn.

No one had gotten much sleep the previous night. They all had tried to find victims and save lives. So far they had found 78 dead and the search wasn't over.

Laura Prescott had finally broken down, sobbing, under a massive burden of guilt. She believed if she had been on board, none of this would have transpired. Eric had carried her to an undamaged building and found a place for her to sleep. Neither had yet made an appearance this morning.

Marilyn Culpepper mumbled something and then raised her voice. "I think I found it, Stoker. Don't know that I've ever seen it myself, but somebody has. Here's a picture of it."

She laid her hand pad on the table and a holo appeared above it. On one side was a close-up of the sculpted leaves surrounding the statue of Ki. Next to it was a slowly turning image of the same leaf in dark green.

"Any idea where that was taken?" the director asked.

"All the info box says is 'foothills of Roc-Ki Mountains,' ma'am."

"That is such a terrible pun," the director said.

They all stared at her questioningly.

"No scholars here? The Rocky Mountains are the largest mountain range on the North American continent of Earth. They are dwarfed by other mountain ranges on the ancient home planet so one wonders why the mountains here were named that."

They continued staring at her.

"Do pardon the digression. I was trying to lighten the mood."

"Who is our botanist?" Stoker Payne asked.

The director checked her computer. "Dr. April Stephans, and her assistant, Dr. Walt Boyes, are our botanists."

"Are they both still alive?" Gorski asked.

"They are on a field trip, so we don't know," the director said, looking up from her screen.

"What's the plant's name, Marilyn?" Stoker asked.

"Kion. Now I'm positive that's the right one." Marilyn grinned.

"So what does it mean?" Melanie asked. "Does it neutralize the effects of the comet gasses or what?"

"We have to find a Kian," Gorski said. "They've got all the answers."

"Since they all disappeared," Stoker said, "maybe they don't want to tell us the answers."

"They've been wonderfully courteous to us for five years," the director said. "Why would they change now?"

"Uh, Madam Director," Dowd said. "Begging your pardon but they haven't told us shi-, uh, anything. We even had four on the dig with us and they never volunteered one iota of information. When asked anything about the planet, their culture, anything at all, they were evasive."

"John's right," Doug Franklin said. "I'm pretty good at drawing people out and I couldn't get anywhere with any of them."

"So what you're all saying is that they have just endured us for five years and now they're going to watch us die?" Amanda asked, her voice full of incredulity.

"That pretty much sums up my point of view," Dowd said, absently rubbing his head.

"So even if we did find them, would they help us?" the director asked the room at large.

"We won't know until we find them," Stoker said. He glanced at Melanie. "How long before the comet gets here?"

"Two and a half weeks, maybe three. It depends on that mix with the atmosphere before…"

"Yeah," Stoker said and looked down at his bandaged arms. Pulling rocks off people throughout the night had made for many scrapes and cuts.

"Could we use the temple you found for shelter?" Chuck

Reed asked.

Stoker smiled inwardly. Chuck would give anything he had to see the Temple of Ki.

"It was sealed when we opened it. But I don't know if there would be enough oxygen if we went inside and sealed the door behind us. We would run the chance of either suffocating or succumbing to the toxic gasses if the thing is vented."

"But we don't know what is in the part Shannon tried to enter," Dowd said. "What if there are oxygen generators in there?"

"Wish for a star ship, too, while you're at it," Gorski said through a smirk.

"John raises an interesting point," the director said. "There could be something in there that could be our salvation."

"And we get to it how?" Stoker said. "I'm not risking one more person in that museum right now. We need all the people we have. Not to mention we suddenly don't have near the number of vehicles we once took for granted." The yawn surprised him. Others followed suit.

"We have too much to do to just be sitting here debating," the director said. "I want you all to get some rest, think about the situation, and we'll meet tomorrow afternoon if we have found all of our people."

"I suggest we all help the security folks search the rest of Siboth." Stoker glanced at his hand pad. "It seems we're still missing about twenty people."

They all silently rose and filed through the door into the sunlight.

73
Ki-Nuuhi Sanctuary

The rising sun wakened Danny. He and Su Laana had spent the night under the tree where she had told him the story of the Kian people. He rubbed at the crick in his neck absently and thought about what he had learned.

Something nagged at the edges of his mind and he knew it would just be a matter of time before it came into the open. Su Laana stretched like a cat and he admired her lithe body. She was everything he had ever wanted in a mate and realized his great fortune in finding her.

She wrapped her chamalla around her and smiled at him. "Shall we go back to the Sanctuary and find breakfast?"

He realized he was hungry. "Yes, I'd like that."

As they made their way to the cave entrance the elusive question popped into his head.

"Su Laana, are the Kians going to allow my people to die?"

"If they don't evac–, oh!" She stopped walking and stared at his face.

He decided she was asking the question of other Kians. Her eyes slightly dilated when she communicated and he wondered if she knew. She blinked.

"It seems you have asked a question that has already started a great debate among my people."

"Among *our* people?"

"Technically, yes. But you won't be a true Kian until you can communicate mentally."

"So if the comet–"

"Yanivina."

"Yeah, Yanivina, wasn't coming soon, I would never be able to become a true Kian?"

"No, I suppose not. How interesting that she is both evil and good at the same time."

"Isn't everything that way? The old yin and yang."

She stared at him and he knew she was pulling the information out of his memories.

"Why don't I feel anything when you do that?"

She smiled. "Because you are not aware yet. Once you become aware you will know when someone tries to enter your mind."

"Will I be able to stop them?"

"Yes. But only a rude person would attempt to enter without first getting your permission."

"So none of you have secrets?"

She laughed. "Your mind is not an open vessel. Think of it as a large house with many rooms. You invite guests into one or two rooms, but not all rooms unless the person is very close to you."

"I don't feel that complex," he said.

"You are, my love, you are."

"Really? Good!"

They moved down the last knoll before the cave entrance came into view. Even Danny could feel dissention in the air.

"What's going on?" he asked.

"The question you asked was asked earlier and has caused a great debate. There are many who would allow the humans to perish."

He felt anger surge through him and suppressed it. If he ever had to rein in his temper it was here and now.

When he and Su Laana came into view a new eddy appeared in the swirl of emotions filling the sanctuary.

Su Laana frowned. "Stay close to me. We must go to Shannon."

Keeping up with her was not easy. He felt that some Kians deliberately tried to block his path. The sixth time someone stepped in front of him his temper rose.

Keep your anger in yourself; they want you to act irrationally so it will bolster their argument.

He could feel the presence of Su Laana in the admonition and it calmed him to know she was there for him. The next male Kian that stepped into his path received a sharp elbow in the ribs.

"Excuse me," Danny said brightly. "I didn't see you there."

The man frowned but moved away.

Danny concentrated on creating optimism and held on to the thought. He wondered what argument she was talking about. The dissention had magnified.

They came to a dark alcove outside which a group of Kians sat staring at each other. Danny could almost see sparks fly between them. As they walked up some looked at him and frowned while others smiled.

He did his best to project acceptance and peace. In the darkest back corner of the alcove Shannon sat huddled against the wall.

"Hey, you okay?" he asked.

"Oh, I'm fucking great. The only person I have ever truly loved gets burned to a cinder in front of my eyes, the local bigots kidnap me from my job and my people, and now they want to let all of us die because we weren't born here. Yeah, I'm so happy I could shit!"

"I wish I could help you through your grief, but I'm not good at that sort of thing. For what it's worth, they aren't going to let us die, as far as I know any way. I've tried looking at this from a Kian perspective and can understand why they are less than thrilled with humans."

"How about explaining it to me then. They haven't said diddly to us in five freaking years and suddenly they want us to die? I don't get it."

"Well, they didn't invite us here. We just showed up and when we couldn't find a government to confer with we made our own. I don't think anyone, especially the Kians, had a vote in the matter. We built a huge compound on the edge of their largest city and proceeded to stick our noses into every aspect of their life. When they wouldn't answer our incessant rude questions we decided they were uncooperative and therefore suspect."

Shannon still stared at him but her expression had softened.

"We were curious about them, dammit. If they didn't want us here all they had to do was tell us."

"And the Coalition would have just pulled up stakes and left? Really?"

"Would have by now," she muttered.

"They were quite ready for us to get back on *Magellan* and go poke around some other planet."

Tears streaked down her face. "Well *that* sure as hell ain't gonna happen now." She buried her face in her hands and her shoulders shook.

Su Laana sat down beside Shannon and began massaging her neck and shoulders. Shannon tensed for a moment and then relaxed into it.

"This is a very complex situation," Su Laana said in a quiet tone. "My people turned away from conflict and strife many centuries ago and we feel we are better for that decision. You are not the first race to come here and impose *civilization* on us."

"I know," Shannon said. "I was leading the team that discovered the remains of your last visitors. They looked like they were nasty. That feels very good, by the way. Thank you."

"You are most welcome. They were not good people. It was easy for us to allow them to die."

Danny blinked and said, "Exactly how old *are* you, Su Laana?"

She laughed. "Not *that* old! But we still have vivid racial memories of that time."

"You are evading the question," Danny said feeling nervous.

"My father and I deduced that I am the equivalent of twenty four of your years. Does it matter?"

"How old is the Mother that helped Shannon yesterday?"

After a few seconds of thought she said, "Perhaps a hundred and twenty of your years."

"Wow," Shannon said. "And she lives in a gravity well at that."

"We enjoy long lives," Su Laana said. "Strife and stress make for short lives and suddenly we are in the midst of both again."

"Thanks to us," Danny said.

She shrugged. "It will pass and we will still praise Ki."

"Yeah," Shannon said. "In a few weeks it will all be over, one way or the other."

74
Island of Nephia

Master Chief Diver Jimmy Mahan scratched his chin through his neatly trimmed blonde beard and was contemplating his next move when the comm station beeped. LCdr Jason Karella, sitting opposite, lifted his gaze from the chessboard and glanced out the dusk-darkened window.

"Who the hell could that be?"

"One way to find out, Skipper." Chief Mahan tapped an icon and a flat panel on the bulkhead bloomed into life. Chief Murphy and Chief Tschurtoff stared out at them. Behind the two men a number of others could be seen.

"Jimmy, is that you? The screen on this boat is a piece of crap."

"Last time I checked, it was me. *Where* the hell are you?"

"We're on *Lifeboat 65.*"

"In space?"

"Yeah. Me and Mongo were giving these kids a tour of the lifeboat deck when everything happened."

"When what happened, Chief Murphy?" LCdr Karella asked.

"You don't know about *Magellan*, Mr. Karella?"

"There was some sort of garbled alert on our com system when we surfaced from our last dive, but that's it. We tend not to contact them. They always want more results than we can produce."

"You all best be sitting down. I'm serious."

Mahan glanced around the building they used as office, communications shack, warehouse, and mess hall. Night had fallen and the rest of the crew sat around the long mess table playing six-handed poker.

"We're all sitting. Tell your tale, Murph."

They heard about the comet, the probe, the change in command, and the fate of the *Magellan*. Patrick was hoarse by the time he finished.

A long silence ensued after he finished speaking. Both chiefs on the lifeboat looked away for a moment or two.

LCdr Karella finally shook his head as if dislodging water from his ears. "Chief Murphy, please tell me that this is another one of your fantastic yarns."

"I wish it were, sir. But it's all as solid as the reg book. I wish it wasn't."

"Fast thinking on you and Mongo's part up there."

"I gotta give Mongo all the credit," he bumped Mongo's shoulder with his. "He sorta kicked us all in the ass to get us moving."

"If what you say about this damned comet is true, we're all pretty much screwed down here," Chief Mahan said.

"Have you folks heard from the Coalition complex on Cimpar, sir?"

"No. Why?"

"They might have a plan, commander. But when we tried to reach them all we got was hash on the screen."

"We'll look into it. In the meantime, you people stay up there in orbit, it's the safest place you can be for now."

"Aye, aye, sir. I sure hope there's a way out of this."

"So do I, chief. We'll get back to you." After he shut the link LCdr Karella turned to his crew. "Thank all deities that we were down here." He wiped a tear from the corner of his eye.

Jason Karella was a big man, six feet of solid muscle and imbued with a sense of adventure and fair play. Chief Mahan thought the lieutenant commander excelled at his job of skippering the *Scientific Submersible Golden Fleece*.

"I can't believe the *Magellan* is gone," Lt. Jaynie Martz, the blonde, sturdy XO, said. "All those wonderful people…"

"Good thing you got the heart replacement when you did," Dr. Sara Mueller said. "This is so *hard* to believe!" Her voice broke and she buried her face in her hands and her long, dark hair shook with her silent sobs.

"Doctor Abrahams and his wonderful staff . . ." Jaynie said through tears.

Chief of the Boat Jimmy Mahan shook his head. "This kinda crap is only supposed to happen in wars, not on scientific missions." He felt a little light-headed and realized he was in mild shock.

"This planet is lucky in a way," Chief Kanoa said. He stretched his tall, slim frame backward until his spine cracked.

"How's that, Keli'i?" Visual Information Specialist Mike Armstrong asked.

"If the *Magellan* had hit the planet we'd all be dealing with a massive radiation problem. As it is, we can hope the propulsion vault wasn't cracked or broken open. How deep is the water in the Eastern Sea?"

"If memory serves," Motor Propulsion Specialist First Class Leo Schmidt said, "about half again as deep as what we have here in the islands. If the vault holds it will be at least a millennium before they have to worry about leakage." Leo's usually smiling, cherubic face looked alien with a frown.

"Chief Mahan," Kanoa said, "how about seeing if you can get through to Siboth."

"Yeah, Keli'i, good idea. You got any problem with that, Skipper?"

LCdr Karella shook his head and blew his nose. "Go ahead, I'm glad someone around here is thinking."

He tapped the icon but the screen remained flat gray. He tapped it again. Nothing.

Mahan turned and pulled the keyboard toward him. "Maybe I can route it through *Mag*–" He stopped moving and stared down at his hands for five seconds before bursting into tears.

A hand clapped him on the shoulder and LCdr Karella said, "This is going to take some getting used to for all of us, chief."

At the back of the table Dr. Annabelle Lee, their waif-like marine biologist, discretely blew her nose and said, "If they land that lifeboat can they take off again?" Her large dark eyes glistened with tears.

"No," Leo and Keli'i said in unison.

"They have verniers, little guidance rockets on that thing, and the regular retro rockets for slowing down, but that's it." Leo loved anything with a motor. "Landing one of those things is basically a controlled crash."

"I'll bet that's why they called us," Keli'i said. "I'll bet they want to put it down on the water."

"They have big 'chutes on them," Leo said. "But that would make for a bitch of a hard landing."

Jimmy shook his head, pissed at himself for losing it. He pushed a different icon. The screen lit up with the countenance of a startled security trooper.

"Who the hell are *you* guys?" the trooper blurted.

"I'm Master Chief Diver Mahan of the *Scientific Submersible*

Golden Fleece, we're down on the coast of Nephia. Who are you?"

"Corporal Jesus Chavez. *Where* are you guys?"

LCdr Karella sat down next to Jimmy. "Corporal Chavez, go get the officer of the watch, *now.*"

"Sir!" Chavez turned into a blur.

Before Jimmy could get rid of his grin a security captain appeared. "Commander, how may I help you, sir?"

"What happened to the communications at the compound?"

"Debris from *Magellan,* sir. Not only did we lose the main array but we also lost eighty-eight people and two shuttles. Did you folks sustain any damage?"

"Negative. We didn't even know the *Magellan* had been lost until apprised of the situation by the two CPOs on *Lifeboat 65.*"

"A lifeboat made it off? How many people?"

"Chief Petty Officers Murphy and Tschurtoff and a class of kids or something, we didn't get a head count."

"Some kids made it off?" The captain sniffed and looked away for a second. "Sorry, sir, it's been pretty tough for us today."

"No apologies required, captain. We need to know what the plan is for getting through the comet visit."

"I don't have any answers, commander. But as soon as they figure it out I'll let you know."

75
Siboth

"What the hell happened here?" Dr. April Stephans said as she and Dr. Walt Boyes limped their damaged utility into town. While searching for new plants they had inadvertently driven it into a rather large rock. Walt had straightened out the forward lift fan enough for it to function but the shaft was no longer in true and it whined and would overheat after fifteen minutes of travel.

Two days ago they had heard something large go overhead and a little later transit closer to the ground. But they had no idea what it could have been. As they had been beneath a dense forest canopy they couldn't see any of the sky.

Something had crashed through the trees and plowed into the ground a half-kilometer away but they hadn't tried to excavate it since they weren't equipped for the task. Walt had made a careful notation of the location on the map in case anyone wanted to study it at a later date.

"Maybe that was a meteor shower we heard the other day?" Walt said.

"I've never heard of a meteor shower coming in two distinct waves," April said. "Have you?"

"No. But what else could it have been?"

"I don't know. Oh, there are some security troopers; I'll bet they will know. Whoa, they're running toward us!"

Walt let the utility stop and shut it down. He could smell something over-heating underneath.

A sergeant and two privates hustled over to them.

"You Stephans and Boyes?" the sergeant asked.

"Yes," April said.

Walt was amazed his or her name was known by anyone. Being a botanist was about as low a profile as one could have on Kiana.

The sergeant spoke into the microphone hooked to his helmet.

"We got the botanists, Colonel Merritt. "Yes, ma'am, right away." He pulled his sun goggles up and surveyed them through squinted eyes. "We need you folks to come with us. The director wants to talk to you."

"Sure," Walt said. "Uh, what happened here?"

"You people been on one of the moons or something?" the closest private said.

"We were deep in a forest under an impenetrable canopy, *private*," April said. "So please answer the question."

The sergeant told them in short, clipped sentences.

Walt thought he was going to collapse. There was, there *had been*, a woman on *Magellan* for whom he had carried a torch for three years. The fact that she never seemed to notice didn't ameliorate his sense of loss.

All the starch had gone out of April. "Nobody escaped?" she said in a small voice.

"The stuff in the probe pretty much killed everyone before the ship crashed, ma'am," the sergeant said in as gentle a voice as he could muster.

A shuttlecraft suddenly roared over and sat down twenty meters from them. The hatch opened and a woman yelled, "C'mon you people. We got places to go!"

Moments later Walt sat strapped to a padded chair as the shuttle lifted into the air.

"You get all their gear?" the colonel, a black woman Walt had never before seen, yelled at the sergeant.

"Yes, Colonel Merritt. We didn't leave a thing in that utility."

Walt leaned over to the sergeant. "That utility needs some repair work before we use it again."

"Don't worry about it, Doc," he said with a quick grin. "As far as the Coalition is concerned it's just junk."

"That's easy for *you* to say. *I'm* the one that signed it out!"

Even the colonel laughed.

"Walt," April said and nudged him, "...look."

He leaned over and peered out the blister window. The city lay broken in many places. Smoke still spiraled up from large deposits of ashes.

"Jupiter and Jove," he murmured. He glanced over at the sergeant. "How many people did we lose?"

"Eight-eight. For awhile, until you two showed up, we thought it was ninety."

"How many Kians died?" April asked.

"None," the sergeant said flatly, "...that we know of anyway."

"How long have you two been in the field?" Colonel Merritt asked.

"Three weeks and two days," April said. "In which time the whole world seems to have changed."

"Landing!" the pilot bellowed.

The shuttle threw up a cloud of dust as it settled and stopped. The sergeant unhooked Walt's harness and helped him to his feet.

"This way, sir. Sorry about the lack of amenities."

Walt gave him a smile. "You work with what you got, Sarge. Thanks for the lift."

Colonel Merritt followed them off the shuttle and directed them toward the open door in the building flanked by two troopers. Both sentries saluted as they went through the door and Walt had to stop himself from returning the honorific when he realized it wasn't for him.

The corridor deemed dark after the bright sunlight outside and both April and Walt hesitated as they peered about. Someone took his elbow and said, "This way, Doctor Boyes."

His eyes adjusted and Walt looked over at the young man holding his elbow. "You can let go now. I can see. Who are you?"

"Doug Franklin, archaeologist, pleased to meet you Dr. Boyes."

"Why does everyone know who we are?"

"Because you're botanists and you're going to help save our lives."

"Oh. I like the sound of that."

In another moment they entered a large room where a number of people sat around a large conference table. Everyone at the table applauded when they entered.

"What the hell?" April blurted.

A dark woman of small stature stood. "I am the Director of Planetary Operations and we need both of you to help us survive the catastrophe we have encountered."

"We would be honored to help," April said instantly, "…in any way we can."

"Please have a seat." The director indicated two chairs.

"You both have been made aware of the death of the *Magellan* and all aboard her?" the director asked.

They nodded in unison.

"It seems that almost as soon as Yanivina, the comet, appeared, the Kians went to ground. Where, we have no idea, but about the same time Dr. Payne and his archaeologists made a stunning discovery. Dr. Payne?"

A tall man with long, blonde hair and a rather chiseled chin sat up in his chair with a jerk. Walt smiled to himself.

This certainly wasn't planned.

He told them about their dig, about Level 6, and about the Temple of Ki. In a more hushed tone he shared the loss of his friend and co-worker, Dr. Shannon Gray. Then he showed them holos of what they had found.

As soon as the image of the statue appeared both Walt and April said, "Kion!" simultaneously.

"Exactly!" the director said. "We think that plant has some sort of prophylactic effect on the toxins in the tail gasses of the comet. How do we find where those plants grow?"

April and Walt glanced at each other.

"Lots of water," Walt said.

"Between three hundred and seven hundred meters in elevation," April added.

"Temperate climate," Walt said, leaning back in his chair. "Not too hot or too cold."

While they spoke half the people in the room busily keyed the information into hand pads.

"Did you capture this image?" the director asked, pointing to the holo.

"Probably. That's how we catalog every plant we find," April said. "Over the past three years we've catalogued about sixty thousand different plants."

"How is it you remember the specifics about this one?" Payne asked.

Before April could open her mouth, Walt said, "This is the one plant that the Kians seem to feel most strongly about. We had two locals who seemed happy to tell us what we had found until we brought this one in."

April broke in smoothly, "We had to be cagey to get this one's name, but we did it."

"And lost our local expert," Walt finished.

"Lost?" Payne said.

"She moved," April said with a shrug. "We had no idea how to find her."

"How would you go about finding large amounts of this plant?" the director asked.

"Spectrum," Walt said.

"Yeah," April said glancing at him. "That would be the easiest."

"But we'd have to search from the air," Walt said.

"Can you set up a program we can use with the shuttles?" Payne asked.

"We already put one together a couple of years ago," April said. "It should be on *Mag–*, oh, sorry."

"Not to worry, dear," the director said. "The reality of our situation is difficult to grasp."

One of the women at the table said loudly, "Computer, do you have spectrum analysis programs for local flora?"

"Affirmative." The obviously mechanical voice bothered Walt. As far as he was concerned the only good thing about AI was they didn't *sound* artificial. This one did.

The woman who spoke seemed to be fighting tears so he looked away.

"Well, that's a relief," the director said. "About time we had some *good* news."

A tall, muscular man at the end of the table stood. "Well let's get after it then."

The director pointed at Walt. "Would you work with Mr. Gorski on setting this up?"

"Of course."

76
Ki-Nuuhi Sanctuary

Danny enjoyed walking with Su Laana. They had fallen into a pattern of hiking around the extinct volcano each day. Each time they changed their route slightly so it would always seem new and different.

"Do all Kians know as much about your history as you do?"

She slowed and gave him a wry grin. "Yes. We all have access to the same knowledge whether it is about our history, the weather, or medicine. New information is always added and immediately available."

"Who holds the information for everyone else?"

"No one person holds it; we all carry it together."

"So it's not like a data bank, or an AI?"

"No. If I wish to know something I ask the question in the, ah, call it a mental plaza, and in time the answer is directed at me."

"You pulled the term 'plaza' out of my head, yes?"

"Yes. If I hadn't put it in your vernacular it would have taken much longer to explain since I would have had to give you a lesson in the Kian language and there is no need."

"I won't have to learn Kian?"

"Dan-nay, you will soon have the ability to share knowledge with us through your mind, and when we answer you will understand."

"How will that happen, me becoming telepathic?"

"Yanivina changes everything she touches. She will change your perceptions and abilities."

"How do you know?"

"That is how we were changed hundreds of generations ago."

"So how will she change you *this* time?"

Su Laana's demeanor changed and Danny thought he detected fright.

"I don't know. We never know. Some die."

"What? Even if you're in the sanctuary smoke?"

"It has happened that even in the midst of sanctuary smoke some have died. Very few, but there is no way to know who will leave with Yanivina."

"Why didn't you tell me about this before?"

She shrugged. "It is not something I wish to discuss. There is no point."

Danny nearly stumbled and fell. It seemed more important to watch her face than where his feet needed to go. He grabbed one of the rough-barked trees and caught himself.

He started to make light of his balance when she blurted, "Dan-nay, do *not* move!"

He froze, not even turning his face away from her to see what she was staring at behind him.

What?

~Make no sound. Slowly turn your head and look to your right. Do not move anything else.~

He complied. No more than four meters away stood an animal that both instantly fascinated and repelled him. At first glance it reminded him of a wolf he had seen on his home planet.

After closer perusal he noticed the wide, thick chest, eyes and ears that sat farther apart than those of a wolf, and the huge teeth filling the wide jaws. He noticed the eyes were red and filled with intelligence. The animal's coat combined mottled stripes of black and a mahogany red.

Without a doubt he knew it was a jingroe. He also knew they could kill an unarmed human with ease; yet it stood there staring at him and Su Laana. Suddenly it crouched and sprang into the woods, vanishing in the space of a heartbeat.

Danny's mouth and throat had never been drier and he fumbled for his canteen. He couldn't take his eyes off where the creature had vanished.

"It won't come back," Su Laana said in a gentle voice behind him.

He turned and looked at her. "Why didn't it attack?"

"Because I asked it not to harm us."

"Are jingroes telepathic?"

"A little bit but their vocabulary is quite limited."

Danny laughed hard and long, to the point he had to sit on the ground. When he finished he felt weak and wrung out.

"By the Great Bear," he gasped. "I have never been so frightened in my *life!*"

"You did not panic and run," Su Laana said in a soft tone. "If you had I wouldn't have been able to stop it."

"Hah! I was too scared to move let alone run!"

"You feel *lessened* by this event?"

"I keep forgetting. I can't hide anything from you, can I?"

"I'll show you how when the time comes. But it is foolish to doubt yourself because you correctly feared a very dangerous animal."

"It's a male thing."

"It's a *human* male thing," she said.

Danny stood and took a deep breath. "I'll always be human, Su Laana. I can't change that."

"I know. I'm not asking you to change, I love who you are. I love that you did what I said despite not agreeing with it."

He moved over and took her in his arms. "You are the love of my life," he whispered into her ear. "I will always do what you ask as long as you keep loving me."

77
Island of Nephia

"You got the lifeboat on line, chief?" LCdr Karella asked from across the room.

"Yes, sir," Mahan said.

"Okay, folks, this is what we've learned. There's some sort of plant that the Kians use to protect themselves from this comet gas."

"Jason?"

"Yes, Sara?"

"How do they know this will work?"

"Oh, yeah, this isn't the first time the comet has been here. They call the comet Yanivina. So we need to find ourselves some Kians and ask them to help us, or we have to get all of us back to Siboth. Chief Murphy, you folks hear all of that?"

"Loud and clear, commander."

"How many souls do you have on board, Chief?"

"Thirty students, two teachers, and Mongo and me."

"You do know that you're the only people who made it off the *Magellan*, don't you?"

"Yes, sir. There've been a lot of tears up here about that."

"Sorry, Chief, I wasn't thinking clearly there."

"Everyone understands."

"Are you all getting tired of emergency rations?"

"The problem is first food," Mongo said, "and then the head just one. No shower they whine, enough almost to give up and bail out!"

"Chute's don't function well in space, Mongo," Chief Mahan said with a laugh.

"Yeah, that's why we don't want to use ours to land."

"Either one of you ever piloted in an atmosphere before?" Mahan asked.

"Hell, Jimmy, of course we haven't."

"I have," a voice behind them said.

Patrick and Mongo both turned.

"Mr. Burton?" Patrick said.

The medium built man moved into close camera range on the lifeboat. His once dark mustache and hair were both flecked with silver. He gave them a self-depreciating smile and nodded.

"I flew sub orbital fighters in the Bohemia-Craddock War. It's been awhile but I think I remember all the important parts."

"Why the hell didn't you tell us before this?" Patrick demanded.

"You didn't ask and I thought you knew what you were doing."

Chief Mahan laughed. "I wish you could see your face, Patrick. I've never seen you struck speechless before."

Chief Murphy grinned. "People *always* think I know what I'm doing. Here, professor, is where you should be sitting."

James Burton sat in the pilot's seat. "Thanks, chief." He looked over the controls and then stared into the screen.

"This is quite a bit simpler than the controls on a Nova Interceptor. Where do you want us to land this thing?"

"You're *Flight Leader* Burton of the 8th Pursuit Squadron, aren't you, sir?" Jason asked.

"Oh, that was a long time ago, commander. A completely different life actually."

"It is an honor and a privilege to meet you, sir."

"Thank you. Where do you want me to put this thing down?"

Jason tapped in the coordinates. "There. I just uploaded them to your navpute. From that spot you will easily see the flag we have flying over our little base.

"There is a long, sandy beach to the right of the flag pole from your viewpoint. Anyone who can defeat three adversaries by themselves can surely land a bucket like that where ever they so choose."

"Commander, you're going to make me blush."

78
Eastern Plains of Cimpar

"Hills straight ahead," Lieutenant Christenson said as he lowered the shuttle's elevation.

Stoker Payne and Chuck Reed both roused from their naps and turned to the laser spectrometer. The lens protruded down through the hull and Chuck moved the lens barrel while Stoker watched the screen and altimeter.

All of them were fighting exhaustion after three days of flying over the Cimparian Plains. Prior to this Stoker had always thought that "plains" equated with *flat*. Not so.

"I'll be damned. The trees ahead are high enough to have Kion around them," Stoker said. "And there seems to be a fairly large body of water, too."

Lt Christenson said, "Did it ever occur to you guys that maybe the Kians are in all these spots we've found but just don't want us to see them?"

"That's a given, Mike," Stoker said. "That's why I'm also checking the areas for body temperature readings."

"But it's so bloody hot out there, how could you tell the difference?"

"Cause they're blobby and maintain a constant temperature," Chuck said through a yawn.

"I'll believe it when I see it," Mike said. "Okay, watch your instruments. We're making the first pass." He reached over and tapped the sleeping copilot on the arm. "C'mon, Patty, wake up. We need your lovely eyes."

Lieutenant Patricia Hull yawned and stretched. "Are we there yet?"

"Yes," all three men intoned at the same time.

"Okay. I'm on the job. Oh, nice trees and water!" She lifted a pair of computer-assisted binoculars to her eyes and tapped a node on the instrument's side.

Lt Christenson slowed the craft to a virtual crawl.

"I have movement!" Lt. Hull said crisply. "Approximately five meters from the water and heading for that large clump of blue trees."

"Camera is on, by the by," Mike said.

"I have your target, Patty. Good work!" Chuck said. "Stoker, what is it?"

"I think it might be a Kian!"

"We have a positive on the plant, too," Chuck said looking at another screen. "Lots of it along the south bank there."

Stoker felt tired, but that damn comet edging closer and closer every minute gave one additional adrenaline to complete the mission.

"Set it down, if you please, Mr. Christenson. We need to check this one out on foot."

The others groaned as Mike located a wide-topped ridge with relatively sparse vegetation and expertly landed the shuttle. He quickly switched off the engines and a bore tide of silence rolled over them.

Patty already had the hatch open and a light breeze moved the foliage and carried the aromatic alien promise of exotic flowers to them.

"I'd forgotten how bad you guys smell," Patty said over her shoulder as she stepped to the ground. The grasses came up to her hips.

Chuck followed Patty out and stopped and looked around.

Stoker stepped out and peered at his hand pad. "The proximity heat sensor says there are five constant signatures within twenty meters of us. They're really small..."

"Stoker!" Patty yelled. "Look out!"

He snapped his head up and saw something rushing through the grass toward him. Without thinking he immediately pulled his laser from its holster. When the "Radar" leapt at his face from two meters he fired three times, hitting it once.

The creature fell to the ground still gnashing its formidable teeth as it died.

Stoker yelled to the others, "There are more of them. I saw at least five on my hand pad. Get back to the shuttle, now!"

Patty turned and ran for the hatch. A Radar shot out of the grass and snapped air where she had just been. Chuck got a shot off but missed.

In moments all three of them were back in the shuttle. Stoker and Chuck stood together in the hatch and watched the grass meadow surrounding the landing area.

"I thought those things were insectivores," Chuck said.

"So did I." Stoker aimed, fired. Another one leaped into the air and fell dead. "I can't figure out why they are going after larger prey."

"Maybe it's a cyclic thing," Patty said from behind them.

"No," Stoker said, wondering where the other three were and how to flush them. "Humans have been around these critters for years and they've never done this before."

Mike, still in the pilot's seat, said, "I just ran an atmosphere analysis and compared it to what has been the norm."

"Yeah?" Stoker glanced at him. "Any changes?"

"Yeah. There are trace elements of something we don't have in our data bank."

"There's a lot missing from our data bank these days," Chuck said.

"All information on Kiana itself had been automatically backed up on the secondary, the one here on the planet," Mike said. "I know that because it was the other part of my job when I wasn't driving this bus."

"Why *were* you guys down here instead of on *Magellan* when it went in?" Chuck asked.

"It was our turn to ferry shuttles down and back." Patty's voice went husky. "This one had just come out of Maintenance. We brought it down to take the next one on rotation back up for its 4,000 hour check."

"Yeah," Mike said. "We were kinda pissed that we got such a late start and were going to have to spend the night in the transit wing instead of in our own cabins on *Magellan*." He sighed and looked through the windscreen. "Uh, we got more company."

Stoker craned his head out the hatch and looked past the nose of the craft. Six Kians were moving toward them, walking abreast with at least two meters separating each of them from the others.

Stoker flashed back to his boyhood on Buhrman's World and, although they were not carrying weapons, he decided they were hunting something.

I hope it's not us!

The Kians walked up to the shuttle, stopped and looked at Stoker.

~There are humans at Nephia who need help.~

79
Ki-Nuuhi Sanctuary

"So what are they going to do with me?" Shannon Gray asked.

Both she and Danny turned to Su Laana.

"I sure don't have any idea," Danny said. "Do you?"

Su Laana made a little frown that Danny had come to recognize as her "asking questions" look. It never took long to get answers.

She shrugged and said, "That is completely up to you, Shannon. You are not a prisoner or anything of the sort. You may stay or you may leave."

"And go where?" Shannon glanced around the clearing where they sat in the shade of a grove of blue trees. Two of the winged mammals the humans called "not-birds" squabbled in the branches. "Siboth?"

"If that is your wish."

"But she can stay here if she chooses?" Danny said.

"Of course. In a sense we brought her here, and that means we are prepared to give her sanctuary for as long as she wishes."

"Why didn't anyone tell me that outright?" Shannon said.

Su Laana shrugged again. "Because you didn't–" She abruptly stopped speaking and her eyes went wide. "Get under the trees, now! Don't touch the trunks, they are unpleasant."

Danny and Shannon scrambled to their feet and hurried after Su Laana. In moments they all crouched near the pungent trunk, peering out at the bright day.

"Do you mind sharing with us the reason for that sudden exercise?" Shannon said.

"The humans are seeking our sanctuaries."

A new sound intruded into the bright day. A deep, heavy hum emanated from the west and slowly grew in volume. Danny recognized the sound of a shuttle at very low speed.

"So why are we hiding in here instead of out there in the open waving them down?"

Su Laana turned to Shannon. "You have a choice and you must make it now. You may stay with us or go back to your people."

Shannon opened her mouth to respond and Su Laana cut her off.

"If you return to your people you will have no memory of anything that has happened since you passed the warning in the temple."

Shannon frowned and looked from Su Laana to Danny and back. "You can *do* that?"

"We can and will. I know you are still grieving for your partner and have reservations about us. But you can have a good life here."

"Wait a minute," Danny said. "Have the Kians decided to allow the humans to die when the comet gets here?"

Su Laana looked away from their intense stares. "That is the predominant consensus at the moment. Opinion is shifting back and forth all the time."

"What are the margins?" Shannon grated.

"It is very close," her voice in a whisper.

"Fuck that!" Shannon said and scuttled out into the open.

"Yeah," Danny said. "I can't do that either." He followed Shannon.

"Dan-nay! Please don't!" Su Laana yelled.

He didn't hesitate. As much as he loved the Kian woman he knew he would not be able to live with himself if he turned away from his own race when its back was against the wall. He saw Shannon running and waving at the shuttle.

The shuttle was low enough that it sometimes touched the top of the trees. It stopped all forward motion and at the same time Shannon tumbled to the ground. Before Danny could react in any way his limbs suddenly froze on him and his momentum slammed him face down in the soft, grass-like vegetation.

He expected a blazing headache at any second. Instead a new presence filled his mind with calm.

~Despite many reservations, we have found your species to be worthy. Much will be given to you, but you must also agree to give in return. Now let us negotiate as equals.~

Danny's immobility vanished and he sat up. Shannon's head popped up out of the grass and she peered around. The shuttle slowly eased down to the planet.

Su Laana walked toward Danny, a beatific smile on her lovely face. From the direction of the great cave hundreds of Kians moved toward them through the trees and grass.

Danny recognized Su Laana's mental presence.

~*You chose the right thing to do! I am so proud of you.*~

He watched her face as she neared. "Was that a *test*?"

She smiled and said, "Yes, and you both passed!"

80
In orbit around Kiana

"Is everybody strapped in, Chief Murphy?"

"Yes, Mr. Burton. You may land this thing."

Burton looked over at Mongo. "Chief, you ready for this?"

"The present is like no better time I am thinking."

"Yeah, I agree."

Lifeboat 65 edged into the thin boundary of the atmosphere and a thin scream of air over the hull suddenly quieted the chattering students. He touched the control panel and retro rockets blazed momentarily causing the lifeboat to shudder and buck before slowing.

"Any idea how much shielding they put on these buckets?" Burton asked.

"No," Mongo said, staring through the windscreen. "For trip only one way is intended. Primary designed for space rescue."

"Probably not much then. At least we have unlimited fuel."

The scream of air increased and fire washed over the windscreen. Chief Tschurtoff tensed and grinned.

"Never in career opportunity before like this! Exciting more than expected."

"Bring up the navpute screen," Burton said as his fingers stroked various retros and verniers. The increased atmosphere and braking actions caused the lifeboat to shudder and pitch more strongly. The blackness of space lightened to a thin milky gray and slowly deepened to blue.

They roared across the continent of Turan losing elevation rapidly. The land mass ended and they could see the island of Mun off to their right and the southwest part of the continent of Cimpar dead ahead.

They burned through a cloudbank and saw the islands of Opiron, Poon, and Nephia. The three islands appeared as one landmass from their angle. Burton dropped lower and they glimpsed a large sea creature just under the surface as they flashed over the Western Sea.

The small island of Poon seemed to separate from Opiron and then they saw Nephia directly behind Poon. The islands rushed toward them and Burton fired the retros again. The water seemed to reach up and grab the bottom of the lifeboat.

Steaming spray boiled past the aft ports in great, loud, sizzling sheets. Nephia hurtled toward them as the craft settled deeper in the water. They slowed as the island went from dark object to mountains, beach and trees.

"Flag is there!" Mongo shouted.

Magellan Lifeboat 65 skimmed across the Southern Sea and shot up onto the sand on Nephia. The craft seemed to slam to a stop and Burton nearly brained himself on the control panel before the top of the control panel spewed out a fat gel-filled pillow that protected his face and the automatic safety harness retracted and slammed him into the back of his seat.

Students shouted and shrieked behind them. All noise and motion abruptly stopped.

Professor James Burton wiped his brow and said, "Damn. I'm glad that's over!"

"Are we there yet?" a student called. Everyone in the lifeboat broke into laughter.

"Professor," Chief Murphy said, "go ahead and open the hatch."

"Capital idea!" He touched the icon and an insistent buzzer sounded. He tapped a different icon and the sound ceased. The bulkhead directly aft of the cockpit jerked in place and with a long, rasping creak slowly opened outward. A number of the students emitted startled cries and others laughed.

"Wow, natural light!"

"Will we get skin damage?"

"The air smells funny!"

"I think it stinks!"

"Do we hafta stay here?"

"Can we get something to eat now?"

"I want my mother!"

Chief Murphy stood up. "I've had all of this I can take!" He bolted through the hatch.

Professor Burton swiveled around in the pilot's chair.

"Listen up!" he bellowed.

All other noise stopped and the group of students stared at him with rounded eyes.

"You people are forgetting your discipline. We are ship wrecked. Things are going to be very different."

They maintained silence and listened with sober expressions.

"We are going to have to depend on the kindness of strangers. Quick now, which character's line did I just paraphrase? Ancient Literature Honors Class?"

Hands waved in the air. Burton pointed, "Tonya?"

"Stella in *A Streetcar Named Desire!*"

"You get one point for getting the play correct." He pointed again, "Maisie?"

"Blanche Dubois, the older sister with reality issues who–"

"You answered the question, Maisie," Amber Nazarrian said.

"Yes, ma'am."

Professor Burton stood. "Never forget, *you* are *Magellan*! Now let's get out of this bucket."

They students followed him out to the beach where they marveled at everything they saw and touched. They tasted seawater and poked at the lines of tide-deposited detritus at various places on the sand. They waved madly at the three vehicles roaring toward them, all with pennants whipping madly in the wind at the top of antennas.

Behind him, Burton heard Chief Mongo say something in Rumanian and Amber laughed. Professor James Burton smiled to himself. A new adventure had just begun.

81
Western Plains of Cimpar

"Are you sure the elevation climbs enough out here to have potential?" Captain Laura Prescott said. She had recovered from her emotional collapse and now forged ahead in an effort to make things right with the universe.

"According to our map," Eric said, "but having never been here before I can neither confirm nor deny the question."

She grinned and briefly glanced over at him. "Hell of a honeymoon, huh?"

"I would have gotten bored with lying about on a sandy beach anyway. You should have a visual on the target area any minute now."

"Let's call it potential," Laura said. *"Target area* brings back too many unpleasant memories."

"You flew combat?"

"I was on Cobalt during the Brotherhood Rebellion."

"You have all sorts of secrets I don't know about."

"If you knew about them they wouldn't be secrets, would they?"

"Was it bad?"

"Very. A lot of Coalition officers belonged to the sect and had been in on the attempted coup from the beginning. People I thought of as friends were suddenly trying to kill me. I don't respond well to that sort of thing."

"I was on a survey ship out in the Horsehead Nebula at the time. We didn't hear much about it until it was over. Not that we understood the situation even then."

"The Coalition pretty much made it a state secret for the next ten years. I'm still not supposed to talk about it."

"You don't seem too worried."

"If we make it through this Yanivina encounter I'll give some thought to worrying about it. Right now I have higher priorities."

"But you saw combat there?"

"Eric, I really do not care to talk about it. I still have some emotional scars, okay?"

"Of course. I'm sorry for being nosy."

"Any other subject is fair game, but not that."

"There!" He pointed through the windscreen.

Almost magically a tree-covered plateau rose from the surrounding sere plain.

"There's the road from Siboth coming down from the north, heading right for it," Eric said.

"Wake up our crew. I want everyone alert when we get there."

He leaned over and kissed her on the cheek. "I hear and I obey, captain."

She grinned and wished they had time to land and make love in those trees ahead.

"Hey, guys, wake up. We have potential coming up fast."

Jenna Freibel stretched and unstrapped her safety harness so she could stand. John Dowd opened his eyes and alertly looked around as if he hadn't been snoring minutes before.

"We've traversed the entire western plain?" he asked.

"So it would seem," Jenna said holding onto an overhead stanchion and looking forward through the open cockpit hatch. "That looks like trees up there to me."

"Right." Dowd loosened his harness and pressed a node to activate the laser spectrometer. "Ready with the gear," he said in an official tone.

Eric dropped into his seat and strapped in before picking up the enhanced binoculars. "We're all ready, Skipper. Do your thing."

Laura pulled back the power feed and the shuttle slowed immediately. She studied the plateau. "That thing is really big."

"There's supposed to be a town on the western edge," Jenna said. "Right where the cliffs drop into the sea."

"Saumin. The town's name is Saumin," Dowd said. "Wasn't there a fish on Earth by that name?"

Jenna laughed. "Pretty close. The fish was a salmon."

"Sounds the same to me," Dowd said and bent to the spectrometer. "We have plants registering the chroma we're seeking, lots of them."

"There's a lake," Eric said. "How freaking big is this plateau?"

"Seventy clicks east to west," Dowd said, "…and forty clicks north to south. It's an anomaly even for this place."

"Why do you think this is an unusual planet, Mr. Dowd?"

Laura asked.

"There's something about Kiana that isn't right. I wish I could explain it but I can't. Ever since we got here this place has rubbed me the wrong way."

"This is the first place I've ever been where a comet is trying to kill us," Jenna said offhandedly. "*That's* different."

"Yeah, that too," Dowd said.

"Lake is coming up. I'm going to fly the perimeter," Laura said.

The shuttle slowed and Laura added power to the lift jets. She hated flying this slow in a craft with the aerodynamics of a brick, since any margin of error bordered on nonexistent.

"There are literally tons of Kion bordering the lake," Dowd said.

"I'm picking up a lot of probable life forms, too," Jenna said.

"I haven't spotted any movement," Eric said. "But with all those trees there could be a complete army below us and I wouldn't see it."

"Secure from your duties for a few. We're going to go look at Saumin." Laura increased power and the shuttle angled across the lake toward the now-visible distant Western Ocean. In the middle of the plateau stood two peaks with another lake beside them.

"That looks like ancient volcano," Eric said.

"It is," Dowd said. "Kiana was tectonically active millions of years ago. I was rather hoping to see an actual eruption while we were here but Dr. Wisdom said we were about a million years too late for the show."

Dowd stared at the spectrometer again. "That plateau is covered with Kion. Just thought I'd mention it."

"I see Saumin!" Eric said, peering through the binoculars.

"Prepare for landing." Laura examined the sprawling town through the pull-downs on her helmet. "They have a lovely square in the middle of the city just perfect for a landing site."

"Any sign of Kians?" Jenna asked.

"None," Laura and Eric said together.

"Then why are we landing in a potentially populated area?" Jenna said.

"Something wants me to," Laura said. "I don't know if it's my gut telling me to or something else."

"You're serious?" Dowd said. "*Something* is telling you to land?"

"Yes to both parts of the question."

"Can we vote on this?" Jenna asked. "*Before* we land?"

"Do you think we're going to be *attacked*, Dr. Freibel?" Eric asked.

"No. I'm more worried about being trapped."

Laura punched in a course that circled over the town and put the shuttle on automatic pilot. She swiveled her seat around to face the others.

"Okay, let's discuss this. We planned on landing near large amounts of Kion, this is actually more open and accessible as a landing site."

"True," Jenna said. "But we now know the Kians have the ability to make people vanish if they don't want them somewhere particular. Right John?"

"Yes, but they warn you first. At least they did with Shannon."

"How do you feel about landing here, Mr. Dowd?"

"You're the captain, ma'am. I have no opinion either way. I just want to find a way to nullify that thing." He pointed through the transparent roof at the easily visible comet overhead.

Jenna followed his gesture and stared at Yanivina. She shuddered and said, "Okay. Let's land."

Laura regarded her husband. "Eric, any thoughts?"

"We're wasting time and fuel. Land."

In moments she had the craft easing down in the middle of the plaza. Small clouds of dust blew up from the jets but nothing like they were used to in Siboth.

"They must get a good sea breeze through here," Dowd commented.

The shuttle settled on its landing struts and stopped moving. Laura quickly shut down the engines and the only thing they could hear was a breeze moving over the hull and the hum of the spectrometer. Dowd reached down and shut off the machine.

"Anyone up for a walk?" Laura asked.

"We aren't going to have to go far," Eric said. "We've got company."

They looked out of the shuttle and saw Kians slowly moving toward them from all directions.

"Seems you were right, Jenna," Laura said, pressing power nodes to start the engines.

Nothing happened.

"Are we in some sort of damper field?" Eric said.

"All I know is the engines aren't functioning. I guess we should go talk to them."

"Do you see *any* weapons?" Dowd said.

"No," the other three said more or less at the same time.

"Then I guess we shouldn't take any with us." He dropped his weapons belt with his lasers and spare power packs. "Sure makes me feel naked."

"Y'know," Jenna said, "oddly enough, I'm not worried about this any more."

Laura snickered. "We must have traded mind sets." She pressed the hatch node. It worked perfectly.

82
Siboth

"Colonel Merritt, have you heard anything from them yet?"

"No, director." Aisha felt anxious almost to the point of fear. "It's like they all disappeared or something. We've got four shuttles in the field and not a peep out of any of them for over an hour now."

The director's light olive skin took on an ashen hue. She cleared her throat. "Do you think they have encountered resistance?"

Aisha frowned, trying to find the right words. "If they had come under physical opposition they would have reported that. All the pilots are highly trained Security Forces and they have the discipline to react and report at the same time. What I am afraid of is that they all stopped for something they thought was curious or non-threatening and got sucked into a situation they hadn't anticipated."

"Here on *Kiana*?" the director said, her eyes wide.

"Here or anywhere. I've been with the Coalition Security Force since I was eighteen years old and if I've learned anything it's that there are always *unexpected's* out there. There is always something new to fear and learn from."

"I have to say, that doesn't sound like a fulfilling life, colonel. Always being afraid and–"

"Excuse me, ma'am, but you misunderstand. We're not 'afraid' but we all have fear and use it as a tool. If you don't know your fear, keep it on a leash and control it, you're going to end up having it eat you alive. I'm probably not saying all this right. I'm a soldier, not a speech maker."

"You're doing pretty damn good from where I'm standing."

"Thank you, ma'am. I appreciate that, but back to the point. I'm considering sending out four more shuttles to check on the first four. What do you think?"

"I think I promoted you to do this sort of thinking for all of us. So far you have shown me clear thinking and an excellent grasp of the situation. You have my fullest confidence and I'm not going to micromanage a situation or process I know nothing about."

The psychic weight on Aisha's shoulders grew heavier. She forced herself to smile and nodded.

"Thank you, director. I hope you're right about all of that."

Amanda Saint-Claire hurried into the room. "Director, Dr. Payne is on the holo and asking for you!"

"The shuttles have holo transmitting equipment?" She gave Aisha a frown.

"Not any that I'm aware of!"

The director left and Aisha followed.

Stoker wasn't the only one on the holo wall. He was surrounded by his crew and Lieutenant's Christenson and Hull as well as scores of Kians.

"Director, Colonel Merritt. How good to see all of you ladies," Stoker said.

"Are you on drugs, Dr. Payne?"

"No, director, but I am so relieved I feel drunk."

"Please share your relief. We can all use it."

"We're all going to live, ma'am. We are *all* going to live."

83
Island of Nephia

Dr. Sara Mueller had held herself in since the previous night when she heard about the *Magellan*. Most of her comrades were out on their own, free spirits, single and alone. She also was single.

But her father, mother, and little sister were all aboard *Magellan*.

And always will be, she thought.

Some of the kids they were racing toward may have known Diana, but she wouldn't ask any of them if they had.

The lifters roared at full fan as they raced down the beach, going up and over a long spit filled with the rank, brittle grass that thrived on brackish salt water, before crossing over sand again. The Sea Survey crew had three of the electric industrial lifters, each of which could carry over a ton of cargo. They had rigged nets along the sides and down the middle of the cargo beds.

"If we can't get all of them aboard," Chief Mahan said, "I'll just walk back."

Sara loved her crew as much as she did her family. In so many ways they *were* family and that would never change. The things they had seen and accomplished together as a team would be vivid in her memory until her dying day.

Although she had grown up in a space faring family her fascination for creatures aquatic bloomed early. By the time she finished basic education the human colony on Poseidon finally reached understanding and accord with the native sentient amphibian species. It seemed obvious to her that she should attend the fledgling university there and learn about the sea from both sides.

When her father, Commander Matt Mueller, shipped out on *Magellan* as Science Officer, Sara happily accepted a survey ichthyologist position on the same ship. After three years on Poseidon, being with her family again turned out to be an unexpected treat. For the first time in her life she understood her mother's mercurial moods and could actually make a difference when they turned dark.

Diana had been the brightest spot. Her little sister was within a year of being the same age as Sara when she went off to work on her professional degrees. Mentoring her sister proved delightful and poignant at the same time.

Diana's schoolteacher was a woman named Shipley. The female teacher aboard the lifeboat had a different name. In all of the chaos the inevitable rosters had yet to be drawn up and tallied.

"There it is, just around the point!" Chief Mahan said.

He piloted the lifter as if it were a combat aircraft from the history holos. First Class petty officer Leo Schmidt sat in the observer seat and Sara and Mike Armstrong sat in the two jump seats. Mike was preparing his holo camera to record the impending event.

"Mike, I'm going to let the skipper get there first, so you might want to brace yourself up where you can get a panorama with that thing."

"Thanks, chief." Mike unsnapped his harness from the seat and stood up in the open hatch next to the heavy laser weapon they had yet to fire. He cross-snapped into the oval and lifted the holocam and peered through the viewer.

"I don't know if the inertial damper will keep the image steady, but I'll do my best," Mike said.

"Your products never fail to deliver," Chief Mahan cheerfully shouted.

"You okay, Sara?" Leo asked.

She wondered how long he had been looking back at her.

"I'm fine. This is going to take a lot of adjustment for all of us."

"That's for damned sure," Chief Mahan said. "I don't know how 'rescued' these folks really are with that killer comet headed our way."

"This has turned into way more adventure than I care for," Mike said. "But I'll get images of everything."

Sara forced a laugh. "Ever the professional!"

The three lifters rounded the last point of land and *Magellan Lifeboat 65* lay within a kilometer in front of them.

"Those things are bigger than I thought," Mike said.

"I always wanted to build a personal space yacht out of one of them," Leo said. "It wouldn't take much modification at all."

"That's what you said about these lifters, remember? It took you months to get them operable again."

"Sure, Chief, but they work better than they did before don't they? Look how fast we're going. They were like turtles before I modified them."

"All I remember is that I did a hell of a lot of backpacking while you dinked around with our only transportation."

"From the base to the dock is only a couple hundred meters. Besides, you needed the exercise."

Chief Mahan slowed the lifter and Sara noticed that Keli'i did the same thing. The military mind fascinated her.

For a brief moment she thought about poor, doomed, gawky Roger Maney.

After giving in to his pleading she had gone to a live musical performance with him. His social skills barely passed minimal but she had felt sorry for him. After he met her in the plaza of the *Magellan* he started talking about himself and didn't stop until she waved farewell after the concert.

Despite rude looks from many he had obliviously talked in a loud voice throughout the concert. As he was tall and strongly built nobody challenged him physically, much to her dismay. His subject did not change once during the entire evening.

For two weeks thereafter he pinged her communicator and she ignored him. Finally one "evening" she was returning home from the clothing kiosks and suddenly he darted out from a side corridor.

"Why haven't you answered my pings?" His tone reeked of hubris and irritation.

"Because I don't want to talk to you, or for that matter, see you."

"What, are you one of those prick-teasing coquettes I've heard about?"

At that she turned, marched over to him and stared up into his face. "For once in your life shut up and listen! I went out with you because you whined and pleaded until I finally gave in. Then you ruined the concert for me, and everyone around us, by loudly bragging about your non-existent abilities and intelligence throughout the entire event.

"I did *not* tease you in any way, shape, or form. I have less than zero interest in you and if you keep stalking me physically and electronically I will report you to security. Now go find yourself someone as insecure as you are. I don't have the time or inclination to teach you social skills or civil comportment."

She didn't hear from him again. But she did hear that he was saying rude things about her. One of the security sergeants who worked with her father overheard him and bounced him off a bulkhead twice before gently explaining he shouldn't talk about a lady like that.

Now they're all gone.

She watched LCdr Karella's floater land and then Chief Mahan sat them down next to it. She couldn't help smiling as she exited. Everyone was laughing and talking at the same time.

Both of the chief petty officers from the lifeboat hugged Mr. Karella. Professor Burton shook hands with everyone from the survey crew, including her.

"So pleased to meet you, Dr. Mueller. Have you seen your sister yet?"

Sara's jaw dropped. "Wha– who, Diana is *here*?"

She turned and a person cannoned into her wrapping arms around her. She stared into the laughing and crying face of her sister until her own tears obscured her vision.

Lieutenant Commander Karella felt good as he watched the Mueller sisters reunite. He turned to the CPOs, "Now we have to get all of us back to Siboth. Any ideas?"

"We sure as hell aren't going in that thing," Chief Murphy said with a wheeze as he hooked a thumb at the lifeboat.

"You okay, Chief?"

"Oh, I'm fine, Mr. Karella. I just seem to have gained some weight since I arrived."

"Hah," Chief Mahan said. "You old farts are just out of shape, that's all."

"Argument to contrary not possible," Chief Tschurtoff said, panting and wiping sweat from his forehead. "Control of climate is great lack I am missing also."

A light breeze wafted over them and both chief's stiffened in alarm for a moment. Mahan laughed at them.

"You've both been off planet far too long."

"Well, that seems to have changed for the foreseeable future, Jimmy," Chief Murphy said in a bleak tone.

"Once we get all this stuff behind us, we need to hold a

memorial service," LCdr Karella said. "This isn't the time to dwell on our losses. We need to be insuring our future."

"How are we going to do that, Mr. Karella?" Chief Murphy asked.

"We know they have shuttle craft at the Coalition compound in Siboth. I think our best chances are there with them. If we stay here we will die for sure."

"Do they know something we don't, sir?" Chief Murphy said.

"I sure as hell hope so, chief." Karella turned to Chief Mahan. "Chief, call up those guys we spoke with last night and see if you can arrange transportation for forty two souls."

"Aye, aye, Mr. Karella. I'll get right on it."

84
Ki-Nuuhi Sanctuary

"I have a visual on the other shuttle," Eric said peering through his binoculars. "It's dropping into the trees up there."

"I had it on the radar ten minutes ago," Laura said.

"Just thought you might like to know," he said in an injured tone.

She didn't know if he was serious or not. If she didn't get some sleep in the next couple of hours she knew she might hurt someone.

~We are nearly to the sanctuary, captain. Would you permit me to clear your mind of toxins?~

Laura suppressed the instinct to flinch when the voice bloomed in her mind. This was something that would take getting used to. For a few seconds she considered the offer, why not?

Instantly her mind felt as if it had dived filthy into a cleansing pool. Sparkling with sudden good humor she couldn't help smiling.

"Thanks!" she said aloud.

Eric dropped the binoculars and looked at her. "What?"

"Do him next," Laura said and cocked her head at her husband.

"Do wha–, oh my God!" He turned to her. "What a rush. That's almost better than sex!"

Laura laughed. "The perfect thing to say to your bride on our honeymoon!"

All twenty Kians in the packed shuttle broke into laughter.

"What's so damn funny?" John Dowd said.

"Share the joke," Jenna said. "Why is everybody laughing except us?"

"Gi Gaann, would you do the same thing for them, Please?"

A moment later Jenna said, "Oh my. That is so nice!"

"That feels so good it has to be illegal!" Dowd said with conviction.

Laura knew they were nearly to the Great Convocation. During this day she had experienced mood swings so abrupt and diverse they had nearly unhinged her. In her service as captain of the *Magellan* she had only met a few Kians while on the planet for R&R.

As her duties had nothing to do with the people of Kiana she had not paid them much mind and learned little about them in passing. When the group of Kians approached their disabled shuttle in Saumin she had feared the worst. Then the "voice" had filled her mind.

~*Be at peace, Laura Prescott, no harm shall come to you from our hands.*~

She had looked at her companions and realized they all had heard the same thing.

~*Our people and your people are to make a pact that will save your lives as well as save our planet. We must go to this place . . .*~

The coordinates for the Ki-Nuuhi Sanctuary coalesced in her mind and she knew this was not a trick or a ruse of any sort. This was the right thing to do. They packed the shuttle with as many Kians as they could.

"I don't have room for everyone. I'm sorry!"

~*Not to worry, they will all be there too.*~

Since they didn't have to see the ground any longer she piloted the shuttle into space and arced over and down to the proper site. What had taken them hours to travel before took less than an hour. One of her motivations had been the lure of a long nap or a night's sleep.

Now she felt more alert than she had since waking up on her grandfather's farm during school vacation. Upon reflection she realized that particular memory spanned forty years. Suddenly she missed her family and wondered if she would ever see them again.

Laura shook her head. "Are you still messing with my mind, Gi Gaann?"

~*No. Clearing the toxins and debris from the mind opens channels and synapses long clogged. You will experience memories long forgotten or suppressed. Some may be painful and I apologize for that. I should have given you more of a warning.*~

"I rather think it will be worth it."

"Did I ever tell you about my best friend from elementary school?" Eric said.

"No, and I want to hear about him, or her, but not right now. Is that okay with you?"

"Of course, Darling. Don't worry. I won't forget."

"Good. There's the sanctuary dead ahead."

Six shuttles sat in two rows of three on the grass of a wide meadow atop a bench in the mountains. Once their craft had landed there was only level ground left for two more of the boxy craft. Off to one side were hundreds, perhaps over a thousand, Kians and humans talking, walking, and watching them come in for a landing.

"If I didn't know better I would say the entire population of the planet was here." Laura said.

~Only a fraction of the population of Cimpar is present. The people of Turan, Antori, Poon, Mun, Opiron, and Nephia are not represented in the flesh but all are here mentally.~

"Are there any humans in those other places?" Eric asked.

~Eight humans operated a research station on the island of Nephia. They were conducting undersea studies of our aquatic fauna and flora. Now they are on their way here with other humans who escaped the star ship.

~There are teams of humans on all of the other continents and islands, but nothing like the numbers here on Cimpar.~

"There were survivors from the *Magellan*?" Laura said.

They all learned about *Lifeboat 65*.

"Which land mass has the highest Kian population?" Jenna asked.

~Turan has half again as many as Cimpar.~

"I wonder why the Coalition picked Cimpar for the majority of the surveys?" Laura said.

~Because the major population centers didn't have a mountain range separating them.~

Jenna chuckled. "I almost asked, 'How do you know?'"

Everyone on the shuttle laughed.

Laura effortlessly landed the shuttle, shut down the engines and opened the hatch. She let the passengers exit first and she and Eric followed Jenna and John down the short ramp. A red-haired woman dashed up to John Dowd and embraced him.

"Big John!"

"Shannon! My God, I thought you were dead!" He hugged her tightly and picked her up and swung her around. Both of them giggled like lunatics.

"Where did you go? Were you still in the temple?"

"C'mon, I'll tell you all about it." They wandered off through the crowd.

Two shuttles came in from the west and landed one after the other. The hatches lifted and over two-dozen young people hurried out onto the meadow.

Laura glanced at Eric. "How are they going to impose order with this mob?"

A pure crystalline tone started in the back of her head and slid forward to stop just over her eyes. The single exquisite note stopped all other thought and completely cleared her mind.

~Please make yourself comfortable in the sanctuary. We have much to discuss and time is very much of the essence.~

Silently, all of the Kians and humans moved into the large cave entrance and found places to sit in the open air next to the large lake. Many humans surveyed their surroundings but no one spoke. Laura's only thought was, *I feel safe here.*

~Who shall speak for the humans?~

"I shall." the director was three to four meters away from where Laura sat. Serenity enveloped her.

~Very well, we shall begin. What you hear in your minds today, as well as your responses, will be heard by every sentient being on Kiana. All agreements made today shall be binding from this time forward until the end of the universe.~

Laura felt rather than heard the finality in the voice.

~Director Donna Henderson, you speak not only for the humans present on Kiana at this moment but also for every human who shall ever come to this place in the future. You are making a binding treaty between Kians and humans.~

"I understand."

~We regret the loss of your spacecraft and those aboard her. We understand that there are challenged individuals in every species and culture. The loss of Magellan *was a tragic aberration that changed a great deal here on Kiana.~*

A collective sigh rose and ebbed among the humans. Pain seeped in around the edge of Laura's mind.

~So be it. We all rejoice in the astonishing rescue of two score humans. It is more than we expected.~ The pain vanished and a sense of expectation replaced it.

~You are not the first alien species to come among us with the intention of dominating our culture and usurping Kiana. The most recent lost many thousands of their people when Yanivina last visited. You have found some of their remains as well as one of our ancient

repositories.~

On the far side of the lake Stoker Payne started at the thought of more than one temple, or repository. Before he could speculate further the voice pushed all else from his mind.

~Unlike the earlier visitors, you have not threatened any Kian with harm despite the implicit threat of your weapons. Yet when you all had boarded your starship to escape Yanivina we planned to send you away unharmed but unable to return. Now that cannot happen.~

Sitting next to Stoker, Melanie wondered how they had planned to pull that off? *Were they able to wipe an AI as complex as Mother?*

~We never meant harm to any visitor, but until now neither have we offered sanctuary. With this offer comes an understanding that future human visitors to Kiana will be just that: visitors. Kiana will not become a part of the Coalition nor will it be used as a base.

~Starships from any culture are welcome to visit, trade, and enjoy what Kiana has to offer. The people of Kiana will continue to serve Ki and keep her planet sacred. All humans hearing my voice, by the will of the Kian people, have the opportunity to stay on Kiana for the rest of your lives.~

A mental catch of breath swirled among the humans and the questioning was almost palpable.

~No one is required to make a choice now. It will become obvious when the time arrives.~

"How can we save ourselves from the – from Yanivina?" the director asked.

~We cannot guarantee that every human will be saved from the ugly death that Yanivina visited on the crew of the Magellan*...~*

An audible gasp and sudden quick conversations broke out among the humans.

~...nor can we guarantee that every Kian will be saved either. Our history tells us that some Kians always perish when Yanivina visits, which is why we fear her.~

"Are there any specifics as to age, sex, or type of person that can tell us who might–"

~No, Madam Director, the chances are even for all. The term I find prevalent among your people which best describes the situation is "crap shoot."~

"What *can* we do?"

~We have prepared a great quantity of Kion for this visit. As soon as possible after this convocation ends we all must begin to inhale the smoke of burning Kion. You will have a sense of euphoria and well being in the initial stages.~

"Many humans still use tobacco and cannabis, even though the effects of both are different. Does Kion affect one the same way as either of these?"

~Cannabis would come closest but it still is not as effective as Kion. Inhaling Kion smoke is only the first step but it is necessary in order to survive the second step; being exposed to the breath of Yanivina.~

"Why won't we die?"

~Our best scientists have yet to answer that question fully. All we know is that Kion acts as a catalyst between the brain and Yanivina's breath that alters the result.~

"Alters?" the director said. "In what way?"

~Most acquire the ability to communicate telepathically. Some also are gifted with telekinesis. Some die anyway.~

"Telepathy. We will be able to hear what everyone else is thinking?"

~As much as another will allow you, yes. As a race thus far untutored in telepathic skills you have some basics to learn. It is possible to block all of your thoughts from any other being.~

"Can you *see* everything in my mind?"

~We can see most of your thoughts, but not everything. Think of your mind as a dwelling. Everyone can see the outside, most can see into the living room. Fewer yet can see your sleeping chamber and only invited guests see your 'bathroom,' which is an interesting term for an elimination chamber. But you do see my point?~

The director laughed along with the rest of the listeners.

"Yes. I look forward to learning these intricacies."

~We should all partake of Kion now. Yanivina's visit is nearly upon us.~

Stoker Payne stood and said, "May I ask a question?"

~Of course you may. Any of you may ask questions.~

"Some of us had an experience with the small creatures we call 'radars' and–"

~Please pardon the interruption. This is an excellent question and pertains to the matters at hand. The jati are analogous to the canary of human history.

~*They are the first creature of any size or complexity on Kiana to be affected by the breath of Yanivina. When the* Magellan *died in the atmosphere the gasses that killed her crew were released into our atmosphere. Even though it was but a tiny sample it affected a number of jati and they now attempt to kill anything that moves.*~

"Is there any way to stop them short of killing them?"

A number of Kians lit long torches and proceeded to set piles of semi-dried mounds of Kion alight.

~*No. Now we must prepare for Yanivina.*~

The mounds combusted with small tongues of flame and heavy smoke rolled off each mound and spread across the area.

~*Breathe in small breaths. At first the Kion irritates the throat but in a few breaths it will soothe. When the irritation ceases take in lungful after lungful and remember that you are among friends.*~

Melanie coughed with the first short breath but fought the response on the second and all breaths thereafter. On the fourth breath all irritation vanished and she felt as if she had been breathing the smoke all her life. Her mental walls receded and she realized she stood on the edge of a totally new universe.

85
Yanivina

The comet's long, timeless swing out of the vast stellar night brought it within a few thousand miles of actual contact with Kiana, passing ahead of the planet's orbit in a cosmic near miss. As a result Kiana passed directly through the massive comet tail saturating her atmosphere with the gasses boiling off the ancient traveler.

The separate gasses by themselves would not have caused more than comment. However, in combination they are exciters of tissue unlike any other and wrought havoc wherever they encountered the brain matter of any creature capable of one.

From the viewpoint of those on the ground the comet swept down and across the sky before racing off into the fancied realm of creatures named for combinations of scattered suns by long-dead peoples. The constellations neither accept nor reject their titles any more than Yanivina is evil or good. It merely *is*.

Within three revolutions of Kiana the volatiles in the gasses have spent their strength and had been completely absorbed by the flora and fauna. Yanivina's breath has departed Kiana for another eight centuries. In its wake large numbers of creatures have experienced instant evolution or demise.

Except for those near Kion, the jati population is near extinction levels that will allow the insect populations to flourish. The flying bird-like mammals, largely unaffected by the comet will also flourish on the increased diet of insects without fear of the diminished jati. Many species used the plant as food and their systems were fortified with the necessary elements needed for survival

New balances replace old and life continues: a very different life for many.

86
Ki-Nuuhi Sanctuary
Day One of Yanivina

At first Colonel Aisha Merritt thought the Kion failed to affect her. Then Grandmother spoke to her.

"You can't go out in public looking like that, young lady! What will people think?"

Aisha laughed and glanced around to see if anyone noticed but the people around her seemed to be hearing their own memories and paid her no mind. Her standard rebuttal to Grandmother had always been, "Why should I care what people think?"

A tear sped down her right cheek, surprising her. For long dead Grandmother had always said, "Because you're walking out of *my* front door, that's why!"

Aisha took another deep Kion-laden breath, wiped at her tears and visited family and friends she hadn't seen for decades.

Dö Laani felt his mind quicken as he inhaled his third breath of Kion. Many decades ago the quickening had nearly occurred unaided but escaped him somehow. Never knowing what it might have meant or how it could have benefited him had plagued him since with conjectures of "what if?" and always wondering "why not?"

Now it ticked in the back of his mind, separate and distinct from the inherited awareness he shared with all Kians. It glowed like a coal in a dark sconce, ready to leap forth in a huge all encompassing flame to throw light into the darkest recesses of his mind and being.

In his innermost soul of souls he always believed it to be the spark of genius. All his long life he felt he should be smarter, more accomplished, perfectly matched to the sharpest wit and deepest thinker. The perceived lack rendered it all the more desirable and it beckoned to him.

Just a few more breaths filled with Kion...

Danny Gordon waited for it. The first breath knifed through his lungs, causing him to gasp in disbelief. He held the pain tightly in his mind, not wanting to alarm Su Laana, or anyone else for that matter.

His body demanded air and he took his fifteenth drink of Yanivina's Breath. It exploded in his lungs like liquid fire and he cried out, despite himself.

Su Laana appeared next to him.

"Dan-nay, you are in pain?" Her large eyes beyond huge with fear.

"It *burns*," he gasped hoarsely. "When does it *stop*?"

~*It should not hurt!*~ Anxiety laced her contact.

Two other Kians hurried over and sat near them. One put her hands on his chest and the fire inside tried to leap through his flesh to sear away the interruption. Danny knew they were talking about him but he didn't care.

~*You will sleep now.*~

And he did.

Jerry Poppert lay in terror, his eyes flicking back and forth. He hadn't wanted to leave the dark of his quarters and come out in the light where people could see his guilt. He wanted to hide forever.

His own troopers had followed that black bitch's orders and bound him up and carried him to this place. He no longer struggled against the restraint of the security jacket; he knew he couldn't defeat it. Enough of what they told him had slipped through his paranoia and magnified it immeasurably.

Everyone would be able to see what was in his mind. All would misunderstand the necessary things he had done. Tears ran from his eyes and the smoke enveloped him.

His mother and wife were waiting.

"*There* you are..."

Molecules he had studied in college long ago took on depth and grew in size and swirled around Stuart Currie's brain. The variety and color quickened and intensified. He laughed as he recognized combinations he had known all his adult life.

Chemistry, always his passion, now seemed to show passion for him. Hydrogen, oxygen, and nitrogen all surrounded him in varying sizes and maniacal intensity. Whirring past his head they felt like old friends.

The progression changed, new atoms created new molecules that he didn't recognize. Abruptly the known friends returned and slowly, clearly transformed into the unknowns. Stuart concentrated, as he suddenly realized the Breath of Yanivina was revealing itself to him.

Briefly he considered locating his hand pad in order to take notes. But the progression of color and new sounds were imprinting their information on his brain. He would never forget any of this.

Amanda Saint-Claire wept. Music throbbed through her body with increasing emotion. Her blood carried the notes and strains to every organ, all four limbs, and infused her heart to the point of bursting.

Many years ago she turned her back on music to follow the Coalition path of administration. But music, her first and close-held love had never left her soul. She listened to the classics in the privacy of her quarters.

Mozart, Beethoven, Copeland, Lennon, Langbein, Yakisama, and all of the other greats from over the centuries, fought for domination in her head. The Kion had broken the self-imposed bonds of her imagination and desires, allowing the music unhindered release.

She sobbed with the beauty of it, for the lost ignored years and what might have been. Amanda wept for her vanished youth as the music took on added dimension. Tactile presence, and cascading color swirled around her while she became transfixed within its geometry.

Jerrol Bainer had serious reservations about this share-your-mind stuff. Maybe his constant self-control wouldn't extend beyond his own mind. Then what? All his life he had depended on his looks, charm, and glib tongue to get him what he wanted.

Pyrocean produced a never-ending supply of courtiers and assistants highly trained in the art of softening an attitude from harsh into smoothly palatable. That these sons and daughters of the Pyrocean League were highly trained in every discipline known to human endeavor never faced serious question. That they constantly vied for dominance by whatever means possible escaped all but the most perceptive non-Pyrocean since those native to the planet excelled at the nuanced climb to power.

Yet somehow in this place Jerrol did not receive his due. With all that he accomplished, Stoker Payne had out flanked him. The smoldering anger he harbored continually grew and fed on the underlying fear that he, in fact, possessed no true professional ability.

He knew many suspected his choice of team members. It wasn't his fault that he was attracted to beautiful, willing woman and they to him. If they achieved their scholarship standing by virtue of their attractiveness, what of it? That was part and parcel of the Pyrocean way.

Those attitudes never enjoyed full broadcast to the Coalition, yet they fell far short of subterfuge. That he questioned one of the tenants of his culture would be obvious to all who beheld his open mind.

The more he contemplated the entire world having access to his thoughts, memories, and want of depth the more strain he felt. His mind remained clenched like a white-knuckled fist and the Kion hammered at him. Something must give.

Stoker Payne forced himself to focus on his surroundings. Kians and humans for the most part lay in attitudes of abject bliss. The majority of faces held smiles, but tears streaked many and rictus-like scowls marred more than a few.

Many slept, and he yawned, feeling totally exhausted. Releasing his concentration he allowed the Kion to take him where it would. The Temple of Ki surrounded him and he floated down the long, perfect hallways to the gallery where Shannon had trespassed.

He again saw the warning symbols and recognized them as the "Trespassers will be transported" alert. He smiled at the efficiency of both the security system and the result of transgression. "Go directly to jail," surfaced in his mind from some long-past source and his grin widened.

He beheld machines and weapons so advanced from his own knowledge and time that he doubted he could operate them safely. Devices encased in translucent metals hung dust-free on racks waiting with sinister patience to once again spew mayhem. There was no question that he passed through a vast gallery of death. The certainty of the postulation pervaded the atmosphere as completely as did oxygen.

Part of Stoker's mind wondered why he was being shown

this vast museum of potential murder. His studied interests lay elsewhere but he thought the history lesson fascinating. He floated into the next gallery and felt stunned with awe.

The gallery dropped far below his vantage point and also soared high above. Held in a massive cradle lay what had to be a space vehicle. No mere shuttlecraft boasted the technology and ability housed in this hull.

Stoker wondered at the antiquity of the vessel and at the Kian rationale for leaving space and turning its cultural back on technology altogether. *There were so many questions yet to be answered and how many more to be asked?*

Taxim Rosta held fast his memories and strained to abjure from the minds he felt bumping into his. He didn't trust the majority of these creatures to understand his motivations and past actions. He held no doubt that he would be stripped of his consciousness and transformed into a slate.

He knew the process was painless and would give him an entirely new personality devoid of the aberrations that compelled him to engage in the actions demanded of him. But the true "him" would be gone forever. Nothing would remain of the real Taxim Rosta.

His mind spun for a moment and tried to follow other thoughts but he bit his lip and the pain helped him focus. The taste of blood triggered deeply buried synapses and the beast in him stirred. Taxim fought two mental battles now, and realized that at least one would be lost. Losing either would mean total oblivion.

He pushed himself up and drunkenly staggered from the sanctuary. No matter what threat waited outside, he could not stay here.

Shannon Gray clung to the love of her life. How Miri could be in her arms didn't matter. She was blissfully happy that they were locked in a naked embrace and kissing.

"I thought I had lost you, love," Shannon said into Miri's neck.

"You did lose me. I came back for you."

After more kisses, Shannon pulled her head back, "What do you mean 'came back for me?'"

"I can't stay here, Shannon. But you can go with me."

"*Where* did you go?"

"To a place where there is no conflict, no turmoil. Where we can always be together."

"I can go there with you?"

"Yes, my little red-headed nymph, you can. Will you?"

"Oh, yes, Miri!"

"Hang on tight…"

Eric Caldwell pushed his helm to port and skimmed along the very edge of the Great Rift. It seemed perfectly natural to him that the rogue suns and burgeoning solar systems rushed past like reefs in a celestial ocean. Centaurus beckoned and he obligingly trimmed his star sails and cut a wide yaw to approach close enough to nearly touch its outermost planet.

This is what he was born to do; sail an ocean of stars. He saw the comet arcing toward him and he changed course to parallel the ancient voyager. It was moving nearly twice his own velocity and creating a vortex fanning out like the wake of a waterborne ship.

Eric turned hard and cut across the wake rather than have it rock him from side to side. The comet tail proved harder to navigate than he had supposed. His craft pitched and bucked through borealis eddies, throwing more of its contents into his face than he would have liked.

The tiller faded from his grip and his star yawl pixilated into tiny fragments to spin away like so much mist. He found himself tumbling through the cosmos, unconcerned and open to the next event.

Then he saw the comet magnified in brilliance and coming at him on a direct collision course.

This could be bad, very bad…

Laura Prescott wept for the lost souls on *Magellan*, for the ship itself, and for her self perceived failure in allowing it all to happen.

I broke my contract with my ship. I allowed my own personal life to take precedence over my command obligations.

She hung in space, far above Kiana, watching the planet and its moons move in their orbits. Guilt suffused her to the point she considered throwing herself into Diana, the closest star. A cry of fear reached her ears and immediately she knew it came from Eric.

Her hesitation and self-recriminations vanished and she moved at speed toward his calls for help. The closer she came to Yanivina the louder his cries. From where her power and speed originated she had no idea, but she accelerated and overtook the rushing comet.

Eric was in the core of the comet. Being held by the icy blue arms of Yanivina herself. The comet's personification had a crystalline beauty that no man, or woman, could ignore.

~*She ran me down, Laura!*~ Eric cried. ~*I couldn't get out of her way...*~

"You've taken enough from me, you bitch!" Laura screamed as she hurled herself into the voluptuous body of the deadly voyager. Coldness suffused her as she grabbed Eric. Icy fingers grabbed at her, clutching and scrabbling to pull Laura in to add to the millions of lamenting souls Yanivina already possessed.

Wrapping her arms around Eric she turned and moved away from the comet. Both of them screamed as they painfully broke free of the frigid presence while pieces of their psyches tore off and adhered to Yanivina like flesh on sub-zero metal.

As they arced back toward Kiana they warmed themselves with each other and relished their future together.

87
Ki-Nuuhi Sanctuary
Day Two of Yanivina

Jerrol Bainer writhed in agony. In his straining determination not to allow others to see the shallow façade he perceived himself, he fought with the effects of the Kion. The result was adversely affecting the very fabric of his brain, which began to tear.

He attributed the delirium sensations to the Kion and clung mentally tighter to his privacy. Finally his brain hemorrhaged so massively he died instantly.

Melanie Frasier opened her eyes and watched sunlight move through the cave door. The speed with which it angled from one side to the other amused her and the rushing sound it made gave her solace. Bright sparkles seemed to be everywhere so she closed her eyes again.

The celestial bodies she had studied for the majority of her life spun around her with unnatural speed, creating a vortex. She felt herself pulled into the spinning wall of light yet she felt no fear, only curiosity.

She wondered if this was how black holes were born or if it would translate into a wormhole or some other means of traveling astronomical distances. The wall of light abruptly vanished and it seemed as if she fell through a tunnel of bright obsidian for hours. Then she entered a solar system totally unfamiliar to her. It was a solar system at war with itself.

She witnessed the inhabitants of the third and fourth planets firing rockets at each other filled with destruction. Instinctually she knew the two planets had orbits of differing speeds and they came within "range" of each other only occasionally. Many of the rockets were destroyed at some point en route but far too many reached their targets.

Smoke boiled from the ruins of many cities on both planets. She swooped down to peer at the belligerents and felt astonishment that she recognized the beings on the fourth planet.

Their remains had concealed the Temple of Ki, and the computer-created reconstruction had poorly captured the ferocity of the fanged creatures. As she watched they prepared for a physical invasion of the neighboring world, filling transport after transport with heavily armed troops. She effortlessly crossed the weapon-filled distance to the third planet and found the inhabitants to be a race of obviously intelligent arachnids.

Melanie knew she witnessed a race war of total annihilation. There would be no treaties between these totally divergent creatures. So much knowledge here would be lost to other races no matter who won.

As she lifted away from the death and destruction she wondered if she had been dispatched to witness this conflagration of worlds. Someone needed to know and only time would reveal the rationale behind the knowledge.

Joyce Mayer and Doug Franklin spun around each other as they swept back over Kian history. Resembling binary stars they unraveled archaeological mysteries. In their all-seeing mode they could look forward or back. They both peered into the future and saw themselves paired for as long and far as the vision permitted.

Then, laughing together, they raced backward in time to seek out even more answers to puzzles.

Jason Karella found himself in the sea once again. This time he achieved a fantasy he had carried for most of his underwater explorer life: to traverse the deeps without benefit of machinery or breathing apparatus. The need for oxygen disappeared and he went wherever he chose.

In the SS *Golden Fleece* they had glimpsed leviathans looming in the distance and no amount of cautious approach would grant them a better view. Now he sought them, more for his own gratification than anything else. While in university he had been privileged to travel to Aquaria, the human-discovered water world that had been populated with every species of cetacean still in existence.

The experience had a profound effect on his life. Prior to that he had intended to go into the Coalition Security Forces Officer Candidacy School. He opted instead to pursue the Survey Corps with an emphasis on underwater research.

After fifteen years and three planets under his belt he felt fulfilled and believed he had done everything he could to further the knowledge of humankind. But he had always dreamed of being able to swim with the creatures he studied without benefit of mechanical adaptation. Whether the Kion granted him that actual ability or merely fooled his brain into believing it, he didn't care; he was down here.

The *Golden Fleece* had been limited in how deep it could travel. Jason had no such encumbrance. Once again he went past reefs of coral, a phenomena they had found on other worlds that boasted oceans. The microscopic life that formed the reefs differed slightly from planet to planet but the beneficial result was identical.

As in all life, a food chain existed down here. They had discovered scores of species of fish, or creatures that extracted oxygen from fresh water and salt water but they had yet to find the top of the food chain. Jason believed the shy leviathans might be the creatures they sought.

What ever the method he traversed the sea, Jason discovered he was capable of great speed. In very little time he was again off the coast of Nephia in the area they had glimpsed the creatures the most. He angled to the bottom and became enthralled with the change in seabed vegetation and species diversity as he followed the sloping continental shelf down into the dark depths.

As on most planets the lack of light reduced the variety and abundance of vegetation down to nil as he went beyond the farthermost reach of Diana's rays. Great shoals of luminescent fish lived in the darkness resembling nothing more than vast, animated star fields moving in tandem and changing direction in spectacular synapse quick sweeps.

Jason decided the creatures that dominated food chains wouldn't be at these depths and he rose toward the unseen light. His visual and aural perceptions performed with more acuity than ever before in his life. He heard eco-location from a distant animal, no, *animals*.

A burst of speed brought him close enough that he saw a pod of the leviathans in the distance. He didn't alter course or slow. In the past he had wondered aloud if the creatures heard them or saw them first when the humans sought them in the *Golden Fleece*.

He was close enough to make out some of their physical characteristics when he clearly heard a whistle that shouted "danger" even to him.

The massive animals fled in every direction. He had the

perception that there were between eight and ten of them. He chased after one, hoping to get at least a good look at it.

Slowly he gained on it, wondering how the animal could move at such speed under water without any body movement. It was as if he were chasing a jet. Suddenly the leviathan slowed, made a tight turn and stopped, facing him.

At this point Jason wondered if the animal could actually see him or just sensed his astral presence? He had no idea how he was alive under water with extraordinary capabilities other than all of this was some sort of mentally enhanced wish fulfillment on a grand scale.

Can I die down here? He wondered.

Jason came to a stop, hung in the water and stared at the most streamlined animal he had ever seen. It resembled an ancient torpedo, with teeth, lots of teeth.

The round snout nearly came to a point and flaps on either side slowly opened and closed. The mouth full of teeth filled the lower portion of the head, and equidistant across the top, were four eyes that regarded him with intelligence.

Something caught in the corner of Jason's left eye and he spun around to see that the pod now surrounded him. He wanted to believe they were smiling, but all he was sure of was the scores of teeth within a few feet of him.

Maxim Rosta huddled, blinking, in a grove of trees three hundred meters from the cave mouth. The Kion had nearly dissipated from his body, his mind slowly cleared of the paranoid fear, and he felt safe. He glanced around to see if any others had followed him through curiosity or malice.

Movement in his peripheral vision startled him and he swung around to see a jingroe racing toward him. The huge jaw was open allowing the knife-like teeth to sparkle in the sunlight as saliva flew from both corners of its mouth. Maxim had never seen one of these creatures before and it took him precious seconds to realize his jeopardy.

He lurched to his feet in new fear and took a deep breath. In that instant the last of the Kion left his body and the Breath of Yanivina found his unprotected brain. A blinding synapse of pain later he turned into hate-fueled energy and charged, howling at the creature hurtling toward him.

Jenna Freibel existed totally in water that continued to change its attitude. When she first inhaled the Kion she had focused on water as a constant in her life. Because it was a huge part of Kiana, her entire being suddenly became a cohesive mass of water roughly analogous to her human form, sliding through the lake toward the small creek where the overflow emptied into the distant ocean.

In all of her years working with water on three different planets she had never imagined water with personality, more than one personality at that. Part of the water sang past her in an oblivious manner as if ignoring her presence although she could tell it of her presence.

In a swirl of bubbles and micro currents a volume of angry water possessing minute teeth and sharp edges tried to tear into her mass. This, she realized, was the water that cut canyons through stone and washed vehicles, homes, and people before it when in flood. As in all things a yin and yang existed in the liquid world.

Dodging the bellicose portions as best she could she dropped over a waterfall and bounced in the spray at the bottom, finding it altogether as much fun as she had thought it would be. Now the riverbed ran downhill to the sea and she wondered if saltwater was more friendly than fresh. Something akin to a flash of lightning returned her to her body for the length of a breath and then she was back dodging rocks on the riverbed again, free as the elements.

The flash seared through Dö Laani's mind, granting him long-sought clarity. He beheld Kiana and the universe in total understanding that dwarfed his lifetime of study and observation. His mind expanded with the inrush of knowledge, thrilling him to his core.

From the depths of Kiana, in the center of the cosmos whirling about the planet, a massive figure emerged and he recognized Ki. His joy merged with acceptance as she opened her arms and took him to her.

Mongo wept with happiness. The realization that he had somehow intertwined his mind with that of Amber stunned him.

As soon as he realized she had sought him, that she was there because she wanted to be part of his life, nearly unhinged him.

Their minds, memories, desires, fears, goals, and passions swirled about each other in an emotional waterspout. That there could be no hiding, no evasions, no lies and no barriers between them turned the pairing into a sacrament.

Each knew the other more intimately than any other human couple before them. Brilliance flickered around them and they accepted it as part of their bond.

Su Laana hovered over the pain of Danny Gordon, trying to absorb as much of it as possible. Tu Annhn, the most knowledgeable healer in all of Cimpar, crouched across from her.

~*The Kion is making it difficult for me to concentrate.*~

Su Laana's immediate rush of despair made the old woman look up at her.

~*He will not die. I promise.*~

~*As Ki wishes.*~

~*Ki and Yanivina have already taken their share, but more will follow...*~

Su Laana looked up. The old woman's eyes were rolling back in her head under the mix of Kion and Yanivina's Breath. All around them Kians and humans writhed and jerked in their mental journeys.

Danny's moan focused her attention and she realized she had also been wandering.

~*Tu Annhn, can you find what hurts him?*~

The healer's eyes snapped open and when Su Laana saw the dilated pupils she realized there wouldn't be much more assistance from her. The woman stared down at Danny and ran her hands over his smooth, bare chest.

~*I can, I can fix, the problem. Allow me space...*~

Su Laana knew she meant mental space and contracted her mind as much as she could. Tu Annhn stared fixedly at Danny as her hands prodded, thumped, massaged, and twisted his flesh. Once Danny cried out and his eyes fluttered open for a moment before he sank back into his induced sleep.

Abruptly the aura of anguish emanating from him vanished and his face relaxed along with his body. For a heartbeat she thought him dead.

~*He lives.*~ Tu Annhn closed her eyes and slowly sank backward to the smooth, hard floor of the sanctuary.

Su Laana laid her head on Danny's chest and surrendered to her dreams.

Tears streaming from his eyes, Jerry Poppert had discovered he could not hide from his fear or his past. He tried to turn away from his mother only to see Cristina.

Screaming in horror he tried to shut his eyes but they were both in his mind which would not shut them out.

"You did this!" his mother yelled, turning to display the abrupt angle to her neck. Suddenly she was at the bottom of the stairs again, bent and broken after he pushed her backward.

"You wouldn't get out of my way," he screamed. "Not then, not now, not ever!"

"You had to atone..." she said, her face so close to his he could smell her dead, fetid breath, "...for the sins of your father of which you are the result!"

Cristina hovered next to him reciting the endless list of wrongs he had committed from the first moment they met until the day he split her head with an axe. After he buried her body and cleaned the wood shed he told people she left him for another man. Everyone believed him. He wasn't the only one with whom she found fault.

The time he had spent with her had been hell and he exulted in his escape from her harpy ways. Now his mother and ex-wife again psychically bludgeoned him and the more smoke he inhaled the more he was forced open to their wrath. He could take no more.

He screamed, "Please let me die!" and discovered that was also an option he could take.

Su Laana nestled in the arms of her mother, weeping with affection, loss, and bliss. Always cheerful, laughing, carefree, and willing to help, her mother had stopped to comfort a child. A large stone, one of many being used to repair a building, had slipped and struck her down at an obscenely young age.

Five-year-old Su Laana was holding her mother's hand at the instant of her death. The instant absence from her mind and life produced a wound that took years to heal. Now they talked, hugged, rubbed foreheads in the Kian manner.

~*I will watch over you. You are blessed, my child, with a good man. You will need him in the days ahead.*

~*You both have much to offer the other. You shall be the mother of a new race as well as...*~ She talked on, revealing much to Su Laana who did not question, only listened and reveled in the embrace of her mother.

88
Ki-Nuuhi Sanctuary
The Last Day of Yanivina

Chuck Reed knew he had bumped into other mental beings while he explored the Temple of Ki. Once he even recognized Marilyn Culpepper who had engaged him in a spirited discourse on Kian body armor from the Third Kian War. So absorbed in the wonder of what he had found, he at first felt nettled when the Great Joining began.

He thought the top of his head had actually opened and he grabbed his scalp with both hands. While his skull remained intact his mind yawned wide to the force and power around him.

Other mental presences jostled and pressed in from all directions. His first reaction was dismay that he would no longer have the solace of his own mind in which to relax. A flash of light so bright he thought it must be atomics swept the chamber.

Once it faded he realized he could identify every person around him for a great distance. They did not infiltrate into his mind but were just *there*. A vast silence settled over the sanctuary as all looked about them with their eyes as well as their minds.

Chuck was afraid to move in either plane for fear of causing a disturbance. So he patiently waited and reveled in the fact that he still lived.

Jason blinked from the bright light and feeling profound detachment pondered on the last moment he had while facing the leviathans. Their presence had suddenly grown within his mind. He knew their unpronounceable names, and that they were at least as intelligent as he was.

With the light came a statement that still rang in his mental ears: ~*We will meet again.*~

For the first time in many years Jason knew he was not in control of his destiny. The thought only brought excitement.

A pure, crystal tone focused everyone's attention on a small, wizened Kian male who radiated peace and the wisdom of ages.

~*We welcome the humans to our family. Be not apprehensive about your abilities or the perceived lack of control. All will be made clear. First we must honor the remains of those Ki took unto her bosom.*~

As people looked around them they discovered the still forms lying solitary on the sanctuary floor. A keening went up.

Danny Gordon held a sobbing Su Laana in his arms. At their feet lay the body of her father, Dö Laani, his staring eyes wide with a look of rapturous joy on his face.

~*How do we honor him?*~ Danny asked. He could feel untold numbers of minds around his and most honored his privacy. The few that intruded were humans who had no idea what they were doing.

~*Cremation is what humans call it. We use the cleansing light of the sun.*~

~*How do you do that?*~

~*You shall see shortly.*~

~*Where should we take him?!*

~*Watch...*~ she stifled another sob and knelt down and kissed her father's forehead. "You are with Ki, my father. Please forgive my transitory grief and know I honor you now as I have honored you always and will for the rest of my days.

"Thank you for your guiding smile and open heart. I am forever blessed to be your daughter. We now send your husk to the next dimension according to your wishes."

Danny realized he had just heard the same salutation from many Kians throughout the sanctuary. A deep sobbing close at hand drew his attention.

John Dowd, consumed with grief, sat next to the body of Shannon Gray. Danny walked over and put his hand on the big man's shoulder.

"Mr. Dowd, you need to look at her."

"Wh-what?" He blinked his swimming eyes and frowned at Danny. "What do you mean?"

"Look at her face."

Shannon's eyes remained half open. A beatific smile creased her face and her hands were crossed over her chest as if something had recently escaped her embrace.

"I don't think she suffered pain, Mr. Dowd. I think she might have willingly gone somewhere else."

"The name is John. I don't doubt she went willingly. She was my friend. I wasn't grieving for her, I was grieving for me."

"Oh. I'm sorry to intrude, John."

Dowd gave him a forced smile. "Thanks for caring, Danny."

The clear tone sounded again and their minds were touched.

~This is for the new members to our family. What you see next is an ability we all possess but some have yet to learn the application. Everyone please follow along to the altar.~

Before Danny could form a question the bodies of the dead all lifted off the sanctuary floor as if being gently carried. People stepped out the way of their passing and all funneled toward an arch in the back of the sanctuary.

Holding Su Laana's hand he followed along with all the others. The arch opened on a large field covered in grass except for the center where a huge expanse of flat stone lay exposed. A ridge created a half circle on the east side of the field.

As everyone moved out Danny was surprised to note that it was early morning. A fine mist hung above the stone slab and the remains of the dead slowly moved into the center and came to rest, side-by-side, in the open air.

~Gather around the stone but do not touch it.~

Danny wondered about the old Kian who seemed to be in charge. Was he some sort of priest or elected leader?

~All will be made known to you.~ Su Laana said in a mental touch as light as a feather.

He reined in his curiosity and watched the bodies silently glide through the air and ease down, shoulder to shoulder.

Telekinesis, he thought. *That's amazing.*

Soon the stone was nearly covered with dead. Only a very few showed other than bliss on their still faces.

~Step back from the stone if you have strayed forward.~

Danny hadn't but he took a half step back any way. Nearly everyone did.

The day grew brighter by the second. A sound up on the ridge caught his attention. A large, bluish rock rose up into view and when it ceased movement the ascending sun caught the very top of it.

Brightness shot through it and the convexity of the huge piece of glass focused the rays on a barren portion of the mountainside that formed the sanctuary. Pieces of rock heated, fractured, and slid down the angular face to join a pile of like debris at the base. As the sun ascended, the focused beam moved down the bare rock. Danny saw that the stone touched the wall at the pile of shards.

Wherever the sunrays touched the temperature elevated quickly and totally. More superheated pieces cracked and fell. The light clatter sounded loud in the total silence surrounding the field.

As the beam moved over the debris pile a mournful chant sprang up. Danny couldn't tell if it was mental or vocal. The chant sounded like nothing more than an extended groan but it moved him to the pit of his being.

He found himself groaning deep in his throat along with the others as tears ran down his face.

The light grew as it touched the stone slab and the first of the dead. The intensity of brightness amplified to the point it transcended that of a welding torch and Danny was forced to close his eyes or risk future vision.

Beneath the continuous chant he could hear a sizzling and cracking that he chose not to dwell on. The sun climbed higher and the light slowly swept the rock and its contents. By the time the focus abruptly vanished only a wide drift of ashes remained on the rock.

The chant lifted into a higher paean, no longer one of lament but a cry of release. The ashes on the outer edge of the rock began to move in a circular movement as a mentally created whirlwind built and intensified. The mass of ash lifted into the air in a tight column of swirling wind and suddenly left the ground to move in a huge boiling cloud up and to the east where the sea waited.

The now shrill cry from hundreds of throats abruptly stopped with a unified shout, "Ki!"

Danny felt drained and allowed himself to drop to the ground to rest. Scores of humans and Kians hit the ground with him. The rock face still radiated massive heat.

Su Laana leaned against him.

"My father regarded you highly, you know," she said in a whisper. "Else you would have never known me as a woman."

"I am honored and I lament your loss."

She flashed a quick, sad smile. "See, you always say the right thing."

The tone captured their attention again.

~First we show you how to achieve alonement. After that we will make you aware of all the rules of mental discipline...~

89
Coalition Star Ship Norman Vaughn

"Captain, we are decelerating from the Davidson Drive," Commander Sarah Barenz said.

"Noted, Executive Officer Barenz. I shall enter the bridge momentarily."

As soon as the one-way holo transmission ended Captain Lee Han splashed water on his face and dried with an old-fashioned cloth towel. Being captain had its perks.

"Confucius, open the log," he said in a conversational tone.

"Log open, Captain Han." The AI spoke in perfect Zhongguo Yuwen of ancient Earth. The one time he visited what was left of Asia and the Chinese Republic he could find no one who spoke in the traditional dialect. He frowned at the memory.

"Ah," said the AI, "visiting Earth again, are we?"

"Your impertinence reminds one of your status of teacher." Captain Han folded his towel, collecting his thoughts.

"I wish to make a note about what I expect to find on Kiana, which is chaos. No subsequent messages have been detected since the last one from *Magellan Lifeboat 65*. This bodes to be a very somber voyage. I hope I am in error. Close log."

"As directed, captain." The AI audibly clicked off.

Captain Han had no doubt that the thing monitored him constantly but at least it was courteously surreptitious about it. After a brief glance in his surround mirror to check for even the smallest imperfection, he walked to the door that opened onto the bridge. As he entered, the AI intoned "Captain on the bridge!"

The voice was not "Confucius," but that of a very officious master chief petty officer, burly and no nonsense. The bridge watch snapped to attention.

"As you were." Captain Han held the opinion that a good captain demanded his crew to show proper respect in a military manner. He felt he was stern but fair.

As the first Coalition star ship captain from the Nine Celestial Orbs, he was creating a tradition within existing traditions. Lee Han was the only person of Chinese ancestry on board *Norman Vaughn*. Ferreting out the provenance of the ship's name had taken him virtually to Earth and to the continents of Antarctica and North America in the early 20th century.

Norman Vaughn had been a dog musher for an Admiral Byrd. Both were citizens of the United States, the first republic on Earth and in North America. Captain Han relished scholarly pursuits.

Through the huge forward observation port he beheld the swirling purple-black on black of the Davidson Portal, the link from one point in space to another. How space and time could be folded and penetrated was beyond his grasp of physics. But he didn't care as long as it was done correctly.

"Not like the *John C. Fremont!*" he muttered to himself. In Cadet Han's third year at the Coalition Academy, the *Fremont* had gone missing, never to be heard from again. Since the AI of the *Fremont* disappeared with it there was no way of knowing precisely what went wrong. As a result every ship captain from that point forward was strict about transit procedure to the point of making it a religion.

He sat in his command module and flattened both hands on the armrests. Small panels under each hand blinked yellow while scans were vetted and the control systems activated in nanoseconds.

Lieutenant Commander Stig M'botti, the navigator, loudly announced, "Clearing Davidson Space in five, four, three..."

Even Captain Han held his breath until the shreds of Davidson Space filigreed out to nothing and normal. Black space surrounded them. With a collective sigh everyone resumed breathing.

Kiana hung boldly in the firmament, slightly eclipsed by a moon and eclipsing in turn a larger moon behind her.

"What do we have, Mr. Nolen?"

"Captain, we're getting a lot of nothing on all frequencies." Lieutenant Todd Nolen could hear conversations where others might hear a whisper or two. "No telecommunications in evidence, either, Sir."

"That is what I feared we would find. Commander Barenz, who is leading the landing party?"

"Colonel Llerena, captain," she said crisply. "They are taking three shuttle craft with minimum crew in hopes of locating survivors."

Captain Han bleakly grinned at his XO. "I certainly would not wager my deployment bonus on them finding anyone."

Commander Barenz kept her face passive. "I never gamble, captain."

"Pass the word for Colonel Llerena to deploy."

"Aye, aye, captain." She tapped an icon on her screen and along with the rest of the bridge crew they watched as three shuttle craft arrowed soundlessly from beneath the observation port in a line and curved toward the planet.

"Secure from transit stations."

The bosun of the watch snapped to attention. "Secure from transit stations. Aye, aye, captain." He touched an icon on his screen sounding the two-tone alert throughout the ship and repeated the captain's order.

Lieutenant Commander M'botti stood and nodded to Captain Han, his uniform tight across his massive chest. The deep yellow eyes in the light maroon face showed no emotion.

"By your leave, captain." He waited for Captain Han's nod and then turned and left the bridge. Other crewmembers followed.

"Are you all right, captain?" Commander Barenz said in a low voice.

Captain Han released the breath he hadn't realized he was holding and glanced at her, willing himself to relax.

"I'm fine, commander. Some things just take time to become accustomed to."

Keeping her voice low enough that only he could hear, she said, "Such as seven foot Altairians with enough strength to break steel stanchions?"

He grinned. "Not for nothing are you the executive officer. Mr. M'botti is the first nonhuman I have served with and I'm surprised at my reserve with him."

"You'll adjust, sir. Altairians have only been in the fleet for five years but their numbers are growing."

"I'll do my best not to let that fact bother me either."

They laughed and Captain Han wondered if he had just passed her latest psych test. He also wondered what it had been that drove Captain Peacock into paranoia and madness. Before the transmission from the doomed *Magellan* had abruptly stopped, the ship's AI had sent the final images from the security nodes.

Captain Han had watched the image of Captain Peacock coming unhinged in the *Magellan's* lab at least a dozen times trying to see something not noticed before. Since the incident psychological evaluations on command personnel had increased. As they had been told in training: Coalition Regulations were written in blood. The same mistake would not be repeated ever again.

He wondered if anyone had been watching Peacock as closely as they now watched him. With a sniff he moved on to other things. The Han Clan of New Sichuan was made of stern stuff and had never failed in their duties – nor would he.

90
Siboth

"Mr. Koly. Inform the other two craft that we will all land together, sterns inward and prows outward in tri-star formation."

"Aye, aye, colonel." Major Steve Koly spoke into his headset and glanced at the holos showing altitude, trim, and all of the other pieces of information needed to keep the craft operational and safe. A grid appeared in front of him with the landing reference for his craft in glowing red and the other two in a muted blue. The real-time display took all the fun out of piloting, he thought, but by the same token it made for safer landings.

With well-practiced motions he set the ship down exactly where Colonel Llerena had ordered. He peered out through the front window. Before this mission they had studied holos of the Coalition compound on Kiana.

The building had sustained massive damage, as had the local structures around the main square where the shuttlecraft now sat, metal hulls ticking as they cooled. Colonel Llerena tapped the comm icon.

"Anyone see anything moving at all?"

"Negative, sir," said Major Kimbrell in Shuttle Two.

"Major Board?"

"If there's anything moving out there it's too fast for me to spot it, sir."

Llerena grinned. "Thank you, Shuttle Three. Let's go on a little recon mission. Open 'em up."

"Do you want me to leave the engines running, colonel?" Steve asked.

"And have someone steal it? No, thank you, sir."

Steve started to point out that they were the only ones with the means to get into the craft but he shrugged and powered down, feeling oddly vulnerable. He raised the main hatch and the lower part of the bulkhead swung out and down to become the ramp. Gunnery Sergeant Dahlke hefted his Personal Assault Weapon and edged down the ramp first.

Steve waited for Colonel Llerena to exit and then pulled his lanky frame out of the pilot's seat. He wore a hand laser on his hip and didn't bother unfastening the cover flap as he ambled down onto the planet.

Fresh air felt good after four months in space. He still started to panic when the breeze moved against his face.

Shipboard habits don't disappear quickly no matter what your circumstances, he thought.

"On me," Colonel Llerena said, holding up his left hand in a fist. In his right hand he held a laser rifle.

Major Kimbrell, Staff Sergeant Davis, and Corporal Helzer moved over to the rest of them. Everyone's eyes continued to sweep the area, watching for movement or remains.

Major Board, Private Doss, and Private Randall came from the other direction. All three carried PAWs that looked ridiculously big in the hands of the two women privates. But Steve had seen both women score top points in the live fire range on *Vaughn*. He wished he could shoot that well.

"Okay," Colonel Llerena said. "I want–"

Steve saw people moving toward them from all directions.

"Sir, we have company."

"Where the hell did they come from?" Major Board said.

Gunnery Sergeant Dahlke and Privates Doss and Randall all instinctually raised their weapons.

"Belay that!" Llerena snapped. "Ground all weapons."

Steve watched the circle of people slowly approach them. Many were human; most were not. They were chatting and smiling, as if out for a walk on a sunny afternoon. As one they all stopped, grew quiet, and stared at the new arrivals.

"We are from the *Coalition Star Ship Norman Vaughn*," Colonel Llerena said. "We are looking for survivors of the *Magellan* expedition."

The people maintained their silence and position as a tall human male with long blond hair moved toward them. He smiled and held out his hand.

"Hi, I'm Stoker Payne, Chief of Archeology. Good to see you folks."

Llerena introduced himself. "Is everything in good order here, Mr. Payne?"

"Yes, colonel. We are quite happy, one and all. How was your trip?"

Llerena frowned and glanced at his team. "Okay. Am I the only one who feels something is off kilter here?"

"No," Major Kimbrell said. "Not even the kids are talking. That's just not human."

"We've been through a lot here," Stoker Payne said, "...and we're getting used to our new home."

"Home? This is not a Coalition world."

Payne handed Col. Llerena a handpad.

"The information in this will explain everything, sir. You will also find the resignation of all former Coalition personnel on Kiana. If you would please take that back to Captain H–, to your captain and analyze the contents we would be grateful.

"We will have a delegation here tomorrow at 1400 hours local time to discuss any points not understood. Until then, colonel." He nodded and turned away.

All of the people turned as one and walked back into the spaces between buildings. They chatted and laughed. Major Steve Koly experienced a flash of memory of his family all walking home from a local outdoor play they had enjoyed one summer during his youth.

"What the *hell* just happened here?" Major Kimbrell blurted.

"What is it you call them walking machines in the vids?" Gunny Dahlke asked.

"Robots!" Private Doss said, her eyes flitting back and forth in her dark face as she watched the departing people. "You're right, Gunny. They all act just like robots!"

"Except there's no robots like those," Major Board said. "I hope."

"Thanks, Cary. We all needed that," Colonel Llerena said. "Saddle up people. Let's get the hell out of here."

"Thank goodness," Steve said to himself. He didn't like the chill he felt creeping from his neck down his spine.

91
Coalition Star Ship Norman Vaughn

"And none of the rest of them said a word while Payne was speaking?"

"No, captain. They just stood there in a huge circle around us and watched," Colonel Llerena said.

"Captain, sir?"

"Yes, Private Doss?"

"It wasn't that they *watched*. It was more like they *stared*. You know what I mean? It was just weird."

Captain Han carefully examined each face of his landing party and realized they all agreed with Private Doss. Every man and woman who went down to Kiana was completely unnerved. There wasn't one person standing in his office he wouldn't trust with his life.

He knew they were each and every one a true professional and most had combat experience. So this wasn't a case where one person got spooked and started a retreat. This was a unique situation that could prove awkward for the Coalition.

"Thank you all for your excellent reports. I sincerely believe what you did down there possesses merit and will prove valuable. You are all excused from duty for three days. Get some rest."

"Thank you, captain," Colonel Llerena said.

"Colonel, I wish a word with you. The rest of you may leave."

They filed out of the office and Llerena closed the door behind them.

"What do you think happened down there, Tony?"

"Skipper, I wish I knew. We were ready for anything be it a firefight or a retrieval of remains. Then we were faced with this." He waved his hand at the handpad lying on the desk between them.

"You were all frightened, were you not?"

"Yes, captain, we were. But it wasn't a fear for our lives. We're used to that in the military. It was more like we were fearful for our souls. There was something unholy about what happened down there. I wish I could be more exact."

"Have a seat, Tony. I want you to watch this with me and a few others."

Colonel Llerena dropped into one of the leather chairs and waited with a blank look on his face.

"Confucius," Captain Han said, "please ask the Committee to come in."

"As you wish, Sir."

The door opened and eight people quietly filed in and found seating on the two couches and other chairs. Once all were still, Captain Han cleared his throat.

"You all just watched the individual reports from the landing party. Now we shall see the contents of the handpad they retrieved." Without further ado he pushed a node and a holo popped into existence above the desk.

An ancient alien stared at them. He displayed no emotion and seemed to stare at each individual in the office.

"I am Qå Naamb. I have lived for most of three centuries, Coalition years, and I am not finished yet." He smiled in such a friendly manner that all in the office smiled back.

"For lack of a better term, I am the Prime Minister of Kiana. *All* of it. As the people conferred this duty upon me, I therefore am their spokesperson in all things legal, diplomatic, and military. I did not seek this position nor did I wish to accept it but when the people speak we must listen.

"Recently we were visited by a comet that carries toxicity in its tail. This toxicity is lethal to all beings with a brain, whether Kian, human, or something else. Nearly a millennium ago our ancestors discovered how to escape the effects of this comet.

"Due to unfortunate circumstances your starship in orbit around Kiana at the time was exposed to the 'Breath of Yanivina' as we call it. The ship and all aboard her were lost. We offer our sincere condolences for this tragedy. As a result we offered rescue to the humans remaining on Kiana and those few who escaped the starship in its final moment of peril.

"As a result we, the human survivors and the Kian people, have opted to form a planetary government. An election was held and as previously stated, I became Prime Minister. We also elected a body of public servants who enact laws and arbitrate issues of concern for the citizens of Kiana.

"We have also formulated an open treaty offered to any and all non-Kian entities wishing to visit our planet. The treaty protocols are simple and non-negotiable.

"We will not now or ever become a part of any Coalition, confederacy, league, federation, or other organization of allied worlds or states. We are neutral and inviolate.

"We offer trade, rest, recreation, medical assistance, and repair facilities for any peaceful beings who visit our planet. Any display of aggression or hostility will be met with overwhelming force and the parties displaying such antisocial trends will be summarily annihilated with no further warning than what you hear now.

"We are a peaceful planet and no amount of military power or posturing will change that. There will be no ambassador admitted or permanent settlements of non-Kians permitted. You are all welcome visitors, but you *are* visitors and will not be allowed to stay more than an Earth year on Kiana.

"Thank you for your attention and may your lives be long and fruitful."

The holo winked out.

"Can they *do* that?" Captain Han asked the room at large.

Colonel Llerena grinned. "Hell, skipper, it looks like they just did."

"Magistrate Botelho. What are the legal ramifications of this situation?"

"Captain, if they have a majority of the beings on the planet who agree with what the prime minister just said, they have every right to invoke the laws he laid down. As a factional leader on ancient Earth once put it; it's a done deal."

"Doctors, did any of you feel this person was under any undue or outside influence?"

"I found him quietly forceful, and in psychiatric terms, a fully functioning personality."

"Thank you Dr. Burke. Anyone else?"

Commander Barenz spoke up, "Do any of you have any idea why all of the human survivors elected to renounce their Coalition citizenships and remain on Kiana? I could understand a few being assimilated, but *all* of them?"

"I have been pondering that very question, commander," Dr. Burke said. "The obvious answer is that since the Kians saved their lives, we have a collective case of survivor gratitude here. I have never before seen so many individuals thus affected, nor have I ever seen all of a group respond in the same way."

"Do you think this is something that will, for lack of a better term, *wear off* after a time, doctor?" Captain Han asked.

"Perhaps after a few years, but there is something about this situation that does not meet the eye. Our only hope is that when all of the data received from the Magellan while in *extremis* is analyzed we will get a better understanding of the situation down there."

The captain nodded and asked, "Magistrate Botelho , do you see any adverse ramifications if we provisionally accept the terms offered by the Kian government?"

"To what end, captain? Are we going to stay here for a year?

"Not all of us. I would like you and two assistants to remain here while we return to Proxima Central. You will make no effort to disguise the fact that you are a psychiatrist and a sociologist."

"The rationale for this request, sir?"

"I want you to study them, both the humans *and* the Kians. Try to figure out why this situation occurred and how enduring you believe it to be. We will present your mission as a mental health gesture aimed at helping any human bothered by the situation."

"How large a staff may I take with me?"

"Whatever you deem necessary. However, remember that you will be the sole Coalition presence on Kiana and whether you carry the title or not, you *will* be an ambassador."

"I will assemble a team by tonight, sir."

"Very well. Tomorrow we will go down to the planet and make sure there are no individuals who wish to return to Coalition worlds with us. After that I suppose the rest of us will go back to Proxima Central and lay this in the laps of the politicians and tacticians. Are there any questions?"

92
Siboth

Melanie lay in the arms of her mate and stared at the stars above their pavilion.

~*Did you ever dream this would happen?*~

~*You naked in my arms, or our communication methods?*~

"Both, I suppose," she said aloud. "I think it's all rather wonderful."

"I sure don't miss the bureaucracy, if that's what you mean," Stoker said. "And I love the iron fist inside the velvet glove we all own."

"The Coalition doesn't know what we have, but they are afraid of it," Melanie said. "Otherwise they wouldn't have left that pitiful group of spies behind. I wonder what they will do when they come back?"

~*There is no way they can undermine the Kian People.*~

He pulled her to him.

Delmar Buhrman

Leonard (Stoney) Compton has had novelettes and short stories published in *Universe 1, Tomorrow, Speculative Fiction, Writers of the Future, Vol. IX* and *Jim Baen's Universe.* His novel, *Russian Amerika* (Baen Books) was published in 2007 and its sequel, *Alaska Republik,* in February 2011.

He is an Illustrator for Chief, Naval Air Training Command, NAS Corpus Christi, TX. Prior to that he was a Visual Information Specialist for the 6th Combat Training Squadron, Nellis AFB, Nevada.

He is a native of Grand Island, Nebraska. He served an enlistment in the U.S. Navy where he had the honor of being a crew member on *USS Yorktown, CVS-10,* as well as in VR-24 Detachment in Naples, Italy.

He is the proud father of Sarah Maisie and Danford Gordon.

His fine art has been included in juried shows from New York to Hawai'i, and Alaska to California.

After 31 years in Alaska he now lives in Corpus Christi, Texas with his wife, Colette, their ever changing number of cats, and Pullo, their energetic Australian Blue Heeler. He is an avid hiker, kayaker, and velocipede enthusiast.

Watch for

Whalesong

and

Return to Kiana

coming soon from

Pullo Pup Publications

Made in the USA
Charleston, SC
17 April 2012